OF SEA AND SONG

Of Sea and Song

Copyright © 2020 by Chanda Hahn

Neverwood Press

Editor: Hot Tree Editing

Cover Design Covers by Combs

Map Illustration by Hanna Sandvig www.bookcoverbakey.com

www.chandahahn.com

978-1950440184 (Hardcover)

978-1950440177 (Paperback)

The Seven Kingdoms

KILN

RYA

BAIST

CANDOR

FLORIN

ISLA

EVILLE'S TOWER

TOWN OF NIHILL

SION

CHAPTER ONE

I fought desperately, plunging my enemy into the water. Thrusting back and forth with a vengeance. Sweat beaded across my brow, and I swore under my breath. I knew it was a losing battle. The sun beat down on my arms as I struggled against the strain, and my breathing turned ragged. I was losing and knew my life would soon be forfeit. My arms trembled, my fingers cold and bruised from the burden.

Finally, I gave up. My hands released the dress in the suds-filled wash tub. I pulled the garment up to inspect the stain and frowned in frustration when I saw it now marred a greater area. I rubbed it between my knuckles and fought the blemish relentlessly. Running it up and down our washboard did little more than bruise my fingers. "Oh, for the love of food," I grumbled aloud. "Maeve is going to kill me."

It's her favorite dress. I spilled a draught all down the front of it, and I was trying to clean it before she got home.

I groaned and flung the garment back into the washbasin, sending a spray of lukewarm water across the ground and startling Hack, our orange tabby. Hack was slumbering in the midday sun. He jumped up when the water sprayed across his fur, hissing at me angrily.

"Oh, calm down, Hack," I chastised. "It's only water. And it would do you good. I know what you've been rolling in." I wagged my finger at him.

Our cat hardly liked anyone other than Mother, Aura and Rhea. He barely tolerated Maeve and downright hated me. Hack arched his back at being so ruthlessly attacked by the sudsy water. He hissed, showing me his displeasure.

"Get over it."

"Mrrreeoowww," he growled and made way to swat at my leg.

"Oh, scat!" I sang a soft note, and a wave of water sloshed out of the basin and completely drenched him. Hack's ears flung back, and a look of utter confusion donned his feline face. Hack scampered off into the underbrush, his tail flicking my way.

Maybe there *was* a good reason he hated me.

I chuckled, unable to contain my mirth, and then it happened. I snorted.

"Oh stars." I slapped my hand over my mouth to contain the unfeminine noise that fell from my lips. It was my curse.

I stood, flung my plaited deep-red hair out of my face, and stretched, surveying my work. There were still baskets of clothes that needed washed that would take me most of the afternoon, plus the actual reason I volunteered to do laundry—to clean Maeve's dress. I glanced over my shoulder toward the tower.

Our home was an old guard tower that had been abandoned and claimed by my mother. Over the years, we added additions that gave us a larger living area and a private workroom for Mother. My sisters and I slept in the cold and drafty tower, but we didn't mind so much.

For we were sorceresses, trained by Lady Eville, one of the most powerful in the known kingdoms. And as much as the world feared her name, they soon cast that same suspicion upon us, her daughters, although we didn't share any blood relation. We were all orphans, abandoned. But then we were bartered for and adopted by her.

I stared at the path that led into the town of Nihill. Years ago, when Mother first moved here to escape her own past, it was a backward town filled with lowlifes and ruffians. Or as Rhea called them, scummies. But over time, it has built up a few fine establishments and has grown in population despite there being a tower filled with sorceresses a few miles away. Last year, they even elected a mayor. Although, he was just a crooked businessman who lined his own pockets with unfair taxes. His son, Armon, was even worse. He used his father's title to bully and steal from anyone he wanted.

Aura left for town a few hours ago to get our supplies for the week, and Rhea and Maeve disappeared into the woods. They said it was to take an old woodcutter ointment for his joints. But I suspected by the amount of basil, nettle, and wormwood they gathered that it was to cast a hex on a particular girl in town. One that had tormented each of our few and far between trips with tossed horse dung and vile words.

Mother had gone to check in with Rosalie in the Kingdom of Baist. There was much secrecy over the birth of the future princess of two kingdoms. Even we didn't know her name nor had seen her. She must have had the baby by now.

Which left four mischievous daughters unsupervised and without a leash.

With a wry smile, I quietly hummed. The water in the tub

swirled one direction and then the other as it listened to my voice. I tossed a handful of soap flakes into the water, and the water quickly filled with suds. I let my magic do most of the work as I hummed a soft lullaby. One I had learned as a child, but not the origins.

The swirling tub of water grew more violent as I lost focus, and the washboard slid into the suds. I stopped the tune, and the water listened. It stilled, and the bubbles slowly popped. I reached in for the dress and pulled out a spotless garment.

"Yes." I ran it through the press and shook it out before hanging it on the line. Magic wasn't frowned upon in our household. In fact, we practiced spells, draughts and curses every day. But I was only good at water spells. Which was how I ended up with the unfortunate stain on Maeve's dress. It was a spelled draught gone wrong. But we were told to not practice magic outside where the townspeople could see us, for they did not understand or approve of us, unless they needed something. A sick child, a loved one who needed guidance or a charm, then my family became indispensable to them. I ground my teeth in frustration.

I had just pulled a second dress through the drying press when a searing pain wracked my skull, bringing me to my knees.

"*Meri!*" Aura's mental cry echoed in my head.

The dress fell from my hands into the dirt. I lifted my skirts and took off running. I darted across the wooden bridge and ran down the gravel path into town. My worn shoes pinching my feet, causing me to grit my teeth in pain. My sister's terror became my own. Her anguish became mine as she shared her fears and emotions with me. Glimpses flashed through my mind, and none of them were good.

The flickers of images I was getting from Aura was that she

was near the butcher's shop. The mental pictures stopped coming. Aura was shielding herself, trying to keep me from seeing and feeling what she was feeling.

"No, Aura," I cried. "Don't shut me out."

But I didn't need much more direction. I ran past the first row of houses and didn't slow until I came to the seedier part of town, where the buildings and shops were derelict and falling apart. Most buildings had faded shutters or missing sections of thatch or shingles on their roofs. The roadside gutters had become a septic waste area, where the poor tossed their garbage and refuse. Even the animals looked sickly and faint from hunger.

Three threadbare children playing in the street saw my approach. They picked up their twine ball and rushed inside their house, calling out for their mother in fear. The fear wasn't new. I was used to being an outcast, but it still hurt when innocent children avoided me.

I burst through the sand-colored butcher shop front doors to be greeted by an empty counter. Dried sausages hung along the rafters, and raw beef lay waiting to be wrapped in paper. Flies buzzed around the uncovered meat, and I covered my mouth from the smell. No one was here or had been for a while. No sound came from the back room, so I left out the front door and ran down the street.

"Aura!" I called out, but no one responded, and the road remained empty.

An opened window across the way slammed shut, the woman inside shielding her family from me. As if the villagers knew something bad was coming and cleared out ahead of time. A muffled cry drew my attention and I turned down a blind alley, the entrance almost completely hidden by a hay-filled wagon.

At the end of the alley, I saw her. Aura trapped against the brick building with three men looming over her. She tried to step around Clive, a known drunkard, but he was too fast. He grabbed her by the wrist and flung her back against the building. Even from this distance, I heard Aura's head smack against the brick, her face pinched with pain as she held in her cry.

The butcher's son, Tobias, took a stick and was trying to lift up her dress. When she tried to get away, Clive hit her in the face. I could see a smear of blood across her fair cheek, and rage built within me.

How dare they harm my sister!

Tears poured from Aura's eyes as she struggled to break free. Not from them physically—but mentally. Aura's gifts led toward empathy. She could feel what those around her felt and at times read people's thoughts. And it was her attackers' horrid and ugly thoughts that had my sister paralyzed with fear.

Aura was the gentlest of all the daughters of Eville, her magic not offensively strong like Rosalie's or mine. She hated crowds and going into town for this very reason. But she was useful in getting the best deals, for she knew if a storekeeper was lying. Inwardly, I fumed that I hadn't gone with her.

"Please stop!" Aura dropped her basket to cover her ears, all of her purchases tumbling into the dirt. The apples rolled into a puddle, and the sack of flour split open and spilled into the gravel.

"Make me," Tobias taunted. He gripped her arm, and I saw Aura wince a second time. He pulled her close and tried to kiss her.

Aura's eyes went wide, and she screamed, clawing at his chest.

"Leave her alone!" I yelled.

Three sinister heads turned toward me. Aura looked relieved but terrified at my arrival.

"Well, looky what we have here," Armon sneered. He was the biggest and richest of the men. He had no problem throwing his name around as the mayor's son and believed himself to be untouchable. "The more, the merrier... and I love redheads. Is it true their kisses are as sweet as strawberries?"

I tried not to show my disgust. Instead, I calmed my features and twirled my finger around a stray lock of my hair. "I surely have no idea. Unless someone kisses me and tells me." I hated that I simpered, but I was only doing what I thought necessary to lure the men closer to me and farther away from Aura.

It worked—sort of. Armon and Tobias moved toward me, while Clive still kept one hand on Aura's elbow. Her face pale, her eyes filled with unshed tears. I could see her nervousness, and she knew what I was planning. She shook her head ever so softly in warning. But I was never the obedient sister.

Her cheek swelled, and I could see the bruise forming under her eye. She tried to wipe away the blood, but it only smeared across her cheek, and now blood coated her white cuff.

I held still. Keeping my hands at my side to try to pose as little threat as possible, but I knew my green eyes glittered angrily, revealing my true intentions.

"Now, Meri, where's my kiss?" Armon shoved his hand into his pocket while he leaned forward. His head swung near mine, and I could smell the stench of ale on his breath. I turned my head away in disgust. His hand shot out of his pocket, and a knife appeared. The tip poked my ribcage carefully. "No tricks. You hear? None of that magic stuff or I'll skewer you."

He dug the tip of the knife into my rib, and I inhaled as it pierced my skin. Warm blood trickled down my side.

Stupid. I'm so stupid. I didn't expect him to be armed. My eyes flickered toward my sister and her tear-stained face. Clive held a knife under Aura's chin, and she stood still as if her life depended on it.

My jaw clenched, and my hands balled into fists.

Aura's eyes widened in fear as she read my emotions. She shook her head a second time, letting Clive's knife slice her chin.

Armon gripped the back of my neck and smashed his mouth against mine. I fought his kiss as he fought to claim me. I heard Aura cry out, and I struggled but felt the knife dig farther into my ribs. The pain was searing, but my anger was worse.

I bit Armon's lip, stepped on his toe, and twisted away. His knife sliced into my side through my shirt. How dare he harm not only my sister but take something from me I had not freely given? When I gathered my breath, I opened my mouth to sing. For it was my gift to sing spells. The sweeter the melody, the stronger the magic.

Except. I didn't sing. I screamed.

A powerful blast of air slammed into Armon and sent him spinning head over heels into the wall next to Aura. His head hit the brick with a sickening crack.

Clive, startled by my attack, dropped Aura's arm and stepped away. It was a mistake on his part. I screamed again, and this time Clive spun in a circle before flying across the alley, knocking Tobias into a barrel. They crumpled in a heap and groaned.

I rushed forth to grab Aura as she curled into a ball. Her

hands over her ears as if she could stop the barrage of feelings and thoughts that came her way.

"Come, Aura. We need to go."

"So much hate," she whispered. Her eyes watered, and she looked up at me and cried. "They were evil men."

"It's over. They'll think twice about trying to kiss us again." I grabbed her hands and helped pull her up.

"Kiss?" Aura blinked in surprise. "No, that is not what they had planned for us. It was much worse. They were going to—"

"Hush now," I scolded, interrupting her. "Don't let their darkness consume you." I wrapped my arm around Aura, and we stepped around the groaning bodies of Clive and Tobias. "If you could block out their thoughts, you might have been able to defend yourself," I chastised softly.

I slowed and tried to not look at the still form of Armon. I covered Aura's eyes to shield her from what I hoped was nothing more than an unconscious man. But when we stepped over his leg, I glanced back at the unnatural angle of his head, the blood that trickled from the corner of his mouth, and I knew.

He would never harm another woman again.

I could feel the magic in the earth recoil from me when I had taken a life. As if I wronged the balance of power. The rejection hurt.

I gritted my teeth and quickly ushered Aura home to the safety of the tower and the protection of our other sisters. I prayed what I had done would not bring down vengeance upon our house.

I would soon learn.

It would not be so.

CHAPTER TWO

Twilight fell over our home, and with it, an ominous feeling I couldn't shake. We cleaned Aura's cuts and bruises, bandaged my rib, and got my sister into bed to recoup. Rhea brewed Aura her favorite lavender tea to calm her nerves and brought her a plate of honey tea biscuits.

"Shush, you need to relax," Rhea commanded, patting Aura's hands.

"But I don't like to sleep," Aura muttered. "My dreams are —" She fingered her threadbare coverlet. "—worse than being awake." Her pale eyes looked at me hovering in her doorway. "Maybe you could sing me to sleep like you used to and spell the dreams away."

My mouth was dry, and I looked away guiltily. "I'm sorry. I don't want to sing right now."

Her pert lips fell, but when she nodded in understanding, I felt even worse.

I quickly imagined a steel trap and closed my mind. Aura could read my thoughts and saw my hesitation and guilt. So, she knew not to push, but if she pried too deeply, she would see the truth—that Armon was dead—and she would only blame herself.

Rhea stroked Aura's hair as I closed the door and headed down to the kitchen to check on dinner. Our kitchen was large, for normally there were eight people, nine when Lorn was visiting.

Our dining table was made of ebony and forged by magic. The legs were twisted roots that held up the magnificent black top. Our fire always had multiple cauldrons on hooks at various levels over the wood. For we were always cooking or brewing multiple things at once.

Maeve poked her nose into the closest cauldron. "So, which one is dinner? I don't want to make a mistake and take a hundred-year nap." She picked up a wooden spoon and stirred a thickening green stew. "It's not this one, is it? Maybe I do prefer the hundred-year nap and can skip this muck." She pointed to the burning soup.

I grimaced and rushed toward our dinner. Using my apron, I quickly pulled the stew from the hook over the fire and almost burned my hands. The soup was not quite ruined. I could save it. I gave a quick taste and added a cinnamon and wine vinegar solution until I disguised the burned flavor.

"Here." I held the spoon out to Maeve.

She flicked her dark braid over her shoulder and glared at me. Her jade-green eyes filled with distrust. In a show of wariness, she pinched her nose and opened her mouth. I watched her take a spoonful, chew, and then look at me in astonishment.

"I will never figure out how you do that."

I grinned, patting my belly. "One should never waste food." I sliced a fresh loaf of bread and laid out three place settings as Rhea came down the stairs.

"Oh good. I'm starving." Rhea hopped over to the table and pulled out her chair.

The table felt empty with three vacant seats.

Rosalie, the oldest and strongest of us, was forced into an arranged marriage to marry the Prince of Baist. What started as hate eventually turned to love.

My sister Eden traveled to Candor and caused quite a ruckus. She not only ended up getting engaged to the crown prince but murdered his family at her wedding. The last I heard, she was on the run with the magical menagerie troupe after having found her birth parents.

My eyes flickered to Honor's seat. She wasn't gifted in the magical arts like the rest of us. Her training was not done around a cauldron or over spell books but up north in the woods with Lorn, an elf, and a dear family friend.

I filled a bowl of stew for Rhea and placed it in front of her. Rhea with her golden-brown hair and tanned skin. Her gift wasn't so much magic but alchemy. She had her own forge out back by our small barn and spent most of her time out there, melting and casting magical artifacts.

Maeve served herself and waited for me to take my portion, and we sat down to enjoy our meal.

"Thank you, Divine One, who watches over us and guides us. Let our paths be true," Rhea prayed.

"So be it," I intoned.

I took a bite and sighed in pleasure. The soup had successfully been saved. I was about to take another bite when a bright yellow light flickered about the room in warning. All eyes rose to the living room fireplace where the ward crystal was flashing.

"The outer ward has been activated." Maeve pointed to the yellow crystal. Each one tied to a ward on our land, and the color told us they crossed one. The yellow was the farthest, the orange the second, and red was the bridge. We armed most of our wards to dispel unwanted visitors with a confusion charm. But we couldn't ward all of them with the same spells. Less we spend eternity chasing down travelers in a mindless fog.

"Maybe it's just a stray animal," Rhea said hopefully.

Maeve shook her head as the second ward activated, and the orange crystal flickered about the room. She and Rhea jumped from the table, their dinner forgotten as they raced to the window.

"Not an animal. This seems to be larger," Maeve answered.

The room flickered as more light danced across the walls. It wasn't from the crystals but from outside our tower.

Pushing my chair out from the table, I went to stand by the window. The night was cloudless. Nothing hid the mob who stood on the other side of the bridge. All of them were wary of crossing into our land without permission.

"Maybe they just came to seek help from Mother," Rhea suggested.

I shook my head. There was no mistaking their intent. They were armed with pitchforks, axes, and scythes.

"They're here because of me," I mumbled.

Maeve's inky hair flowed over her shoulders and down her back. Her eyes glittered dangerously as she slammed her hand onto the windowsill. "Then they shall rue the day they came for a daughter of Eville. I shall make them suffer for trespassing."

"Meri. What's going on?" A soft voice came from the stairwell. Aura stood barefoot on the bottom step, her face pale, her shaking hands clutching her thin shawl.

"It's nothing. Go back to bed," I lied.

Aura looked toward the window, and I knew the moment she opened her senses. Her face crumpled up in pain, and she immediately crouched down on the stairs, clutching her head and tears filling her eyes. "No!" she cried out and rocked in place. "No. It's not true!"

"Aura. What's wrong?" Rhea asked. But Aura was in agony, lost in her mind as she tried to shield herself from the mental onslaught of the mob.

Maeve stood by the far window, staring at the same sight I was. Looking out at the men, her eyes filled with hate as the townspeople kept inching forward, pushing one of their own toward the wooden bridge.

"How dare they come here?" Maeve murmured. "Do they not know that to do so is to exact Mother's wrath? Or worse, my own?"

Aura was still curled in a ball, her hands over her ears. She mumbled out an answer. "So much hate and fear… and something else. I can't quite understand. It's too much. It hurts so much. The agony," Aura cried again.

My teeth clenched in anger as I watched my sweet sister reduced to so much pain because of the men outside. She read their emotions and felt their hate.

"Make them stop." Rhea turned to me. "Make them go away. You have enough magic."

"They will… eventually," I said. "They always try, but they can't get past our guardians." I pointed to the river that surrounded our lands and the wooden bridge, which was the only way to get to our tower. Even from a distance, I could see the shadows under the water, converging toward the bridge, rallying to protect the sorceress's daughters if one so dared to cross it.

A brave soul stepped forward onto the bridge. He was

lanky, in worn breeches, a sickle held out before him in shaky hands. He took two steps, and a purple tentacle shot out of the water, wrapped around his leg, and flung him through the air, his cry echoing into the sky before he crashed into the crowd, knocking the others to the ground.

Maeve chuckled in delight.

Diesel, one of the fae water beasts that lived under the bridge and protected our home from intruders, laughed in return. The water bubbled up and churned, showing his pleasure, as he writhed beneath the murky water. Diesel was only one of our many protectors.

The horde of angry men took the bridge in force, and five men raced across. A great roar came forth as our second protector crawled from the eaves under the bridge to stand in their way.

Traygar, the troll, was an intimidating sight at over ten feet tall, his arms hanging past his knees. In his hand, he clutched a club. The few strands of hair he still had were red, belying that he was of the northern clan who weren't known for being peaceful. His lips pulled back in a snarl, showing his lower tusks, and he let forth a deafening roar. He swung the club, aiming for their heads. One man jumped into the water and tried to scramble to shore before Diesel dragged him under. Two others ducked under the club, one tripped and fell backward, while the fifth man was unfortunate enough to take the full brunt of the swing. He cried out as it knocked him unconscious. Traygar picked him up and tossed him into the other men, knocking them down like a child's bowling toy.

Rhea dragged Maeve back to the center of the room. Rhea's arms wrapped around Maeve in a bear hug. I thought it was in fear, but then I realized she was trying to keep Maeve from transforming and heading out to fight the crowd.

I could still hear the horde of men, and it terrified me. What if they killed the guardians? What if they made it into the tower? What would happen to us? I glanced at the expressions on my sisters' faces. Maeve's anger, Rhea's concern, Aura's pain.

I sang under my breath, intending to send a wave of the water over the people, but then Armon's dead body flashed in my mind—the repercussions of my last attempt at helping. My fear silenced the song, my mouth went dry, and I couldn't sing.

All I could see in my mind was his angled neck and dead body because I used my magic. His death tainted my hands and soul. I knew I couldn't do it again, despite my training.

Aura gasped, her head fell back, and she called out my name. "Meri!"

I ignored my predicament, kneeled down, and grasped Aura's chilly hands between mine. "What is it?"

"Sorrow. Grief. Pain. They have lost so much. Please don't harm them."

I shook my head. "Listen to them. They're angry. They're here to harm us. You must have misheard."

Aura's nails dug into my hand, and her eyes widened. "No, you are hearing wrong. Listen."

I did. I stood and moved to the window and heard the word they were chanting over and over.

"Murderer!"

Aura used the wall to steady herself as she stood and tried to explain what she learned. "When you saved me from those men."

"Hush, Aura. Don't think about it," I soothed, knowing what was coming.

"The one who fell down. He... he's dead."

"What?" Rhea and Maeve gasped in unison and stared at me.

"You didn't tell us you killed someone," Rhea accused.

"Relax," Maeve interrupted. "Meri's not a cold-blooded killer. If she killed him, then he probably deserved it. Now me, on the other hand...." She grinned. I shivered.

Aura's chin dropped, and her hair fell forward, covering her face. "They blame you, Merisol, for his death."

"I know," I said softly. "I used my powers and harmed a living soul, and now my magic has rejected me." I tried to justify that what she said was wrong, but deep down, I could feel the truth.

Traygar roared in pain, and I winced. They shot him with an arrow, and he was now retreating beneath the bridge. The first battalion of men rushed the bridge, and the red warning crystals lit up within the house.

"Why would you do that?" Rhea hissed and lessened her grip on Maeve.

Maeve pulled her arm free. In a flash, she was in raven form and flying out the window toward the bridge.

"It was an accident. I was just trying to protect Aura." I felt sick to my stomach at what happened. "I never meant for anyone to get hurt, much less die."

"I understand," Aura whispered. "But they don't." She turned her face to the window. "They are here, because they have lost someone they loved and are afraid."

Maeve transfigured in a flurry of black feathers back into a woman. She used glamour to cloak herself in darkness, to impose an even bigger threat. Her dress was made of feathers and fur, and black mists pooled around her feet as it curled out like deathly fingers reaching for them. The crowd retreated, not wanting the black fog to touch them. Her hands glowed with magic as she raised them high in the air. I saw her mutter a word, and the sky answered her with lightning, screams coming from the crowd.

"Cower before my wrath!" Maeve flung her hands again, and lightning struck a second time. "Come here no more or I will use your skull for my goblet."

Rhea snorted as Maeve put on a show. "She's always loved theatrics."

"They shall find no sympathy here for what they did to Aura," I snapped.

Maeve walked forward, her long glamoured dress trailing behind. "Leave here. Never return. Or I will curse you and your children's children. Your second cousins, your dog, and even your cow."

Rhea snickered.

"You can't hide her forever," the mayor spoke up angrily. He was a portly man in a suit that could barely contain his belly. "We seek retribution for what was unjustly done. If you won't turn over the murderer. We will send someone who will make you—the bounty hunters. Then you and all your sisters will be cast from the land."

Maeve didn't look impressed. She placed her hands on her hips and dropped her head back. Smoke billowed around her, and she raised her voice and chanted in an ancient dead language.

As she chanted, the crowd clambered over themselves in their hurry to vacate the area.

"What is she saying?" Rhea asked. "Is she really cursing them? This could lead to even more problems."

Aura closed her eyes. The corner of her mouth turned up. "She's reciting the recipe for turnip soup... in elvish."

Rhea snorted. "It seems to be working."

Maeve didn't stop with her silly chant. She sent a few stray bolts after the crowd and heard their cries.

"That should do it." Maeve patted her hands together and nodded at the effects of her spell. I couldn't see the damage but didn't need to. One did not mess with the daughters of Eville and walk away unscathed.

Rhea gasped and ran to the window. "They're leaving."

Aura rose from the stairs and crossed the room to stand before me. She sighed as she listened to their thoughts. "But not for long. They won't give up easily. They will keep coming back until they have gotten justice for Armon." Aura looked right at me. "The mayor has already decreed it so. A life for a life. He will contact the Brunes Guild."

The Brunes Guild were the deadliest of bounty hunters. My heart quickened. I tore my gaze from hers, and I looked down at my hands. Even though they were clean, I couldn't help but imagine the innocent blood that coated them. I murdered someone. I did something forbidden to do, and that curse would haunt me forever. I destroyed the balance of the earth and brought down trouble upon my family. They would keep coming back for me. They would continue to seek justice... unless I left. Only then would my sisters have peace. I had barely come to the conclusion of what I must do when Aura's eyes flickered open and she grabbed my hand.

Her beautiful pale eyes filled with tears, and she whispered so only I could hear it, "Don't do it, Meri. Don't go."

Carefully, I built an imaginary wall in my mind and shielded my thoughts from her. She frowned when she could no longer read me, and I looked away. "Don't worry. I won't let anyone harm you. I promise."

"That's not what I'm worried about," she murmured. "I'm worried about you."

"Well, you shouldn't," I snapped irritably.

Aura winced at my tone.

The witch-hunting horde that tried to attack didn't faze Maeve. In fact, she was closing the door and humming while trying to keep the smile from her face. Only Maeve, our shapeshifter sister, would find pleasure in fighting off hordes of villagers. I shuddered.

The humming stopped as she held up a giant conch shell that was on the floor. "Where did this come from? I don't remember summoning it."

I studied the shell. The shape and color seemed familiar, and I had a desire to possess the strange trinket. Before I could act, Maeve crossed the room, tossed the shell into the trash bin, and sat back down at the table to finish her dinner.

My normally unquenchable appetite was lacking. Dinner was silent, filled with fear and anguish and my own silent thoughts. If only Mother were here or any of my other sisters.

But without Eden, Rosalie, Honor, and Mother, would the four of us have the courage to fight off the town if they came back again, thirsty for my blood? Yes, we were powerful, but it was against our nature to take lives.

My hands shook as I reached for my cup to wet my throat. Our table was too empty. We were stronger together. As soon as dinner was over, we cleaned.

I broke the silence. "We must tend to the wards on our land and give offerings to the guardians for protecting our home." I picked up a basket.

"Now?" Rhea asked.

"Yes, now," I said. I filled the basket with raw meat for the troll, fish for Diesel, gold coins for the gnomes, and flowers for the fae folk and handed the basket to Rhea. Maeve looked irritable and slammed her plate in the washbasin with a loud clunk. I winced at the sound of her displeasure.

"Fine," she snapped. Maeve grabbed her cloak off the hook by the door and stomped out into the night. Rhea followed.

Aura stood by the open door and waited for me. She gave me a strange look as I kneeled by the fire and stared into the blaze.

"Go on without me," I said. "I will be there in a minute."

Aura bit her lip, and I could see her internal debate. "You should come too."

"I will pay my respects to the guardians," I promised.

Aura danced in the doorway and then decided. She grabbed her wool cloak and basket and followed our sisters out into the night.

I kneeled by the trash bin and, using a spoon, pulled the shell out of the refuse.

I recognized the shell from my studies. It was a sacred shell from the kingdom of Isla, said to tell the future to those who sought guidance. I lifted the shell and placed it to my ear, closed my eyes, and listened. Waiting for my future to be foretold. For an omen, perhaps.

At first, there was a low thrum, but then I heard a whisper. Unable to decipher the word, I waited until it came again—though stronger, like a hiss.

"Mur—" It sounded like the shell was speaking my name. I listened closer. "—der."

I dropped the shell, and it clattered to the ground. Deep-red blood seeped from within it to spill onto the stone floor. I backed away in horror, my hands covering my mouth to withhold my scream. It was an omen. A death omen.

I blinked, and the vision was over. The shell lay harmless and pristine on the floor. The blood was nothing more than an omen of what was to come. Murder and death. I looked around our small home and fretted. Was it the townspeople? Would they come back again? Would more people be injured because of my carelessness?

No. I couldn't allow it. I must protect my sisters. Just the thought of Aura being in pain again sealed my decision.

I had to leave.

CHAPTER THREE

The conch shell shattered beneath my fingers. It wasn't enough. I raised the rock again and battered the pieces repeatedly until nothing but dust remained. Leaning back on my knees, I watched as the smallest pieces blew away with the wind. I picked up my basket of offerings and headed to catch up with my sisters as we tended to the wards and guardians.

Even destroyed, I could feel the heaviness of the omen weighing on my heart. It was the driving force that solidified what I needed to do. After our chores were done and we retired for the night, I lay awake watching the moonlight stream through my window and waited until my sisters were in a deep sleep. I was thankful it wasn't a full moon and that no one needed to be up for solstice spells.

I slipped out of my bed and was careful not to wake Rhea or Maeve. Honor's bed was empty, and Aura slept on the floor above where Rosalie and Eden used to sleep. Now there would be two empty beds on each floor, because I doubt Rosalie, Eden, or I would ever come back.

A tear of remorse slid down my cheek, and I brushed it

aside with my palm. I removed the pillowcase and packed my comb, spare day dress, extra socks, boots, my satchel of medicines, a mirror, and money. Tiptoeing down the stairs, I snagged fruit from the kitchen, dried meat, and a few rolls to add to my pack.

Using a quill, I left them a note.

Dearest sisters,

I'm afraid I have become a burden to you and that my presence will bring more harm than good. I know this. Because of my error in using magic, I'm fearful of the repercussions I have brought upon our household. I have chosen to leave to keep you safe, so that the Brunes Guild will never come here.

Please explain to Mother for me.

~Merisol

I stood in the doorway and took one last look around the main living area before heading out of the tower and into the night. I dared not cross the main bridge, in case there were still townsmen out for my head. So I headed toward the northern edge of our property, where the river was nearly impossible to cross because of its fast current.

I took a deep breath, calmed my nerves, and raised my foot over the water. The enchanted rocks sensed my presence, and the boulders rose to allow my passage. They only allowed the daughters to cross here. When I was safe, I waved my hand, and the water receded, covering my escape. But I had not gone unnoticed. The water churned, and a deep-purple head and black beady eyes peered out at me.

Diesel whined beneath the water, and his bubbles burst along the surface.

"I'm sorry, dear friend, but I must go. Please watch over my sisters." I tossed him a chunk of my bread, and he scooped it up with his tentacle and disappeared beneath the water.

I flung my pack over my shoulder and took off into the chilly night. Skirting the town of Nihill, I stuck to side roads. A few miles out, I could hail a passing transport. It didn't matter where I went. I had no destination in mind as long as it was far away from here.

The transports were carriages that had specific routes that traveled between the kingdoms. Fae horses that could travel significant distances without food or water usually pulled the carriages. The transport would fly a banner signally what country it was headed to, and on the door would be another one if they could pick up more fares.

For the first few hours, I was the only passenger. By morning, we picked up two more passengers. The Bakers, an elderly couple, were heading to Candor for their daughter's wedding. They chatted amicably and asked me many questions I was hesitant to answer. They seemed to conclude that I was shy, and they gracefully even offered me part of their packed lunch.

But I was skeptical of everyone who came and went. With magic mirrors becoming more common, it wouldn't be long before others learned of my crime. There may now even be a bounty on my head. I just had to go far enough away that no one cared.

If being snobbish and dismissive kept me alive, so be it.

In the middle of the night, the transport slowed to a stop. My head jolted forward and my bag almost slid off my lap.

The elderly couple continued to sleep undisturbed by the commotion. The wife's head was nestled on her husband's shoulder, his mouth slightly ajar as he snored.

I lifted the flap on the window to peer into the dark, suspicious of anything and everyone. Ominous clouds and constant rain made it impossible to read the town signboard but I could smell the saltiness of the sea, so I knew it must've been a village along the coast. The transport's lantern created a halo that barely illuminated the reason for stopping. The driver was picking up another passenger. I could see a man's black silhouette as he stood on the side of the road. No horse, no bags, nothing in his possession other than the handle of a sword that peeked out from beneath his large cloak that covered him from head to toe.

The stranger spoke to the driver in an inaudible voice, and I strained to hear what they said over the sound of the rain hitting the head of the transport. The handle on the door turned, and I leaned against the side wall, pulled my cloak over my face, and closed my eyes, feigning sleep. The transport dipped as he stepped on the first step, and it swayed as he swung inside to claim the padded bench seat next to me. His leg bumped mine as he settled in and closed the door.

Even with my eyes closed, I could feel his silent perusal of the passengers, and I swore his eyes lingered on me, for my skin prickled slightly, and goose bumps formed along my arm.

The driver climbed back into the box. With a crack of the whip, we were moving again. The jostling of the transport caused the stranger's hip to press into mine, but I dared not move. Instead, I let my hood slide enough where I could study him under lowered lashes. In the dark, I could not tell much, other than he had a straight nose and square jaw and that he was tall, for his legs took up every available inch of the floor.

The rain from his cloak seeped into my leg where his thigh pressed against mine. I couldn't help it—I shivered from the chill.

The stranger must have noticed, because he straightened and pulled away. I used the opportunity to inch even closer to the wall, hiding my face and praying no one would recognize me.

The hand mirror in my bag on my lap hummed as my sisters tried to contact me again. It was an almost constant buzzing I had successfully ignored until now. I wasn't about to answer it in present company. It was safer this way.

I glanced over at the stranger and could feel his eyes on my bag as it continued to hum. His head cocked as he listened. The black hood turned toward me, waiting for me to do something about the noise.

When my sisters didn't give up, I stood, lifted the bag, and shoved it under my thighs, where the padded seat and my bottom muffled the noise. I crossed my arms and turned toward the sideboard, giving him my back. I swore I heard a muffled laugh.

How dare he laugh at me? I was only trying to be considerate. Now I would just ignore him for the rest of our journey. We wouldn't be near each other long. Just until he got off.

It took a long time before I fell asleep. And what seemed like only minutes later, I woke as the driver pulled into a waystation.

The door opened, and our driver stood outside, patting his dusty hat against his side. "We're at the Four Winds Waystation. We will be changing horses and picking up mail. I'd suggest going inside for some breakfast or taking a walk. We will be back on the road in an hour or so."

"Oh, breakfast sounds marvelous. Don't you think,

Jeffree?" Mrs. Baker addressed her husband as she gathered her skirts to exit. The driver extended his hand to help her to the ground.

"Yes, dear," Mr. Baker said through a yawn and hopped out.

The stranger next to me stirred. His legs stretched out and stopped, barring the door. His head was against the rear wall, the hood pulled low, and all I could see was his dimpled chin. I waited for him to move and exit the transport, but he didn't.

"Excuse me, sir. I would like to pass."

Nothing.

I wasn't about to touch him or disturb his sleep, so it forced me to step over his legs and down onto the first step.

I grabbed my bag and a handful of my skirt in my left hand, my right pressing against the roof as I tried to step over the stranger's long legs. I was about to pull my other leg over when the gentleman stirred and turned, knocking me off balance.

I let out a cry and felt myself stumble toward the open door. Firm hands grabbed me around the waist and pulled me back inside. I landed in a very warm lap.

My hood had fallen back, revealing my deep-red hair as I looked up into the bluest eyes I had seen on a man. They were a sapphire-blue and mesmerizing. His lips pulled into a half smile. I blushed.

"Excuse me," I spat out and pushed my hands against his muscular chest. "Unhand me."

"I saved you." His voice was deep; it affected me unnaturally. "You were about to fall out of the transport."

"I wouldn't need saving if you had the decency to move and allow me to pass, you big brute." I pulled my hood back over my red telltale hair.

His eyes narrowed.

The firm hand that gripped my elbow in support now thrust me away from him. I slid off his lap and landed in a thud on the floor. He pulled his legs out of my way and stared at me as I hastily left, my cheeks burning in embarrassment. There was no reason for him to treat me so rudely. I tried to wake him up, and he didn't stir.

"Basta," I uttered the fae curse word under my breath. I took pleasure in Lorn's extracurricular lessons and getting one up on the stranger. For no way could he know fae.

The waystation was one of the larger hubs for the kingdoms, as it was four transport services that shared and serviced one inn. It was the largest inn I had ever seen and served food day and night. Behind the inn were individual stables, all owned by various transport companies. Our transport pulled into the Oak and Leaf building where the stable boys wore green-and-gold tunics. Two came to attend the horses. One unhooked the first horse and led him into an empty stall for a brush down. Another boy carried a fresh bucket of what I assumed was water into the stall, but a pungent smell followed, and I doubted the contents. The fae horse almost knocked the boy over in its enthusiasm to drink the mysterious liquid.

I frowned and tried to place the scent.

"Brandy," a deep voice spoke from behind me. I heard the transport creak as the stranger stepped down. "It's better than water for the half-breed fae."

I refused to acknowledge the man and pretended he didn't exist as I spun and made my way out of the barn and followed the Bakers into the inn. The three-story inn was a large manor with an inner courtyard open to the sky. The north wing was the drivers' quarters, where they could grab a bunk and catch a few hours' rest, a hot bath, and food. The east and south wings were passenger lodgings, leaving the western wing as kitchen and tavern. The Bakers chose one of the open tables in the courtyard next to the fountain, enjoying the sun and food.

I hung back under the interior balcony and kept to a table in the shade, watching everyone with a wary eye. From my table, I could see the drivers come and go into their hall, and each slowed as they came to a notice board. Enchanted scrolls and maps were tacked on the board and were magically updated with current weather forecasts, road hazards, and bandit sightings.

A portly transport driver with a long duster jacket came in from the Wind and Ice Stables. He ran his finger along the map. He tapped it three times over a certain trail and spoke aloud. "Thunder Pass is now open. Rainfall has washed out the smaller trails. Be wary."

A giant red X that was on the road into the mountains disappeared, and the road turned green. The smaller trails along the route turned yellow in warning. It was fascinating to watch the map change as other drivers in the seven kingdoms were updating their waystation maps, and in turn, the one in this station changed as well.

Our own driver didn't even glance at the enchanted map as he rushed up the stairs and headed down the hall marked Bathing Rooms.

"Brekkie?" a soft voice asked.

"What?" I looked up as a youthful woman in a conservative blue dress, apron, and bonnet that covered soft-brown curls placed a glass of water on the table. Unlike taverns where the servants were dressed to ply their many wares, food, and other services, here they were modestly clothed.

"Brekkie?" she repeated. "Eggs, sausage, bread. It's

included in your passage fare. Anything else is an added charge."

"Oh, yes please."

The servant nodded and returned with a small plate of food. My stomach growled. With my spoon, I shoved the eggs and sausage onto my bread and folded it in half, quickly devouring it in a few bites. I worried about parceling out my money for my trip and was thankful for the small meal. After I used my finger to wipe up any leftover juice from the sausage, I felt a pang at the empty plate. I could have easily eaten two more platefuls of food.

A scurry of excitement drew my attention as the notice board changed. The map and weather notice disappeared into the background as papers shuffled to the front to be replaced by the wanted posters. Ferocious mugs of thieves and bandits appeared along the board. Few took notice. A few of the drivers looked up and shrugged.

My hand gripped my spoon. I stared at the board and waited for the inevitable. It was only a matter of time for the news to travel. With how often my mirror hummed in my purse, I knew that eventually someone would get a notice out of Nihill.

Minutes later, the flurry of posters disappeared, and the maps and weather notices fluttered and reshuffled to the front.

I let out a breath I did not know I was holding.

A platter of food dropped in front of me, and I looked up at the stranger from my transport, who took the unoccupied seat across from me.

"Mind if I sit here."

I kept my head low. "I do."

"Well, I don't." The chair scraped across the floor, and the stranger pulled it out and folded his enormous frame into the seat. His long legs again struggled to fit under the table, his knees bumping the top.

What was he, part giant?

"I fear we may have gotten off on the wrong foot," he began.

"No," I snapped. "It's because you wouldn't *move* your foot."

"Ouch!" He laughed. "That's true. But if we will journey together, I fear I may owe you an apology. I'm Brennon." A huge hand shoved across the table over my empty plate.

I still kept my head down, refusing to get a closer look. If I looked at him, that meant he had a closer look at me. He could identify me. It was easier if I ignored the offered hand and any further exchanges all together.

It pained me to do so, but I let the hand linger in the air until he withdrew it.

"I see. Seems there is no repairing what's been done."

"There will be no need," I added hastily. "For we will not be traveling together long."

"Well, we don't know that for sure. Where are you heading to?"

I shrugged. "Wherever you are not." I grabbed my plate and stood up. I decided I had to find the driver and settle up now. This new passenger was way too curious. I couldn't afford to travel farther if he was in the transport. I passed a table full of men who looked like they weren't passengers. Their clothes were dirty, and one was armed with a bandolier of knives. From the amount of empty mugs in front of them, it seemed they were in no hurry to leave. One man had long tattoos that ran up his arm, and when he saw my glance at his arms, he quickly covered them with his sleeves.

I shivered as my senses kicked in. That one had an air of

death about him. He kept his face hidden under his cloak, but I could tell he was watching me.

Instinctively, I skirted away from them. I found a bin and placed my plate there then walked toward the north wing and notice board, hoping to catch the driver as soon as he appeared or to send another driver up after him. Except I didn't remember my driver's name.

Wringing my hands, I paced in front of the boards, and when they changed again, the wanted posters reappeared, and this time the room took notice. I heard the gasps, the change in mood as the scuffling of feet and clatter of silverware paused.

I dragged my eyes to the board, and my heart dropped into my stomach. An enormous banner appeared across the entire board with the words WANTED FOR MURDER.

Beneath it, a very detailed sketch appeared, and I had the unfortunate timing to stand directly next to my portrait. There was no hiding my identity now.

Mrs. Baker pointed in my direction, her finger like a beacon as every eye turned my way. She wobbled, took a step forward, and fainted.

CHAPTER FOUR

Mrs. Baker's collapse broke the awkward silence. Chairs screeched across the floor, trays of food dropped, and many ran for the doors. The sinister-looking men lunged from their chairs after me. From the greedy and desperate look in their eye and the eagerness with which they charged, I knew they were trouble. The closest man pulled a throwing knife from his bandolier, his arm pulling back as he aimed.

I opened my mouth to sing and then froze. Nothing came out. I was paralyzed with guilt and fear. I would not be charged with murdering more innocents. Instead, I closed my eyes and waited for the strike. My punishment had finally come.

A hard body knocked me to the ground as the dagger impaled itself into the notice board with a thud.

"Idiot," Brennon muttered. He dragged me to my feet, his grasp on my wrist solid like an iron manacle, unbreakable. He forced me to follow him up the stairs to the drivers' quarters.

"Let me go!" I yelled.

"I do and you're dead."

I winced as he turned into the first private bathing room. He slammed the door and slid the lock. Heat blasted my face, and steam billowed around us like a white curtain. Brennon didn't stop. He released my hand, went to the copper pipes, and adjusted the valves so that the room filled with even more steam.

The door thudded as a body slammed into it. More banging followed as my pursuers tried to break down the door.

"This way!" Brennon grabbed my elbow. He went to the outer wall, threw open the window, and put his long leg over the sill. He held his hand out to assist me, and we both crawled out onto the thin three-inch ledge. I clung to the window frame in terror. Brennon sidestepped to the right. "Follow me."

I made the mistake of looking down, and my fingers locked up painfully.

"It's just a little farther," he coaxed.

When I didn't move, his hand grasped the fabric of my dress and pulled me after him. The terror subsided as I focused on taking one step in front of the other. Then Brennon disappeared around the corner of the building. When I followed, I saw he turned onto the west wing side and was working on breaking in another window. When it didn't give. He used his elbow to break the glass and reached through to unlock the window and pull it open. His lithe body disappeared into the dark interior.

I stared at the window and then down at the ground below. It was only two stories. I could make it if I jumped. It was either that or follow the stranger into the dark. I was about to make the leap, when he reached back out the window and dragged me inside after him.

I yelped as he caught me up in his arms, my feet dangling below me. His rough hand covered my mouth.

"Shhh," Brennon whispered. "We wouldn't want to get caught now. After all, this is just starting to get fun." His eyes twinkled with mirth.

I glared at him. How dare he think this is fun, and at my expense? I wiggled in protest and pushed at his chest.

He sucked in a quick breath. I stilled as his grip tightened around my waist.

Brennon smelled of cedar, bergamot, and outdoors, which was probably just the scent of his still damp cloak. My body pressed into his muscled chest as he slowly released me inch by inch. His eyes narrowed as he focused on my parted lips. He was hesitant to release me. When my feet found purchase on the wood floor, I put a few feet of distance between us. My heart was racing in my chest at our close contact.

Brennon moved to the door, pressed his ear to it, and listened. His hood had fallen back, and I studied my rescuer from afar. His shoulders were wide and muscled, and he had a narrow waist. His skin was tan, and his disheveled blond hair was bleached by hours in the sun. A single aquamarine stone decorated his right earlobe.

"Let's go." He opened the door. I stood there unmoving, hesitant to go out into the hall.

He frowned and beckoned, and I still refused to go closer.

In the blink of an eye, Brennon was at my side, lifting me over his shoulder like a sack of potatoes, his shoulder jabbing into my stomach painfully.

"If I didn't know better, I would think you want to get caught by those bounty hunters," he said.

Bounty hunters. I should have known they would stalk the waystations, waiting for runaways to come right to them. Brennon flew down the stairs with me over his shoulder, each step causing a painful jab that knocked the breath out of me.

He went through the kitchens, out the side door, and tossed me into a wagon loaded with... potatoes.

"Oomph!" I cried as he threw a canvas tarp over me and climbed into the driver seat. He picked up the reins, and with a cry and a flick of the whip, the two horses took off. I bounced around in the back, the potatoes rolling over and on top of me. But I didn't care. I was too scared to remove the canvas or look out as Brennon continued to drive the wagon at a breakneck speed.

After I was sure we had driven far enough to have lost them, he didn't slow down. I pulled the canvas back, grabbed a potato, and lobbed it at his head.

Thunk!

"Ouch! What was that for?" He glared at me over his shoulder.

"Stop the wagon," I demanded.

"Not until we're safe. That was the Brunes Guild. They will have every available tracker after you. If you even left so much as a piece of hair or article of clothing at the waystation, your fate will be sealed."

My hand reached for my bag, and I groaned. It was gone.

Brennon saw my unease. "What did you leave behind?" he asked.

"My bag."

He cursed under his breath. "Then it's not a matter of *if* they find you, but *when*. We have no time to lose." He spurred the horses on faster.

I tumbled backward into the potato cart. *Gah! I hate potatoes.* I couldn't understand why the stranger was helping me. I wasn't nice to him. In fact, I was purposely downright rude. The only reason he would help me was if he wanted something from me. No, not from me. *Me.* He wanted the bounty on me for himself.

This time, it was my turn to inwardly groan. Another storm system moved in, and the sun set prematurely as the inky clouds hid it. I pulled the canvas back over myself and hunkered down in the wagon as I tried to plan my escape. There wasn't any choice. I would have to jump. But leaping from a speeding wagon didn't thrill me. I could end up with broken bones, or worse, a broken neck.

The path narrowed and the woods became thicker. I heard water and looked up at the oncoming river.

This is my chance. Brennon slowed the wagon down as he forded the river. The water was only a foot deep at first, but then it became deeper. I slid to the back of the open-ended wagon and hung my feet off. I only had a few seconds before the horses pulled to the shallower end and picked up speed again. I took a blue ribbon I had used to tie back my hair and tucked it farther under a sack of potatoes. Laying down a fake trail of personal items seemed like a good way to confuse the Brunes Guild.

Lowering myself off the back, I let my legs drag into the water. I held back the gasp and on the count of three slid out the back. The water pulled me downstream, and the wagon reached the other side of the embankment. Seconds later, it was out of the riverbed and back up at a run. I watched as Brennon didn't look back but kept driving.

I had mixed feelings at seeing him ride away. Part guilt and part relief filled me, but I quickly pushed them aside as I tried to swim toward the river's edge. The current was too strong and pulled me farther downstream.

I was unprepared for the wrath of the river as it flung me about. I swallowed mouthfuls of water and was chilled to the core when it turned at a bend, and I floated past a downed tree.

With numbed hands, I grasped a limb and was about to pull myself out of the river when I heard men's voices. They were shouting, and the sound of running horses drew nearer to me. Using the dead branches as a shield, I swam under the canopy of the leaves and popped up between the foliage, keeping everything but my eyes and nose submerged.

"Here! This is where we lost her." It was one of the three bounty hunters from the waystation. He was the one who threw the knife and missed. A second man rode up, his hood covering his face. The tattoos on his arms were visible as he held up a glowing green stone in one hand and a small compact in the other.

A sorcerer.

I swallowed in anger. He was tracking me using my mirror.

"The water is disrupting the tracking spell," the sorcerer murmured. "She must have crossed the river. We will pick up her trail on the other side."

"I'm surprised the woman is giving us this much trouble. We should have caught her by now," the knife thrower grumbled.

"We'll catch her. I won't let this particular bounty get away."

I hadn't looked at the poster to even see a bounty. How much could the mayor's family put up? Surely, it must've been a mistake. But no. The way the hunters were carrying on, there was more to this bounty on my head than I originally thought.

It was a battle to keep my teeth from chattering loudly and giving away my position.

"Hey, I found fresh wagon tracks. She must have gone this way. Your stone is glowing again," a third man farther up the riverbank called out. The other two spurred their horses, and the chase was back on. I felt bad that the men would be after Brennon because I left my ribbon in his wagon. And as long as I stayed in the water, they wouldn't be able to track me.

I waited in the freezing water as long as I could before pulling myself out to the edge. It was too dangerous to stray from the river, so it forced me to walk in the water until my frozen feet could carry me no more.

CHAPTER FIVE

The Brunes Guild returned. They must have picked up my trail again and followed it back to the river. Each time they drew close, I quickly sought shelter in the rushing water and hid in brush to barely evade capture. But I couldn't hide forever. As Brennon said, they *would* eventually find me. When the coast was clear and the sound of horses faded, I left my hiding place in the water. Boots in hand, I continued to walk along the stony riverbed. A permanent chill settled into my bones, and my feet were numb. I needed to get dry clothes and find a way to avoid the Brunes Guild permanently.

My trek along the river's edge brought me to a water mill, yet it wasn't the mill that grabbed my attention but the farm-house not far away and the line of dry clothes that hung unattended.

Not just any clothes. Boy's clothes.

A plan formed in my head as a smile spread across my face. Leaving the water, I dragged my frozen body toward the line and began grabbing handfuls of clothes before making my way to the mill. The door was unbarred, so I slipped inside, where my body was surrounded by warmth. Inside, the grinding stone was still; the water had been diverted away from the chutes.

I picked up a set of shears from a worktable filled with empty flour sacks and thread. I made quick work of cutting the flour sack into strips. I shed my chemise and used the strips to bind my chest, hiding the fact that I was a woman. The brown pants and overly large gray shirt hid my curves, and the black button-up vest disguised my breasts.

On the floor was a discarded gray knit cap, and I claimed it and tried to stuff my waist-long hair beneath it. My locks were too full, turning the knit cap into a cone. I looked like a gnome. This wouldn't do.

With a dejected sigh. I gripped the scissors in one hand and took handfuls of my red hair. It would have to go. But I couldn't bring myself to shear it all off. I carefully worked with the metal blades and clumsily chopped it off to shoulder length. My head felt lighter than it had in years and easily fit under the cap.

Being careful to clean up my mess, I braided my discarded hair into six thick ropes and shoved them into an empty sack filled with my boots, sack bindings, and an extra shirt. I took a second flour sack and put my wet and discarded chemise and dress inside. I couldn't leave something so personal behind to be found.

Minutes later, I filled the sack with river stones and was careful to toss it into the middle of the river, where it slowly sunk to the bottom.

I headed off with renewed vigor. The current became stronger, and I had to leave the water as it widened and passed under a stone bridge. Leaving the river's edge, I sat on the bridge and quickly put on my stockings and leather boots. I frowned as I studied them, thankful for once for my mother's no-nonsense style. My boots could easily pass for a child's. In fact, when I passed a darkened window, I couldn't believe my luck. I smudged a handful of dirt on my cheeks and nose and knew with my petite height and stature I could pass for a boy of twelve, maybe thirteen.

But the growling of my stomach would be my downfall. I lurked outside a tavern's side door and found it was mostly empty. The town bell had rung out a candle mark ago, so I knew it had to be after midnight.

The barkeep and one elderly server were the only ones left; the rest of the staff must have retired for the night. A table in the corner was full of men who were still eating and drinking. I found my mark in a darkened corner. A bearded man, passed out drunk, his head at an awkward angle on his arm. His mouth cocked open, and a low rumble of snores fell from his lips. The bread from his dinner was left unattended on the plate next to him.

Keeping my head low, I snuck in and grabbed it and ducked under a table to eat my stolen prize, being careful to keep from bumping his knees and awaking the man.

My eagle eyes warily scrutinized the men at the far table. For all I knew, they could be more bounty hunters. But after a few minutes of listening in, I discovered that was not the case. They were sailors on their last night ashore.

"Aye, I'm not looking forward to this next journey." A sailor with cynical eyes and a mustache tapped his pipe before pointing it at the man across from him. "It was a fool's errand to come here. We're no closer to finding answers."

"Captain Pike is nigh a fool, Randall." A white-haired man in a mop cap slammed his fist down on the table. "Just desperate. He's running out of time."

43

"Aye, Howland, that be true, but I've never seen a man more possessed than our captain with finding the missing treasure from the Undersea. You have to wonder if he be right in the head."

"Right or not, he scared off young Caleb with the tongue lashing he got tonight." The younger sailor with a mess of auburn curls laughed.

"That's because when the captain boarded, he was already in a foul mood, and Caleb dropped his dinner... on the captain's lap!" Randall answered, his laughter filling the tavern. "The cabin boy's not coming back. Saw him tuck tail and run as soon after."

"Great, now I got no help in the galley," Howland swore under his breath. "I'm getting too old for this. Look at me." He held up swollen and arthritic hands. "They can barely hold a knife. How am I supposed to peel potatoes?"

"With yer toes." The young sailor cackled.

"Knock off, Jessup!" Howland made a playful swipe at his mate.

"Last call, gents," an elderly server warned them softly. She plucked up the empty tankards and waited for any more orders.

"No thanks, mistress, we be off in a few hours. We should probably get back to the *Bella Donna* before the captain sends Thorn after us," Howland answered.

"Doubt it." Jessup snickered. "He's still in his cabin, nursing that burn he got."

"What can I say?" Howland muttered. "I serve my soup hot." The men slowly stood, stretched, and made their way for the door. I left my hiding spot and followed the one called Howland but kept my distance.

The men headed through town toward the docks. Randall

and Jessup took the lead. Howland with his arthritic and bowed legs lagged behind. I thought I had done a reasonable job at hiding until he spun around and knocked me to the ground. A glint of a metal flashed in his hand as something pressed against my throat.

"Why are ye following me?" he snarled.

I blinked in surprise and tried to gather my wits about me. "I heard you might be in need of a new cabin boy." I kept my voice low to disguise my feminine register.

Howland's white, bushy eyebrows lowered as he studied me sprawled on the ground. "Where's your parents?" he asked.

"Gone," I said. Which was partially true. Mother was gone from our home at the present.

"That's too bad. Why ye want to be a cabin boy? The pay is low, and it's backbreaking work."

"I'm stronger than I look."

"Then ye be running from something." He pulled away, and I saw that what I thought was a dagger was actually a spoon. Howland had taken me down with a dull utensil. I was mortified.

"Isn't everyone?" I sat up and shrugged, hoping to look as pathetic as I felt. "I mean, we're all trying to avoid our past."

Howland rubbed the back of his neck. "Aw heck, yer right. I do need the help." He reached down with his hand and helped me to my feet.

My hands reached up to adjust my cap and make sure my hair was still covered.

"Captain Pike is hard but fair. The *Bella Donna* sails at first light. Don't be late."

"Thank you!" I exclaimed and quickly tried to hide my exuberance.

"Go and get your things and say your goodbyes to anyone

who means anything to you. It will be awhile before we return to Fairehaven Port."

I nodded. Howland turned and headed through the darkened streets toward the docks.

Loud voices echoed from behind me, and I turned in fear. Horse hooves clattered on the stone, and the torchlights flickered on the buildings as they headed my direction. The hunters had arrived like I knew they eventually would. I strayed too far from a moving water source.

Unwilling to give up this easily, I turned toward the docks, hoping to make it to the ocean. But I didn't want Howland to see a bunch of people chasing me. A quick glance over my shoulder told me I would never make it. They were about to crest the hill by the tavern, and when they did, they would have a full view of the city street and me.

Shaking my head and groaning at my predicament, I slowed my steps and stepped into a watering trough, the chill of the water making my skin crawl. I sat down and had to hold back an audible gasp. Taking a deep breath, I submerged my head and waited.

A few seconds later, they passed me.

It was odd to open my eyes and watch the blurred reflection of the riders in black and their horses ride by. I saw the golden flame of the torch pass and the soft ethereal glow of the stone. Then it was dark again.

I stayed still until my lungs burned from lack of oxygen, and finally when I could take it no more, I sat up. Water dripped down my face, having thoroughly soaked my knit cap.

"This will get annoying quick," I muttered to myself. I stepped out of the watering trough and tried the best I could to wring out my clothes.

Dripping wet and alone in the middle of the cobbled

street, I suddenly felt vulnerable and out in the open. Sunrise was still hours away, and I worried about staying hidden until then. Where was I going to hide until the ship set sail?

I turned to the right down a side street and reached into the sack for a braided band of my hair. Clutching the braid, I pivoted, and with a mighty throw, I tossed it onto the roof of what looked like a very large inn.

I grinned and continued to run down the street. Taking shelter in a darkened doorway, I watched as the bounty hunters circled back around, led by the man with the seeker stone. It grew brighter when he approached the inn, and so did his greedy smile.

"She's here, boys."

A second man pounded on the door, and after a lengthy pause, a sleepy innkeeper answered it.

"We have a writ that allows us to search the premises for a fugitive." The bounty hunter flung a yellowed paper in front of the innkeeper's nose.

"A what?" he mumbled. The men thrust him aside as they barged into the establishment.

Cries of distress were heard and lanterns were lit when the search began. Only one man remained outside, and he was busy holding the horses.

"Now, hold on there!" the innkeeper cried out.

Many of the patrons didn't take kindly to being woken and having their rooms searched, and I used the distraction to slink back away into the night, being very careful to tuck and toss my other hair braids into various establishments. Another inn, a pleasure house, and a tavern. Just for fun, I tossed a braid down a latrine.

I snickered when I imagined the men deciding who would go down there to search for me. My mother would be very proud of my resourcefulness. After I laid my fake trail, I slipped down to the pier and found a covered rowboat moored to the stone wall. Grateful for a place that was dry and out of the wind, I slid under the canvas and curled into a ball and tried to rest my eyes. The gentle bob of the rowboat on the water, and the knock of the wood as it swayed into the dock, eventually lulled me to sleep.

But my sleep was restless and my dreams chaotic.

I had never seen the ocean before, and in the light of day and from a distance, the gentle swell looked beautiful. A picture painted by a master's hand, one to be admired from afar. The subtle waves were like a soothing mistress that beckoned to a lost lover. There was no end in sight. The blue horizon went on forever, and on the skyline, there wasn't a speck of land. At that moment, sailing into that unknown seemed unfathomable.

I stepped off the stone pier onto the wooden dock that led to the large three-mast ship, the *Bella Donna*, and my heartbeat thrummed in my ears. The dock moved with the sway of the water, and my mouth went dry in fear. I was wrong. The waves were not a gentle mistress but a tyrannical overlord, and I was the wayward servant about to be beaten down for my failure to bow to its power.

My legs betrayed me, and I collapsed to my knees, my vision blurry, my chest compressing, and my lungs ready to explode. Frantically, I crawled off the dock to the safety of the stone pier and slowly regained my composure.

The *Bella Donna* had already begun preparations for departure. I could see the sailors bringing the last of the provisions on board, and they were unfurling their masts. Once it pulled from the slip and sailed away, so would my escape plan. But the dock seemed too long and the ship so small. Surely it would be battered and tossed about at the first sign of a storm.

"C'mon, Meri girl," I muttered to myself. "Pull yourself together."

I adjusted the stocking cap, pulling it low over my brows, and made sure I tucked all my red hair away. With a quick pat on my vest, I made sure my disguise was still firmly in place.

I tried to take another step onto the dock, but my nerves abandoned me, and I stood frozen for a second time. This time, it was regret that held me back. By stepping aboard, I might never set foot on this land again. I might never see my sisters or adoptive mother.

"Hey, you. Boy!" a guttural cry came from behind me.

"What?" I answered, turning with my head bowed. My eyes stayed on the black boots of the speaker.

"Have you seen this girl?"

He shoved a rough parchment under my nose. I stepped back to let my eyes adjust and took in the Wanted poster with my picture on it. I quickly glanced at the speaker, revealing the uniform of the town's guard. At least it wasn't one of the Brunes Guild.

Keeping my head down, I shook my head.

"Look again," the guard demanded, his firm hand digging into my shoulder. I held back my cry of pain.

"No, I haven't," I said.

I turned, grabbed my sack, and tossed it over my shoulder. No sooner had I turned my back did the guard's boot kick me in the back and sent me tumbling onto the dock.

"That's 'no, sir' to you. You lowlife scum!" he sneered and spat on the wood in front of me.

It took every ounce of self-preservation to keep my head

down in a subservient fashion. His boot to my rump was the final prompting I needed to get moving. I grabbed my sack and picked up my pace, half running toward the ship, not even slowing as I ran up the boarding plank.

In my hurry to board, my foot caught on an excess rigging line. I tumbled forward, landed face-first on the deck, my jaw smacking the wood, and I groaned.

"What in blazes are you doing here?" a gruff voice questioned. A hand gripped my shirt behind my neck, and I was lifted into the air. My feet dangled below me like a rag doll, my teeth rattling in my mouth like dice.

"I think we have a stowaway, men!" The man swung me about, showing me off.

A sea of dirty faces swam before me until I only saw the one who pulled me close and threatened me. "What say we tie him up and give him thirty lashes, eh? That will teach him to stow aboard the *Bella Donna!*"

A roar of approval came from the gathered men. My stomach rolled and dropped, my hands clasping the front of my shirt and vest to keep it from riding up and exposing my chest bindings.

"That, Fang, is the new cabin boy. And I suggest ye drop 'im before he runs away like the last one." Howland came to my rescue. The older man had come from below deck, and in his arthritic hand was his chef's knife.

The deck flew toward me, as I was carelessly dropped without warning. I landed on my rump and had to hold back a gasp of pain. I stumbled to my feet, grabbed my sack, and sought shelter behind Howland.

I looked up into Fang's face and felt fear. His deep-set, shrewd eyes sized me up, and I could tell he found me wanting. Part of his earlobe was missing, and he caught me staring at the deformed ear. He sneered at me in disdain. "Then make sure the rat pulls his weight on board or we will find out if rats can swim."

"C'mon, boy." Howland turned and nudged me toward the stairs below deck. "It's best if we stay out of Fang's sight."

I stood frozen on the step as I contemplated my actions. They had already raised anchor, the gangplank stowed, and we were moving away from the dock. I could still make it. If that was the reception from one man on the ship, Captain Pike surely would be worse. No wonder Caleb, the last cabin boy, ran away.

I dropped my bag and made my way to the railing, my hand grasping the warm wood, and I adjusted my weight, preparing to jump overboard.

Then I saw them.

The Brunes Guild gathered on the dock. The leader, a formidable-looking foe in his dark robe, sat upon his horse, holding the green glowing stone as it pulsed brightly.

"The ship. She's on the ship!" he roared, pointing at our departing vessel.

Others heard him, and they scrambled back down the dock to try to find another way to catch me. A small fishing vessel wouldn't be fast enough, and I knew of the other ships in the harbor that none were ready to sail. If they could find another ship willing to take them, then they would only be a few hours behind me.

But surely they'd give up... right?

I stepped away from the railing and glanced upon the ship. Men climbed the masts and tightened the mainsails. Others were using pulleys to lower the rest of the barrels of fresh water below deck. Fang found another to be the target of his wrath, and I couldn't help but wince when I heard the man yell. His deep voice was made for bellowing orders.

"I wouldn't blame ye if ye jump and swim for it," Howland spoke softly. He had come up beside me and put a reassuring hand on my shoulder. "Stars know I've thought about it a time or two. It's yer last chance."

My breath shuddered as the men on the dock became as small as ants. The threat faded away with each gust of wind that blew into the *Bella Donna*'s sails. "There's nothing for me here."

"She can be a dangerous mistress, the sea."

I gathered my courage and turned to face Howland. "Then teach me to become her master."

CHAPTER SIX

"Ye peel faster than the last lad." Howland whistled when he saw my full bucket of skinned potatoes. My back was sore from leaning over the peelings most of the morning, but I was grateful for the menial task to keep my mind and hands occupied. But the irony of peeling potatoes was not lost on me. Howland tossed me an apple, and I caught it with one hand.

"Let's see how ye fare with that," he teased.

I grinned, adjusted the paring knife in my hand, and quickly took the peel off the apple in one long curl. I held the peel in the air and chucked it into my waste bucket. Then I held out the freshly peeled apple to him.

"Naw, that's for ye, boy."

"Thanks." I tried not to drool as I took a mouthful. The juices ran down my chin, and I used the back of my hand to wipe it away. The apple was heaven, and I didn't realize how hungry I was until I had taken that bite. I made quick work of my snack, tossed the core in the bucket, and went to work on the carrots.

Howland came and took the three-legged stool across from

me. He grunted as he lowered his form onto the seat and stretched his short legs out in front. He wiped the sweat from his brow with a rag and then gave me a searching look. "I never did ask yer name. Have to write it down on the manifest. Can't keep callin' ye 'boy.'"

The carrot almost fell from my clumsy fingers. I hadn't thought of the issue with my name. Meri was short for Merisol, but both were feminine in nature.

"I uh..." I stammered and tried to think quickly. "Merrill."

"Merrill?" he asked. "Ye don't sound too sure."

"No, it's Merrill, but everyone used to call me Meri."

Howland snorted. "Aye, now I understand yer hesitance."

My cheeks burned, but the low light of the galley hid my discomfort.

"I almost forgot. I informed the captain early this morn of your enlistment. He does not want to be bothered. Seems he drank too much last night and is still recoverin'."

Great. The captain is a drunkard. This did not bode well.

"Does he always drink in excess?" I asked hesitantly.

Howland's forehead creased in thought. "No, not usually. Yesterday was different. Somethin' happened that set him on edge. I dare not ask. But just stay away from him when he's in these dark moods, and ye should be fine. In the meantime, I've been tasked with havin' ye sign this." He got up from his stool and pulled out an old leather-bound book. "Sign yer name, birthdate, and age. Contract be for a year and a day."

"What is the purpose of this?" I asked.

"So, when the year is up, ye receive yer wages. And also, if our ship goes down, we know who to inform of yer death."

It was a solemn moment as I used the quill to sign Merrill Nihill, age twenty. A version of my name and my town. Hopefully, if something ever happened to me, my family could figure out the pseudonym.

Howland kept me busy for most of the morning, and I was sweating bullets under my stocking cap. But it wasn't until Howland took me on a tour of the *Bella Donna* and showed me to the berth that I realized how extremely foolish my venture was. I could never pass as a boy.

The crew slept on the wide-open gun deck. Their hammocks hung from the ceiling between the cannons, everyone in the same room. Except for those of higher ranks, who may have shared bunks or had their own private quarters like the captain.

"Where do I sleep?" I asked hesitantly, never having imagined the close and confined sleeping quarters.

"Well, I suppose ye'd take Caleb's hammock." Howland pointed to the jumble of canvas that hung closest to the stairs. "He's not going to need it. Unless ye'd rather be farther back by the infirmary. It can get quite drafty this close to the stairs. But you also need to be up at first light to help the captain."

"What?" I questioned, dumbfounded. "What do you mean help the captain?"

"Are ye daft? Yer his cabin boy. Ye not only help me, but ye serve him meals and clean his room and, when needed, help him dress."

"What? He can't get dressed on his own?"

"That's part of the job, Merrill. Ye wait hand-and-foot on the captain."

I shook my head and backed away. I was a fool. I should have thrown myself overboard and took my chances with the bounty hunters.

"I need air," I blurted quickly.

"Go. Go. Get above deck. You'll get yer sea legs soon."

I abandoned the tour and ran up the stairs onto the main deck and up to the quarterdeck. I didn't stop until I reached the stern of the ship.

There was only blue for as far as the eye could see. I was trapped aboard a floating prison, surrounded by men who would not take lightly to a female if discovered. Maybe I should have taken my chances and waited for a passenger ship to come into dock at Fairehaven. But who knew how long I would have been able to avoid the bounty hunters?

Dread filled my soul, and tears stung my eyes as I dwelled on my circumstances. I killed a man and was wanted for murder. I would face my death at sea or on land. I couldn't run from it.

Movement in the water caught my eye, and I stared into aquamarine depths at the shadows that passed under the keel of the ship. Confused, I watched the shapes move farther back, and then one crested the water.

I gasped.

A silver creature with a horn jumped into the air before diving back into the sea, his massive tail hitting the water play-fully. A second horned creature followed suit, and they jumped and dove, playing in the trails of the ship.

"They're a sign of good luck," a voice spoke behind me. "Which means our voyage will be blessed."

I glanced over my shoulder at the speaker and froze. One of the most graceful men I had ever seen sat on a crate, a short wooden flute in his lap. He was so quiet, I passed right by and didn't even notice him. His long, jet-black hair was tied back at the nape of his neck. He was slim and looked to have been carved out of marble his features were so perfect. His eyes were the darkest green rimmed in gold. Dressed in all black, with an intricate necklace of shark teeth, and the handles of two short swords peeked over his shoulder.

"I didn't mean to intrude."

"You're not. I'm Vasili." He gave me a nod and then fixed his eyes back onto the flute in his lap.

"I'm Mer—rill, the new cabin boy." I drug out my name, as I was still getting used to saying it.

Vasili scrutinized me. "You're awful scrawny for a cabin boy. You sure you can handle the work?"

"I can handle it," I said assuredly.

Vasili's fingers froze on his flute. "Time will tell." He placed it to his lips and blew softly. His eyes took on a faraway gaze as he stared at the ocean.

The creatures in the water drew my gaze.

"What are they called?" I asked breathlessly.

He pulled the flute away from his lips. I could feel the magic in the air lessen, as if magic itself was listening to Vasili's music.

"Narwhals, the unicorns of the sea."

"Narwhals," I repeated. "I've never seen one before. Well, I've never sailed before."

Vasili puckered his lips and hopped down off the crate to stand next to me. I could feel his nearness, and his arm brushed my shoulder. "Then you are in for quite an adventure." His hand came down and patted the top of my head, knocking my hat askew.

I grabbed my knit hat and ducked, backing away to put as much distance between us. "Don't touch me!" I yelled.

My outcry confused Vasili. His green-gold eyes blinked as his hand retreated. "I didn't mean any harm. Believe me."

My breathing ragged from almost being caught, I raced down the steps to the main deck and headed below, searching for a dark corner where I could feel my hair and tuck any stray hairs back under. That was too close. I had only been here a few hours, and I almost blew my cover. I would just need to learn to keep my distance.

"Boy!" Howland's voice carried from the galley, and I took off running, unsure how long he had been searching for me.

"Yes, Howland?" I came rushing into the room and saw a silver tray and dome laid out on the table.

"Take that to the captain."

"The c-captain?"

Howland's white brows furrowed. "Yes, Captain Pike. The captain of the *Bella Donna*, ye twit. He be in a foul mood and is asking for his breakfast."

"It's afternoon," I said in disbelief.

"Don't matter none. It be the captain's orders."

"Right." Rushing forward, I grabbed the tray, and it shook in my hands. Even though it was past noon, I kept the verbal retort to myself.

Howland eyed the trembling tray. "Don't ye dare spill his breakfast on him, or ye may find yerself cuffed on the head or worse, thrown overboard."

I briefly recalled that the last boy Caleb had been so terrified of the captain's wrath that he ran away.

I nodded in understanding and carefully turned to carry the tray past the first mate's bunk room and to the captain's quarters. My hands were full, and I wasn't sure what to do, so I kicked the door with my foot.

"Come in," a deep voice answered.

I eyed the door handle, raised one leg, and batted at the handle, trying to open it with my foot while being careful not to spill the tray or lose my balance.

The door swung inward, and I stood there like an idiot, balanced on one foot, my other hanging awkwardly in the air.

"Most would have put the tray down to open the door," the voice chastised from within the gloomy room, assumingly from the bed.

Terrified I had already made a spectacle and been a nuisance, I entered the room and quickly searched for a place to deposit the tray. Keeping my head down, I attempted to not make eye contact with the owner of the voice.

The captain's quarters were at the back of the ship below the navigational room. The far wall was full of beautifully paneled windows that overlooked the sea. Red drapes hid most of them but one window. The room comprised a large four-poster bed secured to the floor and a long table that could seat six. The room had little clutter, for most of the personal items were stored away in ornate chests and trunks so as not to roll or fall onto the floor. Hooks along the wall held the captain's long, black, hooded cloak and hat.

I placed the serving tray on the table and raised the dome to reveal soft-boiled eggs, warm rolls, butter, and jam. Different from the plain oatmeal the rest had eaten. I boarded after breakfast and my stomach growled. Stepping back, I awaited orders. The captain had not risen from his bed.

I couldn't keep the frown of disapproval from my face. *What kind of captain laid abed all day while his men work?*

He got out of bed, stepped out of the shadows, and passed in front of the great windows to grab his shirt off the back of a chair, and I gasped. One, because when he passed in front of the light, I saw just how tall he was. He was giant, and thick muscles covered his back.

His head shot up at my gasp, and those eyes glared at me. I could feel his anger like a knife.

The captain moved away from the window, and I still couldn't get a good look at his face. His sheer size distracted me. The captain put on his shirt and turned his attention to the food in front of him, his back facing me.

He picked up a knife and buttered his roll. "What are your skills?" he asked.

"Skills?" I repeated numbly.

"You signed on as a cabin boy. I expect you are here to learn the ways of sailing, but I also want to know what else you can do." He tossed the knife back onto the plate.

"Uh, I can mend, wash, clean, and cook."

"Geez, you sound like a woman." He turned around, the light hitting his face just right, and we both froze.

Captain Pike was *the giant*. I mean, the captain was *Brennon*, the traveler who I escaped on the road, only to wind up trapped on a ship with him. Not just any ship. *His* ship.

I was only lucky that it was dark and stuffy in the room and he hadn't given me his full attention until now.

Brennon stared at me. His eyes narrowed suspiciously. "Come into the light," he demanded.

I berated myself for not having the gift of glamour like Eden, where I could easily change my appearance. I hesitated, and he slammed his fist down on the table.

"Now!" he roared.

I scampered forward to the table where the light from the window illuminated me, but I kept my eyes lowered. I couldn't control my hands from trembling, and I clasped them behind my back.

Brennon leaned over the table to study me. "You look sickly."

I sucked my breath in at the insult. "I assure you I am not."

He leaned closer, his face inches from mine. His eyes

scanned my face, and then he looked up at my knit hat. He frowned. He seemed displeased with what he saw, but I hoped the dirt I had smudged on my face helped disguise me. I focused on the white cowrie shells he wore around his neck.

Brennon pulled out the chair, sat, and gestured to the bottle of wine and the goblet on the tray. I stood rooted to the spot for three seconds and saw his fist raise to cuff me, and I lurched forward. Grabbing the bottle, I pulled the cork with my teeth and poured him a glass. The fragrance of the wine tickled my nose. He must've been nursing a hangover for him to need a drink this early.

He swirled the contents in the glass. "It is hard work being a cabin boy. You've signed on and are now tasked with handling all the grueling demands of the ship—" His voice lowered. "—and her captain."

There was an underlying threat to his words, and I knew the color must have drained from my face.

"But take heed. I have been known to be a fair master. I've only had to flog one of my cabin boys in the past." He flashed me a wicked grin, and I was proud that my legs did not buckle beneath me.

When I said nothing in retort, he frowned again then went back to his breakfast. It was an agonizing and silent affair, as he directed me to stand a few feet away where he could watch me the entire time he ate. When he peeled an egg, he would sprinkle it with salt from the salt cellar on the table and eat it in one bite.

I tried to keep my face neutral as he tore into the warm roll, slathering it with the jam, licking the sugary substance from his fingers instead of using a napkin.

My stomach betrayed me with a low growl. Brennon

stopped, the hot roll inches from his mouth. My mouth was watering, and he leaned back and held out the roll to me.

I turned my head and ignored the offering. I didn't need his handouts.

Brennon stood up, his chair screeched across the floor. The roll in his hand, he moved in front of me and put it an inch from my mouth. My eyes and stomach betrayed me again.

I pinched my lips tight and shook my head.

"I order you, as your captain, to eat."

I raised my hand to take it from him, but he pulled it away. He brought it back to my mouth and waited. He would lord his power over me by feeding me. I opened, and Brennon pressed the roll into my mouth. Waiting for me to take a bite.

The warm roll melted in my mouth; the sweetness of the jam made me moan in pleasure. Brennon was watching my reaction closely. I looked at the other half in his hand expectantly and licked my lips.

His mouth parted, and I heard him inhale. "Here." He thrust it into my hands and headed back to his breakfast.

When he was done, he waved me to take the tray away. I was glad to do so and leave the company of the captain.

"And when you are finished in the galley, you are to return here to clean."

"Yes," I grumbled out moodily.

"What was that, boy?"

"I said yes, Captain Pike."

"That's better."

I left the room with a bitter taste in my mouth.

CHAPTER SEVEN

I walked to the galley below the gun deck. It was wide and comprised of a cast-iron stove, built-in shelves, a long wooden table for food prep, and bench seating. Along the back wall were cupboards with slotted shelves that stored the tin plates and serving bowls. Barrels of brined meats, pickled fish, hardtack, bags of flour, beans, oats, salt, and lots of ale and wine filled the rest of the space.

One of the advantages I learned of going to port was access to fresh meat and vegetables for the next few days instead of the normal dried and pickled fare we would all be receiving at sea.

On the far end of the kitchen was a small stall, where a milking goat and chickens in wooden crates were kept. On our earlier tour, I saw there were more livestock kept farther below in the bottom of the boat. But Howland had a soft spot for Pickle, his goat who lived in the galley.

Because the weather was fair, we carried the stockpot of soup and a crate full of bowls up to the main deck and served the meal. In inclement weather, the crew would eat in their berth or cook their rations in cook boxes which were boxes with metal bottoms filled with sand. While I was happy to be in the fresh air, I was in direct line of sight of Captain Pike. Fang was next to him, his voice raised, arms flailing as he vented about some new complaint.

I hoped it wasn't about me.

Howland nodded toward my enemy. "Ye best stay clear of Fang. Ye already got on his nerves and therefore have a target on yer back."

"Why?"

"He be the quartermaster. It's his job to enact the captain's orders and deal out punishments."

"Why is he even on this ship if he's so cruel?" I asked hesitantly.

"Because the previous captain of the *Bella Donna* was Fang's father. The captain didn't want to remove the man from the only home he ever knew."

"How did Brennon become captain over Fang? Why didn't it go to the son?"

"That's not how the line of succession works. The *Bella Donna* is the fastest ship in the sea, and her captain, Captain Saverge, was the fiercest sailor. If ye wanted to learn, ye learned from the best. Brennon worked his way up. When Captain Saverge died, Brennon challenged for Captain of the *Bella Donna*, fought Fang in hand-to-hand combat, and won."

My eyes drifted to Fang, and for a split second, I felt sorry for the man who lost his inheritance, but when I saw him verbally abuse a slow sailor, I changed my mind.

I scooped the soup and held it out as the next hungry sailor approached.

"What about him?" I asked. Pointing toward a bull of a

man with a gray tricorn pulled over his dark and greasy hair. He seemed to be Fang's shadow, never far from the man.

"Thorn, like Fang, is from the old crew. Although I have to say he's nicknamed Thorn because of the way he yields the whip. For each strike is like a thousand thorns raking across yer skin. He could flay a man like a fish and leave him still standin' to within an inch of life."

Vasili came to get his dinner. Even though he had a very relaxed persona, there was a dangerous air about him, like a string of a bow pulled tight. I had no doubt that at any minute he could attack.

Howland followed my gaze, and when Vasili was out of hearing distance, he whispered under his breath, "He's from the Undersea." The awe with which Howland said Undersea wasn't lost on me. I heard they were fierce warriors.

Vasili gave a wary and cursory sniff of the dinner. When he thought no one was looking, he dumped it over the side of the ship.

I pinched my lips to hide my mirth.

To have a member of the Undersea on board the ship and so close to me, made him even more fascinating. There was something in the way he moved; it was fluid, like water, his eyes so dark they gleamed with a hidden danger.

"Why is he here?" I asked. "I mean, aboard the *Bella Donna* and not in the Undersea?"

Howland gave a shrug and dished out another portion of soup and biscuit to the next crew member in line. "He left that place long ago and is the captain's friend. The two are inseparable."

I wanted to ask a zillion more questions about the Undersea, but I bit my tongue. I knew it wasn't the right time or place. I followed Vasili's movements through lowered lashes.

Why didn't he eat any of the meat stew? What about it offended him?

"Look at how happy they be now," Howland said as the last crew member scuttled off with his bowl. "Just wait until the fresh meat is gone and it's back to pickled fish and dried rations. Then they be threaten'n us."

I took a towel, wrapped it around the pot handle, and carried it back down to the galley. There wasn't anything left but scrapings. Just looking at the empty pot made my stomach growl.

"Here." Howland pulled out a bowl of stew and a biscuit.

"Where did you get it?" I asked. It was like he pulled the meal out of thin air.

"Why, I always pull my share out first and hide it before I serve. Otherwise, there ne'er be enough for old Howland." He gave me a sly wink. "Just keep that in mind. Aboard the ship, things aren't always fair. And it's not man's law we follow but that of the captain and the sea."

"Duly noted," I answered and dug into the stew. Even cold, it still had a good amount of flavor.

I went back up on deck to grab the crate that was filled with discarded dirty bowls and took those back down to wash them. When the meal was cleaned up, I grabbed a full bucket of soap, rags, and brush and headed up to the captain's room. Thankfully, he hadn't returned to his quarters, so it left me alone. I opened the door to let in more light and pulled back the curtains over the remaining windows. Letting the light stream through revealed the hidden layer of dust and salt that coated the room. The last cabin boy must have been lax in his duties.

Well, I would give the captain no reason to cuff me or find fault with my work.

I vented all of my frustration about my circumstances over the last few days on the floor. I scrubbed it until it shined and bruises formed along my knees, cursing under my breath at my own predicament. When I was done with the floor, I took the bucket out to the deck and dumped the water overboard. Then I went back and opened up the captain's trunks and wrinkled my nose at how haphazardly the books were tossed in. Brennon had very little personal possessions in his trunks other than the books. It was the nature of the books that surprised me the most.

Books on poetry, history, and myths and legends of the Artilleon Sea. The last volume was called *The Undersea*. The cover was deep-blue and not made of leather but of fish scales with a gold whirl design. I flipped open the book and saw the swirls of colors and dots that perforated the pages. It was like no language I had ever seen or heard of.

But as I held the book, the words blended together, shifted, and changed into a language I could read.

I dove in, skimming to the part that seemed to have been folded back and poured over the most. The book spoke of the sea and how the sea loved her people and bestowed upon them a valuable gift. That gift was a powerful treasure that would protect all who dwelled within and above water. They chose the strongest and fiercest warriors of the Undersea to guard the treasure day and night. They had successfully done so for centuries.

"What are you doing?" Brennon's stern voice startled me.

The book toppled from my fingers to the floor. I winced at my folly.

"N-nothing," I said.

"You are to clean. Not snoop," he reprimanded. Brennon

snatched the book from the floor and pocketed it in his long jacket.

"Yes, Captain." I closed the trunk and looked wistfully toward the book he hid. I wished to know the secrets hidden within.

Brennon spun, and I could tell he was about to lay into me with heated words, but then he noticed the shining and clean floor. "Y-you—" Brennon stuttered and looked around the room. "—cleaned?"

"You ordered me to," I said, confused.

Brennon rubbed the back of his unruly hair and said, "It's never.... I mean, no one has ever cleaned it like this before."

I kept my face still while inwardly rolling my eyes. "Excuse me, for I must help Howland with supper." I struggled to rise to my feet and left without being dismissed.

The rest of the day flew by, and I was ready to fall over with exhaustion from being on the run and having very little sleep the night before in the rowboat. I headed up to the main deck, and the crew was in a merry mood and celebrating with music and dancing.

Three of the crew members brought out their instruments while the rest clapped and stomped the deck in rhythm to the upbeat sea chanty, about ladies, drinking, and the sea.

Jessup was a marvel at the violin, Conroy cut the night air with a melody on his wooden flute, and Adair's sweet tenor of a voice almost made me cry. I found a perch in a coil of rope where I could sit and observe the men sing and dance. The cares of the world were gone, and I could just relax. My scalp was sweaty and itchy from working all day, and I worried how I would keep myself clean once I started to smell.

But not everyone was keen to listen to the music. Fang and

Thorn were having a quiet argument. One that was not meant for prying ears nor mine if I hadn't blended into the shadows.

"I wasn't able to unload the goods," Thorn grumbled.

"Shhh," Fang said. "Now's not the place. Is it hidden?"

"No one will find them. It's fine."

I knew that if they discovered me eavesdropping, I would probably be in for a tongue lashing and a physical one.

When Vasili drew near, they stopped talking and immediately headed below deck. Once they left, the mood on deck lightened.

"How was your first day?" Vasili leaned on the deck rail.

"Exhausting."

"I came to apologize for my behavior earlier."

"It's fine. I overreacted."

"But I should have been more aware. And for that I am sorry." He touched his chest and bowed his head. There was such a refinement in his actions that I couldn't help but wonder why he was working on this ship. He gave me a farewell and headed to his room.

Although the music called to me, exhaustion took over, and I found my head dropping. It was time for me to retire.

I quietly slipped away and headed down the steps and into the galley. I took my sack of extra clothes out of a cupboard and climbed back up to the berth deck. I carefully unwrapped the hammock and attached it to the far hook to secure it. With a jump, I hopped into it, tucked my bag under my head, and wrapped the sides up close over me. Seconds later, I drifted off to sleep.

"Boy!" Howland hissed down at me from the steps of the main deck. "Boy! Look sharp."

Someone grabbed the side of the hammock and lifted. I tumbled out and tried to catch myself as I hit the ground hard.

I sucked in my breath as my wrist bent at an odd angle.

Heavy footfalls stopped, and I saw thick black boots. One lifted to kick me, but I rolled away, knocking into another crew member who was preparing for bed.

"What!" I snapped. Regaining my feet, I cradled my injured wrist and came face-to-face with Fang.

"The captain is calling for you!" Fang snarled.

I blinked and looked around at the cabin full of men who were in various stages of undress as they prepared to sleep for the night. I ducked under my hammock and jumped over Fang's foot as it came around to kick me again, and I scampered up the stairs, using my good hand to slap the steps.

Fang's deep laugh followed my reckless escape as I dashed forth to the captain's quarters. I didn't need to knock, because the door was already open, and the lights were dim.

"Yes, Captain," I spoke aloud to a darkened room.

Brennon stepped from behind the door and closed it. The latch closed with an ominous click.

I swallowed nervously. All moisture had disappeared from my mouth.

Brennon removed his captain's jacket and tossed it over a chair. I moved to hang it up on the wood peg on the wall, and then when I turned back around, I gasped.

He tossed his shirt on the floor, and I stared at his bronzed bare chest. He moved to sit on his bed and tugged at his long boots then stopped and gazed at me expectantly. Waiting.

I hesitated. Catching the hidden meaning, I knew what he wanted, but surely he wouldn't ask me to come nearer. It wasn't proper. But then I remembered—I was a boy. I kneeled on the floor before him, grasped the heel with my hands, and pulled hard. It didn't budge. Panicking, I stood and yanked, throwing my body weight into it. It was impossible.

I glared at the boot. Brennon seemed to enjoy my attempts.

"Maybe if you helped instead of being dead weight," I snapped, losing my patience.

He cocked his head. "Are you saying I'm not helping?" He leaned back on his elbows, and the muscles in his chest flexed.

My mouth went dry.

Oh stars. This is too much.

"How about you point your toes," I said in desperation.

He did. The boot slid off, and I went flying backward, landing on my backside. I cried out as it jostled my injured wrist.

Brennon saw the way I cradled my arm. His eagle eyes locked on the swelling. "What happened?" His voice was a low growl.

"I injured it earlier."

"How?" he demanded. "Did someone harm you?"

My eyes dropped to my feet. "I fell out of the hammock."

Brennon's laugh was deep, from the chest, and his blond head fell back and took full enjoyment at my predicament. "No worries, you'll get your sea legs soon enough. Here." He finished taking off his other boot, tossing it to the floor, and went to the one trunk I hadn't explored earlier. He pulled out a roll of bandages and motioned for me to take a seat at the table.

Perplexed and a little curious, I watched as he inspected my wrist, lifting it one way and then the next.

"Does this hurt?"

"No."

"How about now?" He moved it a few inches, and I inhaled through my teeth.

The sound I made drew his attention to my face. His thumb rested on the underside of my wrist, and his gaze rested on my parted lips.

My heart raced, and I knew he could probably feel it pulse beneath his fingers.

I faked a cough and pulled my hand away. The corner of his mouth curled up as he held back his grin. He took a roll of cotton and carefully bandaged my wrist. Even though his hands were large, his touch was gentle, and I had to focus on a knot in the wood grain on the wall so as not to stare into his mesmerizing sea-blue eyes that kept flickering to me every few seconds.

"There," he said proudly and waited. My wrist was expertly bandaged with enough support and give that I could still use it.

"Thanks," I muttered. "Is that all you need help with tonight?" I asked and stood to escape out the door. My panic must have been evident on my face, because he stopped me.

"Uh, Mer—rill, is it?"

"Yes?"

"Isn't there something you need to tell me?" he asked softly.

"Uh... nope." I said and looked about warily.

"Fine," he snapped. "You're dismissed."

I bowed and left as quickly as I came.

CHAPTER EIGHT

The following days at sea followed a particular rhythm. I would wake up before dawn, get dressed, and head to the galley to prepare biscuits and dried meat and hand out the daily rations with Howland. Then I'd run a tray of more luxurious food to the captain and then return to the galley. By day two, I removed my wrist bandage and was almost back to full use.

Ever since that first day, when I made a fool of myself removing Brennon's boots, he never asked me to attend him while he dressed. And he was always fully clothed when I entered. He ignored me when I brought his food, and I waited in a corner until he finished, and I returned later to tidy his room. I spent the rest of my daylight hours in the humid galley, sweating the days away. It was on the seventh day, when I brought Brennon his dinner, that he wrinkled his nose.

"Boy, you stink," he snapped.

I turned my head and slyly sniffed my clothes. They were ripe.

Most of the crew used seawater to rinse and wash their

bodies and clothes. I had found very little alone time to do so for fear of revealing my feminine features. And whenever it washed off, I would apply more dirt to my face. I didn't think I smelled any worse than the other crew members. In fact, I couldn't walk past Thorn without gagging. But I was the only one who came close to the captain in a small, confined space. Maybe he just had a sensitive nose.

I didn't answer. I learned that the best way to protect my identity was to pretend I was mute. I bobbed my head.

"Tell Crowley to bring in my bathing tub and have the men fill it with hot water."

I was more than happy to oblige, running out to the deck and calling up to the crow's nest where he was on lookout. Crowley was one of the nicer crewmen, and I found him to be jolly and good-natured. He promised to get right on it for the captain.

In a candle mark, they had the large metal tub brought into the captain's quarters and filled with warm water from buckets brought up from the galley. They left, and I was alone in the room with the captain. I stared at the steam rising from the tub, and I desperately wished to be the one soaking in it.

"Strip," Brennon commanded.

"What? No!" I backpedaled away from the steaming water-filled tub.

Brennon shook his head and pointed. "Boy, your stench offends me greatly."

"It's not that bad," I argued.

"I'm your commanding officer, and I say it's bad. You haven't taken off this hat in a week." He made a grab for my hat, and I jumped away, pulling it lower over my ears.

"I've been washing to the best of my ability." I moved to

the other side of the room, putting the enormous table between us.

Brennon was having none of it. In three long strides, he had my arm in his hand and he was dragging me toward the tub. "You've gone nose blind. You can't even tell how much you stink. If you don't get in, I will strip you and throw you in myself."

"No!" I cried out and fell to the floor, grasping my poor vest close to me. "I promise to do better. I swear."

Brennon with his massive strength picked me up and tossed me into the tub. A glorious wave of water splashed over the rim and ran across his floor. Suds and bubbles soaked his boots and ran toward the bed.

I gasped as the water rushed over my head. I sputtered, flailed, and tried to sit up, my clothes clinging to my curvy body. I pulled my knees close and wrapped my arms around them, locking myself into this position to cover my chest. I wanted to scream at the captain, but the room was empty. The door latched with a click as it closed.

"I will be back in two candle marks," he yelled through the door.

I sat in the warm bath and didn't move, waiting for the door to swing open and the captain to come barging back in, but he didn't. I spurred into action, trying to use as little time as I could. I took off my boots and dropped them over the side of the tub and took my pants and vest off, leaving on my long overshirt.

The captain had left me a bar of soap, and I reached out to the table and grabbed it. I tossed my hat on the ground and dunked my head under the water, running my fingers through my locks. Then I worked the soap into a lather. I used it on my hair and then quickly on my body.

In record time, I was out of the tub and using the water to wash my socks and clothes, doing my best to wring them out. I took my clothes, headed to the window, and hung them out to dry in the ocean air.

The breeze dried my hair and shirt. As the bindings around my chest dried, they constricted, and I wished that I dared to take them off. But I didn't have any fresh ones to change into with me.

When I figured that my allotted time was drawing near. I begrudgingly wrapped my hair back up and stuck the slightly damp hat back on. My partially dried clothes clung to my curves.

Using the towel, I wiped up the pool of water that gathered, and then grabbed my boots and socks. I snuck out of the captain's quarters, and instead of heading across the deck in front of all the men to take the steps down to the crew's quarters, I headed to the bow of the ship. Crowley was at the helm, and I assumed then that Brennon was in the navigation room, a place he spent many hours poring over maps.

Among the ropes and storage at the bow, I found a tied-down crate and crawled on top. I turned my boots over and let the rest of my clothes and me dry out in the quickly fading sun.

The wind ripped at my shirt and threatened to pull at my hat, but I just smiled in challenge and laid out. I now understood why my cat, Hack, liked to lie in the sun on the ground. There was something very calming about it. A shadow passed over my face, and I frowned.

"You look like a nixie that got into a pot of blood."

I glanced up to stare into the green-gold pools that were Vasili's eyes. He was leaning over me. His long hair hung loose past his shoulders. I originally thought it was black, but it had hints of green like seaweed. Today, he wore black pants and a deep-emerald-green shirt. He looked daunting.

"If you mean am I happy? For the moment, yes."

"Are you saying you're normally not happy?"

"Depends on the situation, I guess." I sat up and took in Vasili.

His skin was almost a translucent white, his veins laying a cross work of roads that lead to his heart. And even though I had seen him sitting out here day after day, he didn't show a sign of a tan or even a freckle.

"Are you really from the Undersea?" I asked and then quickly covered my mouth.

His smile was sly. "Oh, yes."

"What's it like?"

"Beautiful. Your sea is miniscule compared to mine. The colors are pale, where ours are vibrant and bold. Our gardens are mazes of seaweed, and our whirlpools can transport you to other worlds. Our palace is made of crystalline shells and lava."

As he described the wonder of the Undersea, I could feel my heart beating faster and faster, as if crying out and longing to see it.

"And our sea sings," he taunted.

"No," I said in awe.

Vasili grinned; that's when I saw his canines were a little pointier than a normal human's. As if he was part predator of the deep that prayed on those who came too close. "Yes, it is said that only those born of the Undersea can hear her song." The sun disappeared behind the horizon, and the air grew cooler. Vasili's features seemed engaging. He sat next to me on the crate, his thigh brushing against mine.

"Have you heard it?" I asked.

"Of course."

"What's it sound like?"

"Magic," Vasili answered. He leaned in close and whispered, "To hear the sea sing is an honor."

I took my boots, slipped them on, and laced them back up. The icy air was biting at my still drying clothes, and the chill was working its way back through my bones.

"I wish I could hear it."

"If you hear the song of the sea, you'll never want for anything else in the world."

"That sounds like a tale told to lure children into an unsuspecting trap," I teased.

His face was serious, and he crooked his head toward me. "Is it working?"

"Maybe." I stared off the bow as our ship cut through the water and felt my heart break at my own personal loss. "Do you miss it?"

"I'm not welcome." His voice turned hard.

"Why?"

"Because I failed in my duty as captain of the guard." Vasili stood up and stretched, his long arms lifting over his head, showing off his strong shoulders.

"You mean you guard the treasure of the Undersea?"

"No, I *used* to guard the treasure. The treasure is no more."

"No!" I gasped. "What happened?"

Vasili's eyes dropped in shame. "Years ago, an evil man found the hidden way into the Undersea. Bent on destruction, he destroyed everything in his path as he strived to take the treasure for himself. A perilous battle ensued between the sorcerer's daemon-possessed army and the guards, resulting in the loss of many lives including King Septimus. The treasure disappeared, and since then, the sea has been silent, and our world has slowly been dying." Vasili balled his hands into fists, the knuckles white with anger.

"Can you search for it? The treasure?"

"We've tried. For years, we've searched the seas, looking for the lost treasure, but it's gone. Destroyed by the sorcerer, no doubt. No, our only hope to save the dying Undersea is to strengthen the bond between the sky and sea and hope it is enough." He had retreated into a bleak place. I could see the anger hidden within the set of his jaw.

"How do you do that?"

"Well, that involves the captain, and he has to—"

A clearing of a throat startled Vasili. I swung my head around to see Brennon and saw the slight shake of his head in warning to his first mate. Then he glanced down and noticed how close we were sitting. Brennon's face darkened, his eyes glittering dangerously, his hand reaching for his knife on his belt.

What was the captain going to do, stab Vasili because we were sitting next to each other? Or maybe it was a threat because of our conversation topic.

Vasili just grinned and leaned even closer to whisper into my ear, his eyes never straying from the captain. "Your master calls."

And those words had the desired effect. They spurred my anger at my own circumstances. Going from being a powerful sorceress to a fake cabin boy—I mean *slave*—to a man I despised.

I slid off the crate, marched over to Brennon, and saluted him with as much hate as I could muster.

Brennon ignored me, as he was in a silent battle with Vasili. The two men glared at each other, and I heard Brennon's knuckles crack from his own animosity.

Vasili smirked and rolled his shoulders, focusing his attention back on the sea.

"Follow me," Brennon ordered. His steps were hurried, and I had to take two for every one of his. He stormed into his quarters. The tub of water was gone, along with the wet towels.

He turned to stare at my face. His eyes widened, and I thought he held his breath. I glanced over my shoulder to look into the mirror, and I realized my error. I had forgotten to put dirt back on my face. My skin practically glowed, long, dark lashes accentuated my eyes that were as bright as emeralds, and a soft blush adorned my cheeks. I looked extremely feminine.

"You will no longer sleep with the crew." Brennon coughed. He marched over to the table and rifled through some papers, giving me his back.

"Where will I sleep then?" I asked fearfully. My heart raced, and I stared at the enormous bed big enough for three people.

"There," he said nonchalantly and pointed to a bedroll tucked in the far corner of the room.

"I'm sorry. I don't understand. Why is this necessary?" I asked, feeling heat crawl to my cheeks.

"Because you'll be safe here." He turned and leaned against the table. A lock of golden hair fell across his forehead.

At the moment, being near him at night in the dark was the farthest from safe I could be. Who would keep me safe from him?

I stuck my chin out. "And why wouldn't I be safe with the men?"

His eyebrow rose and he sighed. "Do you really want to play this game with me?"

"What game?" I choked. It had been a week since we set sail, and he had yet to act like he recognized me. In fact, he was cold and mostly avoided me.

"The game where we're the only two players," he challenged and glanced at my hat. I took every ounce of strength to not check to see if the hat moved, revealing the color of my hair. It was still pulled low over my ears. I felt very confident in my disguise.

Brennon rubbed his hand along his jaw in thought. His eyes gleamed in mirth. "All right. We can play this game a little longer. Although, I will warn you. The game you play is very dangerous." He moved closer to me and grasped my forearms.

"Are you saying you will hurt me?" I asked.

"No, but you play with fire that can burn my whole ship down around me, and you will get hurt." Brennon grasped my chin between his fingers. Terrified, I didn't move. "And I never play games unless I can win."

I sucked in my breath, feeling a heat smolder in my stomach. His fingers burned where they touched my chin, half an inch below my parted lips. My eyes strayed to his lips and wished to know what they tasted like.

Steeling my resolve, I pulled away from his grasp and glared up at him, remembering he was the one who was so rude in the transport. He was my captain and nothing further. *Ever.*

"And *I* never lose," I challenged.

"Then we will see who gets the prize in the end."

I stepped back and went to stand by the door, waiting to be dismissed.

"I'm your captain, and I gave you an order." Brennon pointed to the bedroll in the corner.

"I would rather not," I said stiffly.

He pinched his lips into a hard line. "You don't have a choice. It is common for cabin *boys* to sleep near the captain in case I have *need* in the middle of the night."

The way he enunciated *boys* wasn't lost on me. And when he said *need*, I couldn't help but imagine what that need may be. *Am I blushing?* Thank the stars the sun had just set and there was only one lantern lit. Plus, I still wasn't a hundred percent sure he wasn't just testing me. Playing the game to see if I would cry foul or unfair.

I chewed on my lips and debated. Was it worse to sleep in a cabin full of fifty men in one room or with one person?

"Or are you ready to give up?" The corner of Brennon's lip turned up.

My frown deepened. "Fine," I huffed, stomped over to the bed, and unrolled it. It was filled with downy feathers and only had a slight bend to it after I rolled it out flat. I laid on it and glared at him across the room, even making a show of flopping around like a flounder trying to get comfortable.

The bedroll wasn't so bad. It relieved me to not be in the same sleeping space as Thorn and Fang, but I wasn't about to admit it to Brennon.

Brennon's crossed his hands and lifted his shirt over his head, exposing his chest. I couldn't help but stare at the muscles that ran up his stomach and the breadth of his square shoulders. My eyes drank him in, this time unashamedly, as they traveled upward, and I met his amused blue eyes. The corner of his mouth ticked upward.

I made a slight cry of distress and rolled over to face the wall. Now surely my face was on fire as he caught me ogling his chest. *Stupid!* I cradled my head on my arm, curled up in a ball, and waited for him to finish undressing.

My ears tuned in like a bat listening for every creak of a

floorboard or sound of him moving about the room. I prayed he would stay on that side of the room, that he would not come closer, but at the same time wishing it, desiring it. I wanted him to call me on my bluff.

I heard the rustle of blankets as he crawled into his soft bed, and the room went dark as he extinguished the light.

A sigh escaped my lips, and I now waited for him to fall asleep. I hadn't expected him to sleep with the windows open. The night air crept in, and my clothes were still damp in some areas. It was a battle of wills when I became so cold my teeth chattered.

"Only a foolish person would sleep in wet clothes," Brennon spoke up. "We are both men. You can hang them out to dry." He sounded irritable. Probably because I disturbed his sleep.

"Only a foolish person would sleep with the windows open," I snapped back.

"I like the breeze across my skin." His voice was husky.

I closed my eyes and tried not to imagine what he was saying. Instead, I put my finger between my teeth and used it to keep my teeth from clacking together.

Brennon sighed. "But I also value my sleep, and you're keeping me awake." The floor creaked, and I stilled, listening as I heard him move about.

He threw a quilt at my feet, and I grabbed it and wrapped it around me like a greedy child, even covering my head so that if my hat came off in my sleep, I would have another layer of protection.

Brennon retreated to his bed, and I heard his groan as he slipped back into his covers. I focused on his breathing and waited.

After a few candle marks, I heard his breathing deepen,

and I knew it was time. Carefully, I grabbed my boots and tiptoed toward the door. When the floor creaked, I stilled, waiting for Brennon to catch me. When I didn't hear a change, I continued to the door and opened it with only the slightest whisper. Then I tiptoed out and closed it with the softest click. As I headed out of the cabin, I noticed a thick fog had rolled in and worried about sailing in the murkiness. I glanced to the helm and saw an unfamiliar crew member working the wheel. He didn't seem to even notice me. I made my way toward the steps to go below, but a haunting melody caught my attention.

I followed the music to spy Vasili standing at the side of the ship, playing his flute. Magic crackled in the air, and I longed for that connection. But it was the second person standing next to Vasili that gave me pause. It was a figure made of water standing on the ocean side of the railing. Vasili spoke, and the form took the shape of a woman, her hair watery waves down her back. She reached out her liquid hands to him, her mouth opening to speak, but no words came forth.

Vasili spoke, and she nodded, her hands beckoning and pointing to the ocean.

The boot dropped from my grasp, and both heads turned to stare at me. When Vasili stopped playing, the woman opened her mouth to cry out, and she dissolved into a wave that splashed across the deck.

Vasili's face soured. He stormed off, brushing past me roughly to head up the stairs to the back of the ship.

I stood out on deck, staring at the puddle of water that now soaked my feet, and wondered. What kind of magic did I witness? And who was that mysterious woman?

CHAPTER NINE

"Wake up!" Howland hissed in my ear. My hammock swayed gently as he shook my shoulder.

"What's wrong?" I asked. My eyes felt gritty from the salt air and struggled to focus on Howland.

"Everything! What did ye do to the captain?" he accused.

"Nothing," I answered.

"Well, he is verbally tearin' into Crowley, and the man's practically a saint. The captain was perfectly fine until he went to bed last night."

"Maybe he just ate something that disagreed with him," I snapped.

Howland's old face crumpled at the insult to his cooking. He shrugged it off and shook his head. "The last time I saw him this mad was the day he cuffed Caleb and sent him runnin'."

I quietly counted back the days and remembered that was the day I eluded him during his valiant rescue attempt.

I uttered a silent curse and wondered how I could avoid

the coming beating. I disobeyed a direct order and snuck out in the middle of the night. Although, I couldn't hold back the smile that I had gained the upper hand.

"Wipe that smile off yer face," Howland warned. "We've set anchor. And ye slept through it."

"A-anchor," I stuttered, suddenly afraid. "I thought we would be at sea much longer. Are we back at Fairehaven?" I tried to remember where the sun was and wondered if we turned around. I crawled out of the hammock and adjusted my hat. All the hammocks were empty. I somehow slept through the crew rising for the day and walking past me.

"No, it be an island."

"An island? Why? Which island?"

"Maybe if ye make it above deck for the announcements, ya'd know what's goin' on." He took off his own knit hat and swatted me on the shoulder playfully.

I dashed up the stairs hand over hand, racing to the railing to take in the island in front of me. We were still hundreds of yards away, and the men were lowering the longboat to go ashore.

The island was a green utopia upon white sands that stretched for miles. We were anchored in an aquamarine-colored lagoon. Black specks flitted in the air high above the trees, and I wondered what birds and animals occupied the island. Suddenly, I badly wanted to go on land.

But I knew I might've blown my chances by angering Brennon.

A whistle pierced the air, and the crew gathered around. Brennon stood at the upper deck. He was in full captain's apparel. Gray pants, covered in a long navy-blue jacket with gold trim and gold buttons. His hand rested on his cutlass at his hip. His face was an unreadable mask. His hawk-like gaze searched the crowd for me, and I shrank, ducking behind Jessup. Terrified of what might happen if I met his cold blue eyes.

That's when I read the emotions of the crew. They weren't excited like I was; many averted their gaze, shuffled their feet, and some looked downright uncomfortable. Jessup moved to the left, and my shield disappeared.

I knew when Brennon saw me. His shoulders stiffened. His lip curled up in a wicked smile, and I knew he planned to punish me.

He cleared his throat. "Men, we have dropped anchor near one the forbidden isles."

A collective murmur of disapproval moved through the crowd. Their unease became even more evident. Many swore, and I heard their anger and whispers of dissent.

"Which island exactly?" Crowley asked.

Brennon hesitated. "It's *her* island."

The murmur became louder. "It is said that any man who steps foot ashore that place will be cursed," Conroy added.

"He's mad," Jessup said.

"We're all going to die!" Adair cried out.

"Silence!" Brennon roared. "Most of you will stay on the ship. I will only take the bravest of you inland."

"It is not safe to stay in these waters!" Jessup yelled. "The waters run with the blood of those who have never stepped off that island."

"We have been guaranteed safe passage."

"By who?" Conroy called.

"By me," Vasili's voice rang out across the boat. He had been watching the entire affair from the bow of the ship and walked up and placed a ringed hand on Brennon's shoulder.

He plucked a ring with a ruby the size of a grape from his

pinky finger and held it aloft for the men to see. "This ring is the queen of the Undersea's signet ring. By right, it should grant us safe passage."

Barley raised his hand. "I heard tales that there are seven rare treasures on the island."

Vasili shrugged. "We hope so. I can't guarantee what we will find."

The crew, once hesitant, now became filled with lust at the promise of treasure.

"Now, I ask you once again. Who will go with us to the island?" Brennon asked.

A roar of affirmative answers was his reply. Men clamored, jumping up and down and waving their hats; a few even tried to make a run for the lowered longboat.

"Wait!" Brennon roared, upset by how fast his men changed their tune. "I will remind you that this is a dangerous island and that not all of you can go ashore."

"I will go!" Rothbart called.

"No, I will," Swiftly answered.

"Me!" Jessup jumped up and down.

Howland shook his head in disappointment and waddled back toward the steps below.

"Do you not want to go?" I asked him.

Howland pointed at the beautiful floating oasis. "There's nothin' on that island but death."

"Do you mean the island is dangerous?"

"It's not the island itself ye need to worry about," he warned, "but the sea witch who lives on it."

The longboat bobbed against the hull of the ship as the captain organized the offshore party. Brennon ordered Fang and Thorn to stay on board, which I found odd. Many of the same men who only a full candle mark ago cried outrage at going ashore were eagerly climbing down the rope ladder. They lowered a trunk filled with supplies followed by an armory of weapons.

When they were almost loaded to go, Brennon and Vasili were the only two left on the deck, and I could see the worry upon their brows.

"Are you sure the answer is on the island?" Brennon asked. He buckled a bandolier with knives over his shirt and adjusted his cutlass to rest over his left hip.

"I made contact last night with the sea witch. She says she can help." Vasili's eyes glowed with excitement. His dark hair hung long and unbraided, the wind toying with it.

I had to wonder if that was what I witnessed last night— Vasili communicating with the sea witch.

"But those answers have a price, and I only hope this is enough to pay for it." He held up the ruby ring. "She seemed eager for our arrival."

"That makes me wary."

"I know. But we are running out of time, my friend. She says she has vital information on what we seek. Or would you rather agree to the en—"

"Stop!" Brennon waved his hand. "I understand. But that is my sacrifice. Not yours."

"Thank you, my friend." Vasili squeezed Brennon's shoulder. "I know what this will cost you."

"Only if we don't find what we're looking for. It hasn't come to that yet."

Brennon's grip tightened on his sword, and his gaze flickered over to me. He stormed across the deck to confront me.

"Where did you disappear last night?" he whispered heatedly.

"I went back to my hammock," I snapped.

"When I gave you a direct order? Disobeying your captain is punishable by a lashing. You work on my ship. You obey my rules."

"But what if those rules make little sense?" I challenged.

His lips pressed together, and he stepped closer, his face leaning down to where we were now eye level. "I couldn't care less if they make sense. If I told you to walk across burning coals, jump overboard, or even sleep in a perfectly comfortable room, then you better well obey. Or I can find an even less comfortable place for you to reside for the rest of the voyage. The brig." His nostrils flared, and I could feel his anger roll across my body. "Do you understand?" he asked.

"Yes," I said meekly.

"I can't hear you!"

"Yes, Captain," I retorted.

"And stay in my quarters until I get back. In fact, don't come out onto the deck for any reason at all. Even to help Howland." He turned to leave.

"B-but—" I protested.

Brennon spun around. "*Already*, you're questioning my authority."

I bit my tongue and looked out across the water toward the island. Being trapped inside all day while being anchored with no wind seemed like a severe punishment.

I nodded.

"Good." Brennon pulled me forward and pointed at the

bow where Fang was visibly kicking a crate. "And stay out of Fang's sight."

Brennon didn't need to warn me a second time. With a final stone-faced glare, he pushed me toward his quarters and flung his cloak around his shoulders, securing it before disappearing down the ladder.

Vasili watched the entire exchange, and he pursed his lips at me in thought. "Interesting."

From the captain's doorway, I watched Vasili leap over the railing and heard him land in the boat below, surprising the crew. They cast off, and the longboat rowed toward the island. I sighed, closed the door, and began my punishment of waiting.

It didn't take me long to straighten up Brennon's room, since he hardly ever used the room except for sleeping. I rolled up the bedroll and tucked it away in one of the built-in cupboards, since I had no intention of sleeping anywhere near him. No matter how many lashings he threatened me with.

Half a candle mark later, I finished and sat in his chair, drumming my fingers across the oak table. Feeling extremely closed in, I pushed open the windows and went out a side door onto the captain's private balcony. It was small, and because of the way the ship was anchored, I could only see the island from the starboard side. It was here I sat with my knees pulled up and watched the boat, now a speck in the lagoon, row up to the sandy beach.

Even from this distance, I could make out Vasili's dark hair and Brennon's sun-kissed blond. Dark and light, opposite sides of a coin. They headed together up the beach and into the densely populated island.

Hidden by the landing above me and knowing the crew had all disappeared inland, I took off my hat and let my hair fall to my shoulders. I hummed softly under my breath and ran my fingers through my red locks like a comb to try to break apart a few of my tangles, unaware that my singing was attracting attention from below. I heard a whistle in return.

Startled, I quickly tucked my hair up, looked over the balcony, and blinked in awe as a school of undines dancing in the sea's foam. I had only ever read about the water elementals but had never seen them in person. They were blue, no bigger than my palm and sang in perfect harmony.

"Stop that dang racket!" a disgruntled Fang cried out. Tossing a bottle from the upper deck into the ocean, he scattered the undines. I pressed myself against the back wall as I waited to see if he would peer over the upper deck.

"Dang witch," he murmured. "Sending her minions to taunt us."

I snickered and wondered what he would think if he knew that a sorceress was onboard with him. He was too close, so I crept back toward the door and spent my day either watching the island or napping on Brennon's bed.

Being this close to shore, a few of the crew went out in the skiff early in the morning and set out crab traps. By sundown, they brought in full traps. I felt guilty for leaving Howland to prepare the food all by himself, but I dared not go against Brennon's orders and leave the room. I worried about Vasili and Brennon when they did not return by sundown and spent the early evening on the captain's balcony, watching the shoreline.

The fresh crab lifted the spirits, and those who remained brought out their instruments and played. This was a nightly

OF SEA AND SONG

tradition and one I had grown fond of, since I loved music. Except for tonight. There was an odd feeling in the air, a heaviness that permeated everywhere, especially when an overlaying fog rolled in. The others must have felt the same wariness, for once the fog came, the music stopped.

My stomach growled in protest at being forced to stay in solitary confinement, which meant I hadn't grabbed my rations for the day, and I wasn't on deck when the crab was grilled over the fireboxes and distributed. I was not one to miss meals, and therefore my temper was rising and my fuse was very short.

Feeling vindictive, I raided Brennon's stores, opening up his trunks to where I had seen he had his saved rations. In a fit of anger. I decided I would revenge eat through his food. I poured myself a cup of his best wine. After a sip, I decided it was not meant for me. Instead, I took it and dumped it out the window. All drinks on the ship were wine, rum, or mead, for fresh water went stale fast.

I found a sweet dessert cake in a tin, ate all of it, and put the tin back in the cupboard, leaving not a single crumb. With a full stomach, I crawled onto Brennon's bed, leaving the heavy drapes pulled back and the window and door to the balcony open to the island. Tucking my hand under my head, I waited eagerly for the sound of oars on the water, Brennon's booming voice commanding the rowers, or the boarding party.

Those sounds never came.

In the middle of the night, something cold brushed across my cheek, and I gasped. Sitting up in a tangle of blankets, I slapped and punched the air and met nothing. The room was black, the cabin door still locked from inside.

Gently, I touched my cheek and felt cold water drip down my skin. I lit the bedside lantern, held it up in the air, and almost cried out in fear, for a set of wet footprints trailed from the balcony to my bed and then back out.

I grabbed a blanket off the bed, wrapped it around my shoulders, and followed the wet trail out the balcony door, where it disappeared over the side into the sea and to where I only assumed it came from—the sea witch's island.

CHAPTER TEN

B y the second day, I became impatient. Surely, Brennon did not mean to keep me locked up here permanently? What if he didn't return? I would have to leave eventually for food.

The floor in front of the balcony windows would probably have a permanent wear pattern from my pacing feet. My stomach betrayed me, and it growled in hunger. I had already eaten through Brennon's lovely rations yesterday, and there wasn't anything left in his room.

To try to take my mind off my hunger, I dug through his trunks again and searched for the book on the Undersea. It seemed to have changed since the last time I held it. It was a deeper hue, and the colors were more vibrant. I opened the pages and stared at the swirls and whorls and shapes that made up the dead language.

I traced my finger around one particular shape that looked like a vortex. It glowed faintly, and then the glyph soaked into the text, disappearing into the pages. Another glyph looked like a drop of blood or a tear, while one I was sure symbolized waves. I spent a few candle marks studying the book and was fairly sure I understood a few of the more cryptic lines.

But they were ramblings of dire warnings.

Something of blood and song, of seas and shells.

I studied until my eyes were crossed and I could feel the beginnings of a headache forming. I tucked the book back into its place in the trunk, being careful to put everything back exactly how I found it. Then I saw a few shirts that needed mending.

Yes. It was the perfect excuse. I grabbed the shirts, tucked them over my arm, unlocked the door, and stepped out onto the deck. I headed out in search for a needle and thread.

I tiptoed across the deck, heading straight for the stairs below. There was quite a lot of idleness about the ship, since there weren't any sails to man. Two of the crew were making light repairs with pitch. The ship's carpenter Barley was reinforcing the decking under the cannons. Swifty was asleep in the crow's nest, while Fang and Thorn were nowhere in sight.

Once below, I headed past the berth where the rest of the crew was resting in their hammocks and headed toward the galley.

The old man was sitting on his three-legged stool, near the larger of the two porthole windows, his sore leg stretched out before him. His arthritic hands kneaded the muscles in his knee.

I rapped lightly on a wooden beam to get his attention. His red-rimmed eyes looked up at me, and I saw there was something wrong. He looked off, sad.

"What do ye want?" He turned his attention back to the window.

"I'm sorry," I mumbled. "But he ordered me to stay in his room."

"Sure, and leave poor ol' Howland to do his work alone." He still didn't peel his eyes away from the sea.

"Maybe I could help now a little before the captain gets back, as long as we don't tell him."

"I don't feel like workin'." He scoffed. "Nor cookin'."

"Is something the matter, Howland? You seem different."

"I'm just not sleepin' well. That's all." He rubbed his eyes with the palm of his hand, and I felt sorry for him. Sorry that I abandoned him. He had every right to be angry with me, and if he wasn't planning on cooking, then I would have to grab my own rations from my hammock and bring them back with me. But that still didn't deal with my boredom.

"Howland, do you know where there might be a mending kit?" I asked.

"What for?"

I held up the stack of Brennon's shirts.

His forehead creased as he reflected. "Well, most of the crew do their own mendin'. But those be nicely tailored, and ye not wanting what we use on the sails. Ye may find some thread and needle in our medicine stores." He patted his hip to grab his key ring and thumbed through them. Holding the small iron key in the air, he pointed toward the bow of the ship.

"I'm too tired to escort ye. Head toward the bow, past the spare rigs and the cargo hold, and you'll find the ship's stores. They're locked up, and look for a chest yay big." He gestured with his hands. "Ye might find what ye need in there. But lock it up when yer done. Ye hear? No one's allowed in there except for Fang. But Brennon gave me a spare key."

Nodding, I took the ring of keys and headed out of the galley. The ship's stores were on the same level but had the smallest windows, and light was scarce.

I hadn't brought a lantern with me and didn't trust magic

to answer me if I sang. When I found a lantern, I scavenged for a match. Striking it and lighting it the old fashion way seemed lackluster. The lanterns illuminated the dark and humid cargo hold. At the very end, I saw the heavy wooden door to the ship's stores.

I placed the key in the heavy lock, and it became stuck. I jiggled it and it turned. The door swung inward with a creak and entered the locked storage.

Bolts of the finest fabrics, silks, and brocades leaned in the corner. I could easily smell the exotic spices of turmeric, cumin, and curry, along with the supplies that were needed to keep the ship running. I accidentally knocked over a folded rug, and it unrolled, revealing another hidden layer.

I raised the lantern to study the furs. Gray and speckled, the furs were warm to the touch as if they were alive. It couldn't be. My mouth went dry as I closed my eyes and tried to find the source of the magic.

There was something wrong. Darkness and pain. My skin felt like it was being torn from my back. I sucked in a painful breath and backed away, staring in horror at what I believed to be the items Fang and Thorn had stolen and were trying to unload.

"Selkie furs," I whispered, knowing I was correct. These were the living skins of selkies, seals that could turn into humans by shedding their coats and vice versa. But I could tell from the pain emanating from the skin that they weren't removed voluntarily.

"What evilness is this?" I cried, knowing they had taken the selkies' magic furs by force. But for what purpose?

I knew I needed to leave before they caught me.

I quickly located the trunk of medicine by the healer

symbol etched on the outside and searched the contents for needle and thread, which I easily found.

No sooner had I closed the lids of the medicine box was I discovered.

"What are you doing in here!" Fang growled from behind me. His eyes went to the exposed selkie fur. He grasped my arm and yanked me out of the storage room roughly, his fingers digging into my flesh.

"Ouch!" I cried, and quickly tried to muffle my outcry.

"Stealing. That's what you were doing."

"No, I swear."

"Liar!" Fang flung me to the floor. His hand reaching for the knife on his belt.

I rolled over and ran, scrambling to run past the cargo hold, up the steps to the main deck, but I didn't get far. Once I hit the main deck, Thorn blocked my way.

"Seize him!" Fang cried out.

Obeying, Thorn grasped my other arm and yanked me back to his side.

"Ten lashes for stealing."

"I wasn't stealing!" I hissed. I dug my nails ruthlessly into Thorn's hands, but he didn't let up.

"I caught you!" Fang snarled. "No one's allowed in those stores."

Thorn dragged me across the deck and ripped off my outer vest, the buttons popping off and rolling across the deck. He left my oversized shirt on. With practiced hands, he tied me to the mast, my back facing the crew as they came to watch the beating unfold. Most of them were strangers, and none came forward to speak on my behalf. Howland was down below in the galley and probably hadn't even heard the commotion. Of the few men I saw, they seemed dazed, clouded, and half asleep.

"Stealing! What about what you have hidden in the stores? The furs. I saw the—" He stuffed a rag into my mouth, cutting off my cries.

I tried to keep the anger from boiling over, but the weather had other ideas. As soon as they placed the slip knot around my wrists, the sea churned and the sky darkened. My anger caused the water to act up. But I waged an inner war within myself. I could, with a few words, destroy Fang and Thorn and let them feel my wrath, thus exposing I was a daughter of Eville and a woman. Which would lead to the discovery of the bounty on my head. They might then kill me and claim the money. I couldn't find it in me to destroy everyone aboard the ship. What about Howland? My other option was to bite my tongue, accept the beating, and pray to the stars above that my ruse was not discovered.

Fang handed the whip to Thorn. He gave it a cursory practice snap, and the crack was inches from my ear. The sound made my head ring, and I felt my knees go weak. I wouldn't be able to do it. I couldn't take the punishment like a man. I would fold and scream out at any minute.

"Do it!" Fang ordered.

Crack!

My back arched, my mouth fell open in a silent scream, and pain racked through my body, paralyzing me. My back was on fire.

"One!" Fang yelled.

One. I wouldn't survive. There was no way I could survive nine more lashings.

I clenched my teeth and jaw, squeezed my eyes closed, and prayed. Prayed that I would black out by the second lashing then maybe I would survive the others without an ordeal. But my fear overcame me, and a silent tear trickled down my face. I swallowed, my mouth dry and lips chapped. Then I realized it wasn't a tear but rain trickling across the deck, thus disguising my tears.

"Thank you," I whispered aloud and buried my face into the wooden mast.

"Two!" Fang screamed. His enjoyment was clear in his evil laughter.

Crack!

"Mmmfff!" I bit my tongue and could feel the warm copper trickle of blood in my mouth and a second running down my back. My bindings. Anymore lashings and my chest bindings would be exposed for all to see.

"What is goin' on 'ere?" I heard Howland's voice but could not turn to look at him. "Fang, what in the hell are you doin'?"

A verbal argument ensued, but it was like bees buzzing in my ears. The sea cast her displeasure by rocking the boat, sending a few running for the lines and others to the railing for support. I only hoped it knocked Thorn down. But I saw him out the corner of my eye.

Thorn turned, the whip in his hand raised toward Howland.

I tried to help him, tried to stop it, but I was powerless without my voice. He cracked the whip, and Howland fell backward. Thorn returned his attention to me. His arm pulled back for a third time, and I braced myself but could feel my knees give out as I gave in to the fiery pain and blacked out.

Crack!

CHAPTER ELEVEN

The strike of a match and its light burned my eyes as I adjusted to the darkness that surrounded me. I was lying on my stomach on the wood floor, my back on fire with pain. I tried to push myself up. Searing agony raced across my back and I almost passed out again.

"So, you're awake," a voice pierced the darkness.

The match moved, and my eyes followed the light as it touched the wick of a lantern and lit. The speaker adjusted the knob, and it flared even brighter to reveal the bars that surrounded me. I was in the brig.

"Who are you?" I asked, already knowing I didn't recognize the strange person kneeling before me.

I turned my head to take in the silvery-white-haired woman with the eyes so dark they looked like endless pools of nothing. Her hair was braided with seashells, her skin pale like moonlight, and her dress made of kelp and seaweed.

The woman plucked a strand of seaweed from her dress and placed it against my injured and bloodied back, and I cried out—partially from pain and followed by a sigh of relief.

"You know who I am?" she asked.

"The sea witch," I said.

She frowned and shook her white hair. "I've never been partial to that name. You may call me Sirena."

"That's not your true name, is it?"

"Of course not. For you know very well names have power. Maybe the question you should ask is who are you? Hiding your true nature from these men. You shouldn't hide from them." Her hands made quick work. She plucked another strand of seaweed from near her leg, rubbed a poultice on it, and placed it on another red cut. I shivered as she continued to apply the poultice. With each strand she placed, my pain dissipated. I could feel the muscles in my back begin to reknit and heal.

"I know who I am," I answered, not pleased by the games she was playing.

"Ah, yes. A daughter of Eville. The one whose name means 'Of the sea.' Do you know why you were given that name? Do you know anything about where you came from?"

"I was adopted," I said stiffly. "My father was a lowly fisherman; my mother was ailing and could no longer take care of me. They brought me to Lady Eville, and she took me in."

"Yes, yes, yes." The woman rolled her eyes. "That is your after. But do you know your before?"

"I don't understand. Why are you talking in riddles?" I asked.

"Maybe because I rarely get visitors, and when I do, I like to keep them awhile." She smiled, revealing small, pointy teeth like a piranha. "Do you know I met another man with the same surname of Eville? Let's see—what was his name? Lazlo? Lake? No, now I remember. Lachlan."

"No." I couldn't believe what I was hearing. Lachlan was

Mother Eville's father.

"Yes," the woman purred and closed her eyes as if savoring the memory. "He made a deal with me long ago. But he couldn't keep up his end of the bargain, and therefore I took it all." She snapped her fingers. "First, his ships, and then his life."

The pain in my back subsided as I put the pieces together. Mother Eville was once engaged to a prince, but her father lost all his fortune when his ship sank at sea. Destitute and without a dowry, the prince broke off the engagement, and Lachlan died of a heart attack shortly after.

With a painful grunt, I pushed myself up to a sitting position.

"Was that you?" I accused. "Did you cause the misfortune to befall my family?"

"Which family, dear? You must be more specific." Her knowing grin was annoying me. She was baiting me with information, and I knew better than to fall in her trap.

"What did he want?"

The woman leaned back, running her hands through her hair seductively. "The same thing every man wants, dear girl. The same thing these men who invaded my island want." She stood up; the seaweed draped elegantly down her body. On each of her fingers was a glittering ring that glimmered. She picked up a conch shell, placed it to her lips, and blew. Nothing came forth, and I blinked, waiting to hear something, but I was deaf to whatever magic she displayed.

She stepped to the side of the cell, leaving behind watery footprints in her wake. The same watery prints I had seen in my room the night before. She stopped at the bars and looked over her shoulder at me. "If you want to save them, you need to find me."

"What do you mean save them?"

"I have them. Their hearts belong to me now."

She turned, beckoned with a black-painted finger, and I felt the black magic spill forth as I shivered.

"Come to me, daughter of the sea," she whispered. "Come save your measly humans. For where they are, they won't last long." She walked backward through the cell bars, and as she did, she dissolved into a wave of water that splashed down and soaked the floor.

The water turned black and pooled around the bars, and I stared at the footprints she left around my cell. There were no doubts in my mind about the woman who mysteriously disappeared before me. Nor her underlying threat.

She had Brennon, Vasili, and the others, and she made it very clear that I would have to save them.

My hands trembled as I reached around to grasp the iron bars, closed my eyes, and reached for the magic. Magic I had been terrified to use. During my initial testing as a child, Lorn said my powers were that of a muse. For my voice controlled water and sometimes air because of the condensation within it. Any other magic, I had to lean onto Mother Eville's lessons, but they weren't my strength, and I failed more than I succeeded.

I needed to draw a sigil. I saw the glittery reflection of the sea witch's puddle. I dipped my finger into the trace of water leftover, easily drew the symbol on the floor, and pictured the spell in the air.

"*Incendium.*"

The iron door exploded outward, bending the hinges and frame. I waited for someone to come running toward me with swords drawn, but all was silent. I limped out of the brig past the empty galley. Food still littered the table, knives and biscuits left out. Howland never left the galley messy. I quickened my steps to pass through the berth and listened for the chorus of snores and whistles that always punctuated the night. But every hammock I passed was empty. Not a single soul was asleep, even though I imagined it to be the middle of the night.

I gasped and made my way to the upper deck, and the ship seemed deserted. My only clue to what transpired was the silvery trails of footprints illuminated by the moonlight that ran across the deck.

A sail had come unfurled and flapped in the night air. One of the lower ropes was tangled around something large, and it kept making a thudding noise. I followed the sound to the fore course sail, walked around the mast, and gasped.

Jessup hung upside down, his foot caught in the sail's rope as he swung slightly, his body slapping against the sail. There was no mistaking the water that pooled by his fingertips. His sword was on the deck just out of reach, and I could see water coated it. He must have fought against the witch's magic and paid the price with his life.

I clapped my hand over my mouth and ran to the railing. Great sobs racked my body as I cried out in anguish. When the tears slowly passed, I heard a raspy breath and looked out at the head of the boat. Howland stood on the forecastle deck. He was using his entire body to turn the capstan to bring the anchor up. His face ruddy, his chest heaving, he cried out in pain.

"Howland!" I cried, running to him. "Stop. You mustn't. You'll injure yourself."

"We must leave this cursed place!" he cried out, his hands bloody, and so were the handles of the capstan.

"You can't do it alone. It's made for six people."

"If I don't, we will all die. Ye didn't see them. An army of watery bein's with colorful hair, all of them climbin' aboard and lurin' the men into the water. One after another, they jumped overboard. Ye didn't hear their cries. Poor Jessup tried fight them to no use. But he... he...."

"We need to leave!" Howland pushed on the capstan, his boots slipping along the deck, unable to find purchase.

"No, Howland." I grasped his bloody hands between mine and forced him to look at me. "We need the crew to sail the ship. We can't survive on the open sea alone. We have to go find them."

He shook his head and looked at the island in fear. "Impossible. No man can survive the lure of the sea witch's power."

I took a deep breath, pulled off my knit hat, and shook out my long red hair as it tumbled free.

Howland made a noise of surprise and pulled away from me in fright.

I stood tall and looked him dead in the eye. "As you can see, I'm no man."

"That ye aren't, lass. I can't believe I be so blind." I gave him a wry smile. He reached forward and gave me a hug. "But I still can't let ye go. How are ye going to battle a witch?"

I turned to the water, raised my hands, and sang. The sky darkened, and the waves rose in answer to my song, pounding the side of the ship. When I stopped singing, the water settled down.

"How's that in answer to your question?"

"I can't believe it." Howland burst into an enormous grin. "I think yer right. The only thing that can beat a sea witch be another sea witch."

With Howland's help, we lowered the smaller skiff into the water. I told him to stay aboard, but he refused to leave or let me go by myself.

"No, miss. I don't dare. Ye may be the captain's only hope, and it wouldn't be right of me to let ye go without an escort." He reached for the two oars, and I could see him struggling.

"It's not miss. It's Merisol. Or as my sisters call me, Meri."

"Merisol," he repeated. "That's nice. Better than Merrill. Has a regal sound to it."

"Let me," I answered, and began to sing. The water pushed against the skiff, and we sailed easily through the waters.

"Praise the stars!" he crowed and grabbed the oars so they wouldn't slip out of the rings and into the ocean.

I wasn't sure how I felt about being called a sea witch. My gifts had always leaned toward the two elements of water and air, which were two compatible gifts. I didn't believe I was anything like the watery creature who could dissolve into a puddle at will.

I closed my eyes and opened myself up to the magic of the water. It was soothing to my soul. The largest body of water I ever controlled was the lake near our home. I could see the allure of living near the sea and being able to control the ocean. It was heady, it was powerful, and I felt invincible.

We were approaching the beach, and the waves weren't slowing our approach.

"Careful!" Howland warned. The wave we were riding crested, and we lifted into the air.

I stopped singing a while ago, and it was the echo of magic that was pushing us into the white sands.

"Hold on!" I cried in warning.

The wave crashed into the shore, and we surfed along the

sands until the nose of the skiff was slowed by earth. Even though I was prepared for the landing, I still went flying and banged my knee on the forward bench. Poor Howland lost his hold on the oars, and one was floating away in the water.

Quickly, I hopped out and trudged back into the surf to retrieve the oar. The water soaked my pants, and I shivered as the cold bit into my skin. I flung the oar over my shoulder and walked back to the boat. Now that I was here on the island, I was rethinking my plan. Maybe I wasn't the best choice to save a bunch of men.

Howland secured the boat to a palm tree and made his way over to the abandoned longboat. He walked around the boat, studying the sands, and then he frowned.

"What's the matter?" I asked.

He wiped his brow, and I could see his nervousness. "From the looks of the undisturbed sand around the boat, none of the men have returned to the beach. That was two days ago."

"They've been taken prisoner," I said. "By the sea witch."

Howland's hand went to his heart, and I saw him falter.

"It's okay," I tried to reassure him. "You don't have to go with me. You can stay on the beach. Maybe some of the men will come back."

Howland nodded. "I feel like such a failure not comin' with ye."

"You've got me this far. I will do the rest." I took my hat out of my pocket and tucked my hair back inside. Before I left him on the beach, I reached out to give him a hug.

"Y-ye better come back now." He patted my shoulder, and I heard the emotion clinging to his voice.

"I will."

I slung my pack of supplies over my shoulder and turned to face the enormous island alone. It was a daunting task, one that I wasn't even sure I was prepared for. How did one search for a sea witch on an island? Did I announce my presence with a hello?

I skimmed the abundant vegetation, saw a freshly cut path, and knew that was probably where the crew cut their way inward. I guessed the fastest way to find the witch was to follow the trail the men forged.

When I was out of sight of Howland, I looked around in despair as the darkness of the island swallowed up the little moonlight that made it to the island floor. At first, it was easy to see the boot prints left behind by twenty men, but then the path dwindled. I pulled out a torch from the pack of supplies, and instead of using flint and steel, I breathed out one word. "*Fiergo.*"

The torch flickered as it tried to light and then fizzled out. I frowned. If Mother had seen, she would've been quite displeased with the attempt.

Water is the antithesis of fire, and I always struggled with fire spells. Giving up, I reached for the flint and quickly brought forth a bright flame the old-fashioned way. I grinned in triumph. Swinging the torch above my head in an arc, I searched the ground for tracks. Nothing. There wasn't a single heel print, bent bush, or foliage out of place. It was as if they disappeared.

I bit my lip in thought. I dropped my sack and carefully reached under my newly stolen shirt. Thorn destroyed my other one, and after Howland helped rebandage my back, I slipped on one I had taken from Brennon's room over my body.

It wasn't the easiest angle, but I could pull a piece of the seaweed bandage still wrapped around my back. My back healed, skin perfect and smooth. It had come from her dress, and I could easily do a reverse tracking spell on it. If the bounty hunters used my stuff to track me, I should've been able to use this to track down the witch's lair. If I had an object of power, like a quartz crystal, I could've amplified its abilities and used it like the bounty hunters. But I didn't.

The piece of seaweed had already dried out. It was now brittle and falling apart. I doubted it would hold together long enough for a simple spell, but I prayed this would work.

I tossed it into the air, giving it the command to "Seek."

The dark seaweed fluttered once, twice, and almost dropped among the foliage when it took off in the darkness.

I followed, my torch held high. Twice, I almost lost it to the shadows of the night, but it led me deeper into the island and then dropped into a hidden oasis of water. As soon as it touched the water, it broke apart and dissolved. The tracking spell had gotten me this far. Now, the rest was up to me.

The pool was black and still. None of the surrounding palms were shown in its reflective surface. Only the moon itself shone brightly, not giving away any of the secrets that were held within. But I knew the power of moonlight and reflections, for I had been taught well.

Even in the midst of night, there should've been sounds of life, birds, the wind rushing through the trees, even the ocean. But here by the inner island, there was a void of sound. Nothing existed.

I kneeled next to the water, took a pebble, and tossed it into its depths.

The stone sank. No ripple marked its passing.

"Interesting."

It was a well-designed trap.

I walked the length of the pool, looking for each of the hidden sigils I knew would be there. There was a moon, mirror, trap, and another I couldn't quite understand.

After I thoroughly inspected the magical pool, I sang—softly, waiting for the water to answer me. At first, it resisted, because it had already been given an assignment and wanted to fulfill its duty. But water was fluid and could be easily influenced. I sang notes of freedom, strength, reality, and finally door.

The water receded bit by bit to reveal a set of stone steps that led down into the earth. How far down, I didn't know.

I grabbed my bag and torch and took the steps one at a time, being very careful to hold my command over the water. The steps leveled off, and an impressive underground room appeared. One foot in front of the other, I continued until my boot crushed what I thought was a shell. I lifted my foot and looked down in horror at the human skull I trampled. I spun, and the torch illuminated the cavern floor covered with hundreds of skeletons.

I held back a gasp, covering my cry with my hand, my heart aching for the remains that would never return home. I prayed they weren't the remains of Brennon and the others. Warmth filled my mouth. I had bitten my cheek in anger. I let that anger fill me, the rage at the senseless deaths fueling me, and my fear dissipated.

This couldn't continue. I couldn't allow the sea witch to murder anymore.

"Obliviate."

The skulls became white dust, and I marched forward down the tunnel with a renewed sense of purpose. My mother trained us to be powerful, but my guilty conscience weakened my confidence in using magic. Fueled by anger, I had only one desire.

To not have my skull added to the ones on the floor.

CHAPTER TWELVE

The creepy tunnel went on forever. I'd been walking for two candle marks and had yet to find another passage or turn. Maybe I'd been mistaken in my quest? Maybe I failed at the seeker spell? For surely I would have encountered something by now?

The path ascended, and the ceiling rose higher. My boots echoed loudly off the cavern walls. The air took on a salty yet acrid scent. One I associated with black magic. I stepped into a wide-open cave with an underground pool. Torches blazed and reflected the watery surface onto the walls.

A chair made of stone covered in strands of pearls sat on a naturally formed rock dais overlooking the deep pool. The waters inside lit up with colorful algae. Sitting on the edge with her feet dangling in the water was the sea witch, Sirena. In her lap sat a wooden bucket full of mussels. She was tossing them into the water.

I strayed closer and glanced into the pool, and I held back my gasp of surprise. For at the bottom of the pool, their feet chained to heavy weights, was the crew of the *Bella Donna*.

Instantly, I recognized Brennon's light hair and the darker-hued shade of Vasili's deep inside the watery prison.

"Are they dead?" I asked.

Sirena was watching me out of the corner of her eye. She plucked a mussel from her bucket and, using a knife, slipped it between the shell and easily pried it open. She offered me the raw mussel. I shook my head. The sea witch shrugged her shoulders and tipped back her head, eating the contents and slurping the shell clean.

"They're under a spell and are safe." She tossed the broken shell behind her. "For now."

"Let them go!" I demanded.

"Let them go?" She scoffed. "They trespassed on my island. They left me no choice but to imprison them. Especially since one of them brought that horrid ring into my home."

Vasili's ring must have upset her and may have even had the opposite effect of helping.

"What does that ring do?" I asked.

"It's a painful reminder of a past long forgotten," she answered. "You're welcome." She gestured with her knife. "If I hadn't given you the bandage, you probably wouldn't have found me."

"Thank you." I scoffed. "But why did you take the crew when they came here for answers?"

She waved her hand in the air dismissively. "I lied. Because my daughters were hungry. I've kept them at bay... for now."

"Daughters?"

The sea witch placed a mussel on the edge of the pool and knocked it into the water. The shell bobbled and floated to the bottom near Vasili. A blue-and-green blur swooped out from under a hidden shelf and gobbled it up before turning its attention on us at the surface.

I sat awestruck as a mermaid with blue hair and a shimmering green tail swam upward. Her head broke the surface, and her piercing black slitted eyes watched me warily. The witch stepped away from the pool and placed the second mussel in front of me.

A deep wailing cry came from within the water, and then the mermaid propelled herself out to sit on the edge. She tried to reach for the mussel, but it was just out of reach. Frustrated, she turned and let out an inhuman cry at her mother.

"I told you, Grotta, if you want it, you need to use your legs."

Grotta made a grunt, her mouth unable to form words out of the water.

The mermaid turned those silky eyes my ways and blinked, her arms pleading with me to give her what she wanted. I picked up the shell and was about to hand it to her, but her beauty distracted me.

Apparently, I didn't move fast enough, because Grotta let out a high-pitched scream, and I covered my ears in pain. In a blinding flash of magic and light, her tail was gone and in its stead a pair of human legs as she propelled herself out of the pool.

Grotta was on me, her hands clawing at my face, her pointed teeth snapping at me and almost taking a finger off as she snagged the shell from me. She turned, raced back to the water, and dove in, her legs transforming back into a tail. It splashed the water with a thump.

The mermaids were very dangerous creatures, and now that I knew what I was looking for, I could see the witch's other daughters swimming in and out beneath the hidden alcoves. Bright, silky manes flowed behind them.

"How many daughters do you have?" I asked the sea witch.

"Seven. One to rule every sea." She grinned and tossed a few more mussels into the pool. Her smile faded as she watched her daughters bicker and fight amongst themselves like dogs over the scraps she was throwing them. Another silky head popped out of the water, and this time a woman with hair the color of wine and stormy gray eyes cooed at me. "But my poor daughters are cursed. If they take human shape, every step they take is like walking on knife blades, and they cannot speak out of water."

"Who cursed them?"

Sirena's eyes glittered dangerously, and she stroked the silky hair on her daughter's head. "A very bitter woman. I took something precious from her, and in return she took something precious from me."

"My mother," I whispered in realization. "In retaliation for what you did to her father. She cursed your daughters."

Sirena's fingers dug into her daughter's hair, and the girl squealed and tried to dive beneath the water to safety.

Sirena's face turned moody. Her white hair moved on its own. The waters in the pool rippled as she directed her anger at me. She had not meant to reveal that tidbit to me.

"Yes, and lo and behold, the captain brought you right to my very island. So now, I have something you want. And you have something I want." Her pointed teeth seemed to gleam at me. She held out her hand expectantly.

"I-I don't have anything."

Sirena blinked at me. "Then they die." She waved her finger in the air, and I saw the seven daughters begin to circle the crewmen. Grotta drew close to Brennon, and her webbed fingers traced down his chest hungrily. She brought her sharp teeth close to his lips.

"No. Stop!" I cried out. "What could you possibly want in return for all their lives?"

"I think it's obvious," she hissed. "I want the curse lifted from my daughters."

"I can't. I don't know how," I said dejectedly. And it was the truth. I didn't know how to lift a curse placed on them by my mother. There were secrets that even she never shared.

"I do," Sirena said sweetly. Barefoot, she tiptoed across the cavern to me, the trail of water lingering behind her. It was as if she was made of water, and a trail was always flowing from her and her daughters. "All you have to do is make a deal with me. One little, itty-bitty deal. A contract that is binding. It will free my daughters *and* give you what you want."

"How could you possibly know what I want—" I raised my voice. "—when I don't even know what I want?"

"It's what everyone wants." Sirena brushed her icy fingers across my shoulders then trailed a finger across my cheek and under my chin. Slowly, lifting my face to meet hers, her bottom lip tucked under her front teeth as she whispered, "Freedom."

"Freedom?"

"I know what you did, Merisol. I, too, know how to scry the kingdoms. You who thought yourself so high and mighty used your powers and murdered a man. Now, you can never return home or see your sisters ever again because of the bounty placed on your head."

My eyes dropped to the floor with guilt. Sirena gripped my chin and made me look into her milky eyes.

"I can make all of it go away."

"How?" I asked.

"I'll take away your magic."

"What?" I snapped and swatted at her hand. "That's impossible."

"No, you see. If your magic is gone, then the bounty hunters can't track you. It means you'll never be able to use magic again, but then you can live your life. Free of all constraints."

"It doesn't undo what I did."

"No, but that is the price you pay. Plus, you will save them." Sirena waved her hand at the floating bodies below.

I shook my head. How long would Sirena's spell last? Would they awaken chained to the floor underwater? Would they drown if I didn't free them? A feeling of dread overcame me. "There must be some other way. I can't give up my magic."

"I wouldn't waste time if I were you. My daughters are getting hungry." She pointed into the pool, and I could see seven girls swimming closer and closer to the men, a few even taking playful snaps at their fingers. If I didn't agree to her demands....

My heart beat wildly in my chest, and I knew my mother would never agree to what I was about to do. She would have found some way around it. Or used her magic to destroy the sea witch, but as Aura constantly reminded me, we were not our mother, despite how she wanted to raise us. We created our own merit and that drove us. We may have been raised to be bringers of evil, but I had already done that and didn't like the repercussions.

Curses were one thing. I was a murderer, and mother never told me the heavy burden that guilt caused. It was suffocating. I felt like I was the one on the bottom of the pool chained to the floor. What I wanted more than anything was a chance at redemption.

"Okay," I muttered.

"What was that, dear? Did you say something?" She grinned.

I knew darn well she heard me, but she was enjoying the gloating.

"Fine," I snapped. "I will give up my magic."

"Excellent." Sirena moved behind her throne and pulled out a conch shell. She carried it over and held it out in front of me. "Put your hand inside."

"What?" I asked in confusion.

Her lips pinched together in frustration. "I said put your hand inside. We must seal the pact."

My right hand trembled as I slid it against the cool shell. My fingers followed the curved form, disappearing as it dipped downward.

"Ouch!" I cried and tried to yank my hand back. It was trapped within the conch. A searing pain bit into the tips of my fingers, and I could feel my warm blood drip down into the shell.

The sea witch's head dropped back, her eyes closed, and she moaned under her breath. "Yes. Yes!"

I fought the shell one last time, giving it a hard shake, and it released my fingers and fell to the floor. The conch rolled, and blood—my blood—dripped from within and pooled on the floor. My heart pounded loudly; my breathing stopped as I saw the omen come to pass.

I backed away, tripping over the discarded mussel shells as I clasped my injured hand to my chest. My fingers still bled, but it wasn't horrible. What scared me was the white lines that ran from my fingertips up the inner palm of my hand, like white veins that looked like coral.

"What did you do to me?" I accused, showing her my hand.

The witch rushed forward, scooped the shell into her hands, and cradled it lovingly. "I did a binding contract in blood." She kneeled by the pool and held the shell up. A daughter with soft-lavender hair broke the surface and grasped the conch shell. Her lips sought it hungrily.

Sirena held the conch and let her daughter drink deeply from it. I watched in horror as my blood dripped down the side of the mermaid's face.

After she drank, the mermaid wiped the drip with the back of her hand. Her mouth pursed as she tried to form words. "Th-thank you, M-mother," she whispered before diving back into the water.

The sea witch clasped the conch to her chest and visibly wept.

"Did you hear her? Did you hear Velora? She called me Mother."

Quickly, the other six sisters rose to the surface, and each one of them reached for the conch greedily.

"Not yet, my sweets. Soon, soon. We mustn't take too much now or we will kill her, and you won't be healed." The sea witch's eyes glittered dangerously at me.

"What did you say?" I gasped.

The sea witch held the conch close to her body protectively and stepped away from the hands of her six daughters who were now all reaching out of the pool. Their cries were painful in pitch and desperation. Their eyes fastened on the magic conch.

"Your magic is in your blood. For me to break the curse on my daughters, they need a continuous supply. Which is why we will be slowly taking it from you over the next few weeks. You've already been linked and can see the mark."

I looked down at the coral white lines on my hand and could already feel a weakness in my body.

"When the curse mark reaches your heart, it will heal all seven of my daughters, and you will be dead."

"Dead. You never mentioned I would be dead when this is over!"

"Oh, didn't I? Silly me. Yes, of course I said you'd be free. And the greatest freedom is death."

"No, you deceived me!"

"I only did what your mother did to me! A curse for a curse," she hissed. Her eyes went black as her pupils widened. "Her sweet lies that cost me so much. Now, it is my turn to take something away from her. I will have my revenge." She curled her hands into fists as she cackled.

I felt so helpless, trapped by my stupidity because I wanted to be the hero. I wanted to help others and therefore guaranteed my death.

"No, this can't be," I whispered.

A loud, haunting whisper rose out of the deep of the cave. A man's voice that sounded like it came from beyond the grave gave a creepy warning.

"You promised," the haunted voice called out. "You promised." The two words repeated as if spoken by a thousand voices.

The sea witch cocked her head and listened. She gave me a sly smile.

"That I did," she answered.

I didn't think she was speaking to me.

"There *is* a way to break the curse." She twirled a finger around a pearl bead braided in her hair. "It should be easy for you, since you've already done it once before."

"What? What must I do?" My world was closing in on me, and I was struggling to breathe.

Her eyes glowed with excitement. From the folds of her seaweed dress, she produced a sheathed dagger, and embedded in the handle was the ruby ring Vasili brought to the island.

She unsheathed the deadly blade. "The heart stone in this dagger will glow red when presented with the one acceptable as a sacrifice. If you plunge the blade into the heart of them, it will break the curse." Sirena sheathed the dagger and placed it in my palm, wrapping my fingers around it and giving my hand a reassuring pat. "A life for a life."

"No." I tried to give it back.

"Really? I'm surprised at you. You call yourself a daughter of Eville, and yet you balk at this simple task."

"Taking a life is never a simple task. It's murder."

"Yes, and your hands are already stained with blood. What's one more life? Especially if they are as evil as Armon? I'm sure the world will be better off without another rapist. Ask yourself, aren't you glad he is no longer alive to terrorize your sisters and other young women?"

"Yes." My fingers hurt as I grasped the hilt, my knuckles turning white.

"Then maybe you would do the world another favor. Take the dagger, take a life, and save yourself."

The weapon dropped to my side, my shoulders slumped, and I stared at the water puddles that covered the cave floor.

She leaned close to me; her breath came in excited whispers. "But you need to do it before this—" She touched the white mark on my hand. "—reaches here." She jabbed my heart. "Or you'll be dead." She cackled. In a whirl of seaweed, she spun, holding the conch shell high above her head like a prize. "Oh, and I forgot to mention something else. You cannot speak to anyone of our deal or your mouth will burn with fire."

My blood turned cold in my veins. My body shivered as I realized my plan at redemption had failed. I would need to murder again, not to protect someone, but to survive. My legs gave out, and I collapsed, bruising my knees on the rough stone, feeling alone and defeated. I was too shocked to even cry at my misfortune and fate.

"But a deal is a deal." She snapped her fingers, and I felt a wave of power emanate through the room.

Then I remembered why I had come. I crawled toward the pool and looked into the water, and what I saw terrified me. The crew was waking up. I could see them struggling against the chains. Brennon's eyes were open, and he was swatting at the mermaids who were coming and tormenting him. Vasili was clawing and pawing at the water, trying to swim to the surface.

"Let them go!" I screamed.

"I did." Sirena stepped backward, holding the shell as she retreated to the far end of the room. "I released them from the spell that kept them asleep." She pulled an iron key from around her neck and tossed it into the pool. The key floated to the bottom, just out of Brennon's reach.

"Now, the rest is up to you." She waved at me.

I reached for magic, opening my mouth to sing.

"Ah, ah, ah!" Sirena held the shell in the air. "If you use your magic, your curse spreads faster! It could kill you right now, and then where would your friends be?"

I swore under my breath, dropped the dagger onto the cavern floor, and dove straight into the pool. The cold hit me like a slap to the face as I dug with my hands and kicked like a madwoman. A blur of motion swam past me, and I remembered I was down here with seven carnivorous mermaids.

My eyes on the iron key, which sat partially submerged beneath the sand, I could already see that some other crew had yet to awaken from their spell. Either that or they had already drowned.

No! Don't focus on the negative.

Finally, I reached the key and swam over to the heavy padlock on the anchor stone beneath Brennon. The water kept wanting to pull me upward, and I had to kick to stay near the bottom. I pushed the key in the lock. Desperately, I tried to turn it, but it wouldn't budge.

Then someone else was there. Brennon grabbed the key from me. His mouth was pinched in a hard line, his brows furrowed as he tried to use his exceptional strength to turn the key. During our endeavor, the knit hat slid from my head, and my red hair floated in the water like a cloud of blood.

Vasili, chained five feet over, had stopped swimming and now floated in the water, his body motionless.

"Mmmph," I cried out in distress. Air bubbles escaped my lips, and I focused back on Brennon. He hit the lock a few times and tried to turn it again. That's when I realized it was the wrong key. Sirena never intended for me to free the men. It was another trick. And I was the fool.

Brennon realized the key didn't work. He could see the panic in my eyes. My lungs were burning, and I desperately wanted to abandon him and swim to the surface for air.

He grabbed my shoulders and placed a palm against my cheek. He pointed up, and I shook my head, refusing to leave him.

His eyes darkened, and he gripped my shoulders and tried to use his massive strength to propel me to the surface. I fought him tooth-and-nail, kicking and fighting to stay near him. Then, the unthinkable happened. Brennon's mouth opened and he gasped. I could see him convulse as he began to drown. His eyes filled with pain.

I couldn't let that happen. I had to save everyone. I had to save him.

No matter the cost to myself or the sea witches warning. I kicked to the surface and broke through the water, gasping. Exhausted and half choking, I focused all of my power and sang a clear note, followed by a second.

I continued to sing and used my hands to coax the water to my bidding, sending it into a vortex, pushing against itself. Note after note, it followed my commands. As the water receded, we all dropped to the sandy floor, a wall of water now rushing around us like a hurricane and we were in the eye.

My hands pushed out as I focused on holding the water back, knowing that if I lost my concentration, the water would return and hit us like a wall, crushing and possibly killing all of us.

Brennon lay immobile on his back, and I desperately wanted to rush to his aid, but I couldn't. I had to continue to sing. My hands trembled under the strain, but I needed help. A few of the men stirred, their spell having worn off, but neither Vasili nor Brennon moved.

I saw a purple blur watch me through the rushing waters, and I silently pleaded with her, motioning with my head to help Brennon. The mermaid nodded and stepped through the wall of water. Velora's long lavender hair covered her naked chest and legs as she tiptoed over to Brennon's side. She leaned down and pressed her mouth to his, and I thought she was killing him.

My singing faltered, and the water rushed in a few feet.

She stopped and glared at me angrily. "No, stop! Sing," she commanded. "I help."

I had no choice but to watch as the beautiful woman leaned back over Brennon and pressed her mouth to his. A few seconds later, Brennon coughed. She backed away, and water spewed from his mouth. She rolled him over on his side to help clear his lungs.

"There." The mermaid pointed through the moving wall of water to a dark cave. "Safety. There."

Understanding, I used my hands and pushed the water farther back, revealing an exit at the bottom of the pool. Where it led, I didn't know. But I knew enough that the mermaids wouldn't want me dead. Not yet. Not until all the sisters could walk and talk.

Velora motioned with her hands to her other sisters, and they came through the water wall. "Come. Help!" She pointed.

The girls hissed and cried out in pain as they walked along the floor. Each one grabbed a half-enchanted crewmember and carried them out of the exit. Despite their stature, mermaids were incredibly strong.

I couldn't help but wonder if they were taking them away to eat them or imprison them again.

Velora easily lifted Brennon. His head fell back on her shoulder. "We help." She turned and walked after her sisters, her long hair covering her backside. I could see that, unlike the painful steps of her sisters, Velora's were long and confident. It even seemed that the more she used her voice, the more eloquent she became. And it was because of the promise of the curse being lifted that the others were helping me.

What seemed like forever, but was probably only minutes later, the sisters returned and helped another seven men out of the cavern. After a quick count. I saw it was more than the twenty men who had originally come ashore. It was our entire crew.

A mermaid picked up Vasili on the second rescue wave, and after the fifth wave, I was the only one left, and by then, my throat was burning. I ran after the girls into the dark tunnel. It was slippery but had natural worn steps that led upward. When we hit dry stone, I knew we had reached above sea level, so I stopped singing and turned to watch the water rush in after me.

A great roar filled the air as a mighty wave rushed down the tunnel and splashed up the steps to hit my knees.

A chorus of cries came from above, and six colorful heads came running back down the steps. One after another, they dove back into the water and transformed into mermaids. Their green, blue, and rose-colored tails cut through the wave and disappeared into their home.

Only Velora stood at the top of the steps, waiting for me. When I reached the top, I saw we came out behind a waterfall, and it was midmorning. Most of the crew were still asleep under the sea witch's enchantment and were curled on their sides, sleeping along the bank of the waterfall. Vasili was sitting on an enormous boulder, his head tucked between his knees. Brennon was sitting on the ground, his back to me. Velora pointed through the palms, and I followed the direction of her finger. Beyond, I could see the white sandy beach and the longboat. She handed me a wet gray mass, which turned out to be my hat.

I wrung it out and then tucked my hair back in, not even sure why I bothered anymore.

"Thank you." I turned around, but she was gone.

CHAPTER THIRTEEN

The reunion of the crew was not the triumphal event I thought it would be. I retreated through the underbrush and watched the men from a distance as they recovered from the aftereffects of the spell. I wasn't ready for the questions or accusations that would come my way once they learned of my deceit, and second that I was a sorceress.

Most of them never remembered even encountering the sea witch nor sleeping in their watery prisons. They only remembered walking up on the banks of the waterfall.

"What a waste," Adair muttered, kicking a stone. "We didn't find any treasure."

Vasili, who looked like he had the biggest headache, looked around in confusion at his surroundings. "I don't remember. Where are—?"

"Where's the woman?" Crowley called out.

"What woman?" Adair asked.

"I remember the most beautiful naked woman." He wrapped his arms around himself. "She was embracing me."

"You're a nut. No woman would want to embrace you!" Swifty muttered.

I believed Brennon and Vasili remembered more. Although, I wasn't sure. Brennon kept pacing the clearing, searching the surrounding foliage, even going waist-deep back into the pool of water to dive below.

"What are you doing?" I muttered. My hand had been hurting ever since I sang back the water wall. I flexed my fingers and looked at my palm. What had started as a few white markings along my fingertips now spread through most of my palm and a few inches above my wrist. Like a disease that was spreading through my body.

At least I wasn't dead... yet.

Just the thought made my mouth go sour with fear. No, I would reverse the spell. I had to. But then, the image of Velora walking without pain and speaking to her mother was beautiful. It had even created a bond between us.

I sighed and wiped away the tears that threatened to spill forth. Taking a deep breath, I headed through the palms and went back to the skiff. Howland was sitting on a fallen tree, watching the waves crash against the shore. I made plenty of noise as I came out of the dark.

"Meri!" Howland called out in surprise when he saw me. "Did ye find everyone?"

I grinned and waited until I was up close. "They're all safe and will head back here shortly. But we should head back. They'll be hungry."

"What about the witch?" he asked. I could hear the fear in his voice.

"She will not bother you again," I said, knowing that it was me who had to worry about her from now on.

"A-are ye sure?"

"I'm sure." I stepped into the boat and was about to open my mouth to sing but then looked at my white palm and shook my head. It wasn't worth it. I sat down and eagerly tried to get the two oars under control.

"Slow down. If I didn't know better, I'd think ye be running away from somethin'."

I looked back at the island, and my heart hurt. "I just want to get back on board quickly, Howland. Please." I touched my hat, and his eyes went wide.

"Oh, that be right. Let's get ye tucked away." He swung his leg over the boat and sat next to me on the bench. Tuckered out, I did my best to row as fast as I could. We had just gotten to the ship and were tying off when I saw the shadows of the crew head out onto the shore.

Fang and Thorn stepping from below deck startled us as we boarded. They both froze and looked surprised to see us. Fang's face turned into an ugly snarl, and he stormed across the deck.

Howland stepped in front of me. The old man puffed out his chest and tried to stand up to Fang, even though he only stood a few inches over me. He pointed to the oncoming long-boat. "Ye best prepare for the crew's return."

"The crew's back already?" Fang asked in surprise.

Fang and Thorn glanced over the side of the ship at the longboat, and they seemed shocked. If I didn't know better, I would've thought these men were in league with Sirena. For how else had they escaped her clutches?

"And the captain."

Thorn cussed under his breath.

"How did ye escape the spell?" Howland asked.

Fang reached up and pulled out chunks of wax from his

ears. "Something my father taught me when under attack by sea folk."

"Ye coulda shared that knowledge with the crew," Howland growled.

Fang shook his head. "You seem just fine."

Howland lunged and I grabbed his arm, holding him back. The old man sighed before backing down. He patted my shoulder, shoving me toward the galley away from danger.

Howland and I quickly prepared the rations. We would probably sail away fast, and the men needed sustenance while they worked. I used the time to explain to Howland what I discovered in the storeroom, what I believed to be selkie furs.

"So that explains why Fang reacted the way he did. I bet he hoped ye woulda died and their nasty secret with 'em."

I grimaced, thinking back to the painful lashes. "I'm not sure how I didn't either."

"Well, ye only received three lashes before a mighty storm came. Scared the men, so they threw ye in the brig. I'm so sorry I couldn't help ye, Meri."

I heard the commotion and the confusion when the captain and crew came aboard.

"I best go hand out the rations." Howland sighed, putting down his knife. "I'd stay down here if I were you until this business with Thorn and Fang is over."

"I know," I muttered.

I listened as Howland limped out of the galley and headed up to the deck. I could hear muffled cursing from the men. The ceiling sounded like it was caving in as heavy footfalls ran down the steps and toward the galley.

Brennon burst through the door. "You're here!" he gushed when he saw me sitting at the wood table.

"I'm here," I replied softly, waiting for him to yell, curse, or cuff me for leaving his room.

He blinked and looked at me in confusion. "You've been *here*." He pointed his finger at the floor. I could tell from his dilated pupils that he was still under the effects of Sirena's spell. He was probably still in shock from dying and being revived. It would've been easy to pretend I had never left the ship at all.

"I was here in the *brig*, actually," I said.

"The brig? Why were you in the brig?" His hands fell to his sides.

"Fang and Thorn," I said sourly. "Fang gave me three lashes for stealing."

"Did you?" Brennon's voice was stern.

"No," I snapped as all the emotions from the last few days came pouring out of me. "I found what I believe to be selkie furs."

Brennon's look of concern turned to one of suspicion. "Selkie furs. Are you sure?"

"Yes. I overheard them earlier say they were trying to unload them in Fairehaven but could not. They're hidden inside an ornamental rug."

His lips pressed into a vindictive line. The muscles in his jaw clenched angrily. "A pirate. Just like his father. I will deal with both of them shortly."

Howland returned carrying an empty crate. He moved to the other side of the long worktable and watched the captain warily.

Brennon paced the galley in thought. "So, you weren't on the island? I could have sworn you saved me. That you...." He ran his hands through his hair.

"I wasn't on the island," I repeated firmly. "I never left the ship."

He shook his head in disbelief and reached for my hat, and I pulled away from him. "Don't touch me," I warned.

Howland came to my rescue and stepped between us. "Ye heard 'im."

Brennon's face turned hard. I saw the clench of his jaw as he glared at me and shook his head. "I must have been mistaken then." He had to grip the pillar for support as he swayed slightly.

"Are you okay?" I asked worriedly.

"No. I mean... yes, I will be as soon as we leave this dreaded island. It was a mistake to come here." Without further accusation, he spun and stormed out.

"Merisol," Howland muttered. "Why would ye deceive the captain like that? What good would come from lyin' about bein' on the island?" Howland was the one to turn distrustful eyes my way. "What happened in that place that has everyone actin' all crazy?"

"You were right. It is a cursed place, and for the sake of the men and myself, I cannot speak of what transpired. It's safer for me if they don't know what happened. Can you trust me on this?"

He scratched the shadow of a beard along his chin and sighed. "I'll trust ya, but just to let ye know, I won't be lyin' for ye. If he asks me straight out, I will tell 'im."

I nodded and accepted the peace and comfort that gave me. Sailors were a very superstitious bunch, and if they knew I was a sorceress, I'd be tossed overboard. That's why I hid after rescuing them and why I would continue to hide my identity. Brennon called for all hands to go on deck and drop sails. Everyone was in a hurry to leave. I was wrong about saving the whole crew. Despite my rescue attempt, there were seven members missing. Not all of us escaped the sea witch's clutches. I prayed they were still alive and ended up marooned on the island, but then I remembered the cave full of skulls and I knew better. They were gone.

Without their help, they tasked me with climbing the chains to the foremast and dropping the top-gallant sail. Being as small as I was, I felt like a spider clinging to a web for dear life. But I feared failure more. I, too, wanted to leave this dreaded place.

Once I unfurled the sail, Crowley began securing it. I threaded my arm through the rope chain as we sailed away. From my perch by the crow's nest, the island slowly became nothing more than a black speck on the horizon. When it was the size of a marble, I finally felt the weight lifted from my chest.

Brennon was a different man after he returned. Not once did he comment on my vacancy from his quarters. In fact, it was as if he forgot who I was completely and the game he accused me of playing. I counted my blessings and went to sleep in my hammock. Though the eight empty hammocks next to me haunted my sleep.

I dreamed of men drowning, of a shell piercing my hand, of being eaten alive by mermaids. And finally, I dreamed of the sea witch. Standing over my hammock, touching my face.

Gasping, I sat up so fast I almost rolled out of the hammock. My breathing was ragged, salt crusting my cheeks from silent night terrors. In my hand, I clutched the dagger— the same one I had abandoned in the cavern when I dove underwater to save the crew.

I pulled the dagger from the pearl sheath and gazed at the deadly double-sided blade. Sheathing it, I glanced over at the floor below me and saw the footprint-sized puddles that led from my hammock up the stairs.

CHAPTER FOURTEEN

Our course and speed were nigh impossible. Brennon had become a man possessed and hardly left the helm, determined to put as much distance between the island and our ship. We had even dumped non-essentials to lighten our load. Only when the fog became too thick or the seas became too rough for the knots we were sailing did he slow.

They had tried Fang and Thorn at sea and found them guilty. The captain sent them to the brig for the rest of the journey. They were lucky they weren't tossed overboard, for Brennon was angry enough he could have killed them.

Since the island, I threw myself into work so I wouldn't have to worry about the curse. I had to mop out Brennon and Vasili's cabins, polished their boots, and spent the rest of my time mending sails or running up and down the chains. It was backbreaking work, but I dared not appear weak or risk drawing attention back to me.

But then I would chuckle to myself. I was a powerful sorceress. I didn't need protection from a man. Yet, using my magic terrified me. Multiple times a day, I would stare at the coral pattern and trace it on my hand, wondering if it had grown any larger since the last time I looked. I kept telling myself that maybe if I didn't use magic ever again, I would never fully be siphoned.

But I knew it to be a foolish dream, for each day the white poison marker moved an inch up my arm. Some days, I was the barrelman and had to sit in the forward crow's nest. I could see seven shadowy figures following in the *Bella Donna*'s wake. I was so fixated on what was following us that I didn't notice the temperature rise, the wind change, or the wall of white clouds until I heard the most dreaded call.

"Squall!" Crowley cried out, pointing toward the oncoming storm.

"All hands on deck! Get the sails stowed! Batten down those hatches!" Brennon roared.

I scrambled out of the crow's nest, climbed down to the top yard, and crawled out to the end. Securing my feet in the footropes under the yard, I frantically tried to stow the sails. Crowley, Swifty, and Adair quickly climbed up and joined me on the yard.

"We won't get them all secured," Conroy warned. "Do your best, boy, and when the storm gets us, tether yourself to the ship and hold on for dear life. Do you understand?"

I nodded while clinging to the yard. My hands clawed at the sail as others pulled the ropes to secure them. I worked at a frenzied pace while continually glancing up at the white wall we were sailing into. I tried to hide my fear from the others as we secured one sail. In front of me, I could see others on the fore mast doing the same thing. If we left the sails up as we went through the storm, they could be destroyed, and we would be left adrift at sea.

Howland and Barley were scurrying across the deck, using

batten rods to close and secure the hatches that led below. Vasili and Brennon were discussing the storm. I could see Vasili using his hands to direct the best sailing route. Brennon shook his head and pointed to the west.

The storm was a good ways away, but on a normal day, it could take a full day to stow the sails; we knew they wouldn't all survive the coming storm. We did our best. But my best wasn't good enough for me. When the others had made their descent, I struggled with my section of the sail.

"C'mon, boy! Leave it. It's not worth yer life," Howland cupped his hands and yelled up at me.

The crew tied themselves off using spare rope to the sides and the masts, in case they were thrown overboard. I knew I had forgotten something as I rushed out onto the yard. The closer to the storm we came, the more the end of the sail flapped out of my reach. I just needed to secure this last bit. My fingers worked at the knot as the waves got rough.

Brennon turned the ship to hit the waves at an angle, the waves knocking into the ship, the wind whipping us relentlessly.

I clung to the yard, too scared to shimmy back down to the mast.

"Merisol!" Howland yelled. "Get moving. Now!" He stomped his foot.

It was my actual name that did it. I abandoned the corner of the sail and, hand over hand, my ankles wrapped around each other, I pulled myself toward the mast.

We crested another wave as I was going down the rope chains. I missed a step and felt myself fall. I screamed and reached out, clawing for purchase. My face smacked against the chains, the rope burning my cheek as I slid and tumbled down. My arm caught on a cross hair of rope, and I slowed. My hat disappeared in my tumble.

Warm blood trickled down my face, and fear paralyzed me. If I let go, it would fling me into the sea. I could sing, but then I could also die. The wind and waves beat at my heart and soul as I contemplated just ending it all. Letting go. And then I wouldn't have to kill anyone, and the sea witch couldn't claim my powers for her daughters.

One by one, I worked my fingers loose, and I was about to release, when a hand clamped over mine.

"Don't you *dare* let go!" Brennon growled. I looked up into his stormy eyes. His blond hair was pulled back, but the wind whipped out tendrils. Rain and water dripped from his nose onto my cheek. He had scrambled up the lines and placed himself over me, pushing me farther into the chains. "Tie yourself to me," he ordered.

"I can't move," I cried out.

Brennon wrung one hand in the rung above me then quickly worked a rope around my waist. He brought his face low to my waist and used his teeth to tighten it. He came back up, yanking on the rope, and gave me a sly grin.

His warm hand wrapped around my waist and pressed me closer to his chest. As I followed his lead, Brennon and I took it step by step. When we made it to the deck, he wasn't ready to let me go. He gripped my hand and pulled me into an embrace, as if he tried to shelter me with his very body. I shivered against the cold and against the heat that burned between us.

Vasili had taken the helm. Man against the sea, man was losing. Crowley rushed to his side, and both men struggled to keep the ship steady as we hit another massive wave.

One of the partly tied sails became unfurled.

"Watch out!" Brennon pushed me to the deck as the wind snapped the closest sail, and it flung around. The end of the sail was like a snake with its head cut off, whipping in the air, catching a few off-guard, and sending one man into the sea.

I could hear his scream, and then it stopped.

"This is not a natural storm," Brennon cried.

I closed my eyes and listened to the sea as Brennon's words rang through me. It wasn't a normal squall. Magic created it, and I knew what was happening. The sea witch sent this. She wanted me to save them again. If I used my magic, she could syphon me faster.

I pushed against Brennon's warm body. "Untie me," I said.

"Are you crazy? If I do, you'll die."

"We are all going to die if I don't do something crazy." I placed my hand on Brennon's arm and gave it a squeeze. "Trust me."

He looked at me and nodded. He untied me from his waist, and I walked out onto the deck. I stumbled a few times but then quickly regained my footing.

I couldn't hide who I was anymore. There was no shame in being a daughter of Eville. There was no shame in being me.

I pictured the emblems in my mind and sang them into being. My hands, first lifeless at my side, raised as my voice crescendoed. Instead of looking at the glowing white markers that were slowly burning up my arm, I closed my eyes and sang.

Sang a song of *silence* to the wind.

A song of *obedience* to the waves.

My arm burned, and I could feel the mark burning up to my elbow. But I would not give up until the ship was safe. The sea, at first, didn't want to listen, like a petulant child, but I could feel the authority deep within myself. I had only briefly touched it in the cavern. The power came.

I commanded.

The sea obeyed.

Then it was over. I opened my eyes and saw the boat was sitting on a still ocean. The sky was clear and the sun shone across my face.

Never had I used so much of my power. Never before had I sung until my voice was raw. Even though the storm passed and the boat was still, the deck rocked beneath my feet.

I saw Brennon's white face, and I tried to move toward him, but my world slid out of focus as I blacked out.

I awoke disoriented with a pounding headache. As my eyes adjusted, I realized I was in Brennon's bed without a single window left cracked open or a lamp left to give me light. Stumbling through the darkness, I found the door and turned the latch. He locked it. My fists nor my voice brought anyone to my aid. How dare they lock me in like a prisoner? From the position of the sun in the sky, I slept through the night and it was past noon.

A candle mark later, I heard the click of the door, and it swung open as Brennon stepped inside with a tray of food.

"Why do you lock me up like a criminal?" I asked with venom in my voice.

I had taken Brennon's chair at the table and sat facing the door. My knees were pulled up in front of me. It wasn't very ladylike, but since I was still wearing pants, I didn't care.

Brennon wouldn't make eye contact with me. He placed the tray on the table and removed the lid. I had seen the fare

Howland and I prepared for Brennon and his officers. This was nothing more than my daily rations. Dried biscuits and fish.

"Because you *are* a criminal," Brennon answered. "Or is there a different reason the men were chasing you at the waystation?"

I wrapped my hands around my knees and refused to answer him.

Brennon slammed the dome lid back on the tray. "I'm doing this for your protection."

"By keeping me a prisoner?"

"By keeping you alive. Most of those on board don't like your kind and would sooner put a knife in your back."

"My kind?" I asked, dumbfounded.

"Many blame you for what happened on the island. That you bewitched and killed their comrades. They are calling you a witch."

"Sorceress," I corrected. "I was not born a witch. I had a gift for sensing water magic and was trained in its control. Just as someone trained you to see the wind and sail on the sea." I snorted and looked away. I was in a foul mood, and Brennon's mood echoed my own.

"Nevertheless, you shall remain here."

"What have I done that deserves this?"

He turned and gave me the full force of his gaze, and I trembled under the weight of it. I could sense his impatience. "You lied to me."

"I-I... uh...." I couldn't correct him. My shoulders dropped, and I nodded.

"You *were* on the island. There's no doubt about it. I remember you, but you did something to our memories. Now I have to figure out what part you played. If you were in league with the sea witch the whole time."

"No, Brennon. I'm not."

"That's Captain Pike to you!" His voice was hard.

I shook my head. "I—" My mouth burned as I tried to explain what happened with the sea witch but couldn't speak of it.

"Explain to me what I saw. What transpired in that cave? Or I will have to think you were in on it."

"I-I—" I stuttered and grimaced in pain as my mouth refused to speak. I tried to rethink my words that would satisfy him and not enact the spell on my mouth. "I went there to *save* you."

"Liar!" He stormed over to me. Leaning over me, he had a hand on each armrest, trapping me between his arms. "For you're determined to destroy me."

"What?"

"First, when I lost you in the woods, I thought for sure the bounty hunters captured you. Then in the cave, when I couldn't save you, and a third when you almost went over the side of the ship. The thought of losing you... it-it almost destroyed me."

My heart beat wildly in my chest.

"Meri, I blamed myself for losing you in the woods. Then you show up, disguised as a boy on my ship." I sat up, and he shook his head. "Don't fool yourself. I saw right through your ruse. I even thought it fun to tease you. To watch your cheeks bloom like a rose whenever we came too close."

He brushed his fingers across my cheeks.

"I-uh...." The blood rushed to my cheeks, and I pulled away. He had played me.

"Even when I'm away from you, I can't stop thinking of you." He paused and shook his head.

"You think of me?" I asked breathlessly.

"I'm going crazy." He ran his hands through his hair in frustration.

"Brennon," I whispered his name. I almost broke down and told him everything.

When I said his name, his face turned to one of desire. "You are the *very* thing I want yet can't have. Even now, I want nothing more than to kiss you."

My heart beat loudly. Surely, he could hear it. My lips parted as I sucked in my breath.

It was his undoing.

Brennon reached up and ran his fingers through my red hair as it fell about my shoulders. He cupped the back of my neck and drew me close, his lips claiming mine in a kiss.

It was not a gentle kiss but one of passion and desire. My response to the kiss caught me by surprise as I hungrily kissed him back. Our lips parted, and he moaned.

Wrapping his arms around me, he lifted me up out of the chair, and our kiss deepened. I dug my hands into his hair. Not wanting it to stop and fearing it would, I met his desire with my own.

Brennon broke the kiss. I could see the heat still burning in his eyes, the way he couldn't stop staring at my lips as he set me down on the floor. My own ragged breathing matched his own as we tried to control ourselves. I didn't want to. For once, I wanted to be daring and take what I wanted. I wanted Brennon. I reached for him a second time.

"No," he breathed, and my hands dropped to my side. "This cannot happen again. I was foolish to allow it."

"What?" I could feel my newly awakened desire fade.

"There's no question I desire you, Meri. But desire isn't enough, because of who you are and who I am and of my own obligations."

I inhaled. His words cut through to my soul. To be all-consumed in a kiss and then immediately tossed aside was painful. A stab to my heart.

I placed my hand upon the table to steady myself. I felt like he had given me the gift of the universe to only have it ripped from my grasp.

"Tomorrow morning, we will land in Isla."

"Isla," I breathed out the word of the mystical kingdom, and I felt a momentary thrill of excitement.

"But mark my words, Meri. Don't even think of trying to escape. We must discuss your punishment." He tossed his captain's hat on the table and left. I heard the key turn in the lock.

I couldn't stop the room from spinning, and I collapsed to my knees and felt the oncoming tears burn my eyes. Then, as quickly as they came, they stopped. For now, I understood my mother's rule against love and how it made you weak. I would not let him see he hurt me. I was strong, for I was a daughter of Eville and I could face rejection. For I had lived with it my whole life.

The white markings on my arm tingled, and I traced their pattern with my finger. I wouldn't dare use magic to escape the room.

Maybe I could save myself. I reached into my boot, felt the hilt of the dagger, and wondered.

Could I take another life to save my own?

CHAPTER FIFTEEN

The *Bella Donna* made port at Isla a little after sunrise. I headed out to the balcony and watched with interest. The docks were teeming with life, tired men loading and unloading cargo, young women with ribbons in their hair, carrying trays, selling samples of meat pies and pastries with promises of more to come in the taverns beyond the docks. Various birds dotted the skies, more than the white gulls that sometimes flew inland back home.

Even the sea foam sparkled, and the water was crystal-clear, so I could see indigo and blue starfish clinging to the stone pillars and columns. But the chief glory of Isla was the tall spiral towers that shimmered like pearls in the morning sun, and the waterfalls and mystical pools that surrounded the palace. Each waterfall poured into the one below, like a tiered fountain that spilled into the sea. The falls' spray floated up to give the impression the palace was floating on a cloud. I could hear the rumble of the mystical waterfalls even though they were over a mile away.

"It's so beautiful." I blinked away the tears at seeing the

magical city.

Thud. The gangplank lowered, and rumbling and rolling sounds followed as the supplies I had seen locked up in the stores were being unloaded. A few candle marks later, I heard men come and go from the ship, but no one unlocked my door or came to release me.

Was Brennon waiting until all the crew left before he let me go? Did he have an ulterior motive? Was I really not safe as I was first led to believe? Left alone with my thoughts, my mood darkened, and my outlook turned bleak.

My neck ached from watching the pier. But my ears didn't deceive me when I heard the thundering sound of horses, nor the unmistakable sound of armor and shields clanging together. They were coming down the ramp built into the wall that led to the docks on sea level.

Soldiers. The royal banner depicting a gold trident on a field of aqua waved freely before the troops.

Brennon was going to have me arrested.

"That jerk!" I spewed.

I backed away from the balcony railing and panicked. I needed to escape and escape now. I looked down at the shimmering water below me. It was quite a fall, at least forty feet, but I would have to chance it. I heard the key rattle in the lock and glanced over my shoulder.

Brennon entered the room wearing a blue-green cloak. He frowned as he searched the interior darkness of his cabin, but then his eyes went wide when he saw me with one leg over the outside balcony and poised to jump.

"No, Meri don't!" He rushed forth. His steps resonating against the wood, drawing closer.

I hesitated as I remembered our shared kiss. But then I recalled his rejection. I didn't think.

I jumped.

The water rushed toward me. I kept my arms to my sides and shot straight into the water like a needle piercing fabric. Unlike our lake at home, the island water was the temperature of a tepid bath. Thankful I wasn't wearing a dress, I kicked my legs out and dove deeper, swimming under the ship to hide my shadow as I strove to put as much distance between me, the troop, and Brennon.

In the ship's shadow, the water became cooler, and I continued to swim, proud of how long I could hold my breath. I didn't come up for air until I was under the wooden dock, but that was only for a split second as I dove back down and swam parallel with land. When my lungs burned for air, I broke the surface and turned back to try to get a bearing of my surroundings.

I swam farther than I thought, pushed by the sea, or magic, but I was at least three births over from the *Bella Donna*. Brennon was a speck, but I still recognized his giant frame as he ran down the gangplank toward the troops. I took the southern ramp up to the streets and ducked down an alley, working my way through the city, being careful to turn every few streets to make it harder in case someone was tailing me.

As I moved through the streets, I saw an abundance of fountains placed every block. Within them, there would be a multitude of water fae. The fountain closest to me had two naiad girls standing within the shallows, holding up home-made necklaces made of shells and pearls. A faun with a broken horn stood on the street outside and helped them by resizing any of the jewelry on his portable stand.

But among the people of Isla were various castes and accents. I could hear those with a thick Islayan accent, while some had very little. Most of the natives had golden-tan skin, and their hair was a rainbow of colors—fuchsia, aquamarine, plum—but I couldn't tell if it is natural or dyed. My deep red didn't seem to stick out when next to the sky-blue mohawk of the fish stall owner. Trident-shaped tattoos covered his chest, and he wore a necklace made of net and hooks.

The hairstyle for the women was braids with beads and shells throughout. Almost everyone included an aquamarine stone somewhere on their body or hair. Whether it was an aquamarine necklace, beaded bracelet, dyed shirt, or bracers, aquamarine seemed to be the royal color of Isla. It was easy to identify outsiders by their lack of color.

Soaking wet, my hair in knots, I was obviously an outsider. My stomach growled loudly from hunger. I looked at the man with the mohawk and desperately wanted the fish he was serving on a giant palm leaf with papaya and pineapple. It seemed that no matter what, I was always hungry, and food was my biggest temptation.

But I had nothing other than the dagger in my boot, my belongings lost on the ship, and I had not yet finished out my contract nor earned my wages as a cabin boy. I was contemplating stealing the food, when a hand gripped my shoulder and pulled me into the shadows.

"Caught you!" someone whispered.

Fearing it was a bounty hunter, I spun and kicked my attacker in the shin.

"Ouch!" Vasili released me and clutched his bruised leg. "Okay, okay. I surrender. You caught me then." He raised his hands up in the air and gave me a smile. His dark hair covered one eye, making him look playful. "I saw your brilliant exit from the ship. Bravo!" He clapped.

I blushed.

"Brennon is beside himself with frustration and has set out

to searching the entire island for you." Vasili grinned, showing his canines.

"It seems you take pleasure whenever Brennon is put out."

"Of course, but only because we have a longstanding rivalry. And I love getting one over on him. What say you become my guest while you're here? I will grant you my protection, and therefore you will have nothing to worry about."

"You're protected? But aren't you from the Undersea?"

"Yes, but I am held in high esteem with the Prince of Isla," Vasili answered and held up the red ruby ring on his finger. Now that I was closer, I could see the inscriptions in the gold setting. It was the same in the book of the Undersea, which meant it wasn't the same ring in my dagger. Maybe I was mistaken about Vasili being in league with the witch.

"I would be grateful," I said.

"Then come, we must get you out of those clothes and into something more comfortable and let Brennon fret for a while longer."

I was cold, wet, and tired, so I let Vasili lead me through the winding streets. I inwardly groaned each time we passed a food stall.

But the slight pressure he put on my back every time I slowed was enough of a warning that he didn't want to stop. Vasili passed through an old iron gate and came to a fountain of a mermaid in the arms of a king with a golden trident. Vasili pressed his ring against an old emblem in the fountain, and the statue moved back to reveal a swirling vortex of water.

Vasili gave me a slow smile, his eyes twinkling with excitement. "Come with me to the Undersea. Let me show you the wonders of my kingdom."

"But isn't it forbidden?" I asked in awe.

"To mere humans, yes. You would be a special guest of mine and be one of the few who would get to visit the kingdom."

"Only on one condition," I stated, holding my finger in the air.

Vasili's green brows furrowed. "What's that?"

"That one, you promise to bring me back when I say, and two, you feed me. I'm starving."

Apparently, those were not the conditions Vasili expected, because he doubled over in laughter. "Deal, little one. Deal." He wiped the tears from the corners of his eyes and held his arm out to me.

The clear water turned dark as the whirlpool opened up to reveal a dark hole that could span for miles.

"Is this a mythical whirlpool that leads to the Undersea?"

"Yes, there are only two that are still active. This one, which leads to the outskirts and one other that's hidden within the palace. They are both protected by this kingdom."

I carefully stepped over the edge of the fountain and wrapped my arms around Vasili as I looked into the darkness. The wind was powerful and whipped my hair around. Water sprayed up into my face.

"I have to admit. This is terrifying."

"I'd say there's something wrong with you if you weren't terrified of jumping in. You ready?"

I buried my face into his chest. "No!" I murmured.

"Too late." Vasili wrapped his arms tightly around me and yelled, "Hold on!" He leaped into the vortex, and I screamed.

His shirt muffled my cries as we fell.

Into darkness.

Into nothing.

Into the Undersea.

CHAPTER SIXTEEN

M y first impression of the Undersea was that it was cold and dark and lacked the expected seaweed smell. I shivered, and Vasili ran his hands up and down my arms. I waited to let my eyes adjust to the lack of light.

"Careful." He held my hand, and we moved out of the water.

After a few seconds, I could tell we were in another fountain. I would have thought it was the same one, except instead of the king with the trident being the center feature, the Undersea fountain featured a woman holding the trident while the male sat by her feet.

"Why is it so dark?" I asked.

"Because it's night here."

"Really?"

He laughed. "Really. It's daylight in the Overkingdom, but night here. Our kingdoms live in symbiosis of one another, except for a few exceptions, one of them being the passage of time."

"Overkingdom?"

"That's what the people of the Undersea call the Kingdom of Isla."

"Ah, I see."

Vasili dropped my hand and pointed to the sky, or what would have been the sky in our world. The ceiling was a black wall of ocean, and instead of stars, it was lit with floating jellyfish and bioluminescent fish.

"How is it we...?" I pointed at the wall of water.

"Aren't drowning? Magic." Vasili ran his finger over his ring, and it glowed and lit up. He held it up, and I could see it reflect against the magical barrier that held the water back.

An ominous shadow passed overhead, and I stared. My mouth hung open as a whale swam just feet outside the sphere of magic. Surely, it would crash through the watery ceiling, but it continued to swim and ignored the underwater city.

"This is amazing," I breathed.

"Come, I promised you food." Vasili led the way through the dark streets. At first, I thought it was gloomy. But that was because the city was asleep. When he walked past a coral formation, the coral woke up to his presence and began to glow, lighting the path in front of him. With each step we took, more rocks and even underwater plants came to life, reaching out to touch him and then going back to sleep once we made our way safely past.

Undersea guards stopped us in front of the red coral palace gates. Black shale and dark-green algae uniforms decorated their bodies that were accented by their muted purple-and-gray hair.

"Who goes there?" the white-haired guard challenged.

"It's me, Warren," Vasili drawled out lazily.

"Sorry, Captain." Warren quickly opened the gate. "Did you find what you were looking for?"

Vasili's shoulders dropped. "No."

The coral gate swung inward as more troops lined the inner courtyard. Lanterns filled with colorful orbs of green magic lit the path. Where Isla's palace shimmered with light, the Undersea's dark stone palace glowed like a burning ember lit from within. The upper floors glowed purple, while the lower floors shimmered in colors of green. A very calming effect for the night.

Vasili came to the main doors, and he pulled out his flute and played a tune. The doors lit up from within, and traces of magic symbols ran along the frame. They swung open with a click.

Vasili tucked the flute into his pack and gestured to the foyer. "Welcome to Loch Lair Palace. The only palace completely created by magic and music."

With every step on the marble floor, a musical note followed. Not loud and overbearing, but faint like a whisper.

I studied my feet and the glow that surrounded them. I took another hesitant step, and the marble tile lit up again. Then the inner child in me came out, and I began to hopscotch across the floor, the floor chiming with my dance.

Vasili shook his head in amusement. "You're easily amused, aren't you?"

Not caring. I turned around and raced back, this time sliding across the tiles, creating a cacophony of sound. The room lit up with a prism of bright light.

Vasili covered his eyes, as it was almost blinding.

"Enough already, before you wake everyone and get me in trouble," he teased.

"Sorry, I forgot," I whispered. Immediately quelling my

antics, I tucked my hands in my pockets and tiptoed, staying dutifully behind Vasili as he led me down a hallway then up a flight of stairs. He came to a room with double doors and opened one for me, gesturing for me to enter before him.

I expected depressing colors, but I was pleasantly proven wrong. Furniture made from living coral filled the room, giving the impression of living in an underwater flower bed.

Tables and chairs were formed from yellow bamboo. Each piece of coral had a function and added to the beauty of the room, and the darkness of the wall only amplified their glow. The lamps again contained glowing algae, and along the walls hung various instruments including lutes, harps, and whistles.

"You can stay here. I will send some servants with food and clothes for you. Can't have you looking like a boy upon introductions."

"Introductions with whom?" I asked.

"A friend. Then we will head back. There's someone who will miss you despite what he warned." Vasili gave me a wink and closed the doors.

I took a turn about the room, studying the paintings on the wall. They all depicted previous queens of the Undersea. The first portrayed a woman with hair as white as milk, a black crown upon her brow, a conch shell horn in her hands. The second image, another white-haired queen on the back of a shark, a spear in her hand, a pan flute around her neck. The last queen looked forlorn, a harp cradled in her arms, her face looking down.

The doors opened, and a trio of naiads swept in with dresses, combs, and—thank the stars—food. Made of water, they were full-size water sprites. The closest one pulled at my clothes, but I ignored her and followed the tray of food. When she removed the lid, I hungrily grabbed the colorful and neat finger foods provided, shoved them in my mouth, and chewed.

And almost spit it out.

"Mmmfff!" I clapped my hand over my mouth and looked around the room in panic.

"Here." One naiad sensed my discomfort and handed me a cloth napkin. With little grace, I spat out the food and made a face.

"W-what is it?" I asked, wiping the flavor from my tongue.

She pointed to each one with enthusiasm. "Raw snail soaked in cod oil, fresh octopus with caviar, and shark wrapped in seaweed."

I became queasy as the octopus limb crawled across the table.

"Is there anything else? Maybe cooked food?"

The naiads looked at me like I was crazy. Apparently, these were the delicacies offered in the Undersea. Now I understood Vasili's expressions when he tried Howland's food. He was probably used to very *fresh* kills. Thankfully, eating the snail in cod oil had killed my taste buds and ended my immediate hunger pains.

The naiads were gentle as they used a powder shampoo, rubbed it into my hair, and brushed it. I sat on a coral stool and let them work on me from head to toe. As one massaged my scalp, another filed my nails with a shell, while the third took my measurements and disappeared out of the room, only to return moments later with a dark-green dress with feather capped sleeves.

"That's beautiful!" I exclaimed.

Their laugh was the sound of crashing waves. I couldn't tell the women apart even though I tried. One looked to be a little more substantial while the other two were lighter, possibly younger.

I allowed myself to be dressed in the dark-green gown. My hair was curled and pinned with pearls and a jeweled starfish. Black gloves covered my hands and the white marks on my arms.

When I finished, they brought me to Vasili, who was lounging in a chair, his long legs draped over the arms. He sat up when he glimpsed me. He used his finger to direct me to spin, and I obliged.

"Perfect," he exclaimed. He held out his elbow, and I rested my palm on his arm as he led me into a music room. An older woman with white hair sat at a piano bench. Her black dress had tendrils of black beads that ran up the sides, creating a hidden pattern within the folds. There wasn't enough reflective light to see the pattern from across the room. A black coral bracelet enveloped her slim wrists.

"Who is this, Vasili?" The woman sitting by the piano glowered at us.

Vasili crossed the room and gave her a kiss on the top of her head before leaning on the piano. "This is Merisol, a friend." Vasili smirked.

"We strictly forbid outsiders, Vas. You know that."

"I do. But she's not an outsider, per se."

"What do you mean?" she asked.

Vasili plucked a dead piece of coral off the fireplace mantel and placed it within my hands.

"What do you want me to do with this?" I questioned.

He leaned close and whispered, "Sing."

"I can't," I said softly and held the coral toward him.

Vasili's lips pinched together in impatience. "Yes, you can. You calmed the storm."

The dead coral shook, my hands trembling with fear. "You don't understand. I can't."

Vasili pinched the bridge of his nose. "Are you purposely trying to make me look like a fool in front of my mother?"

Now, my hands not only trembled; they became clammy.

"Your mother." I turned to the woman at the piano.

When I addressed her, she smiled, and I could see the same pointy canines Vasili had.

"Darya, Queen of the Undersea." She held her hands out as if addressing the room. She sauntered over to me and looked at the dead coral in my hands.

"It seems you were wrong about her, Vasili."

Vasili stood at attention, his eyes focused on a spot across the room. "I'm not wrong."

"Please, believe me. I can't do what you're asking."

Darya pulled a gold chain around her neck and lifted a pan flute to her lips. She blew across the top, and the flute glowed. The coral slowly changed colors and came to life in my hands. Colorful flowers sprouted along the edges, and I could feel the warmth and magic flow through my fingers.

She tucked the necklace away and gently took the coral from me, stroking it like it was a pet.

"Well, whatever you thought you saw, you must have been mistaken, because you are wrong... again." Her tone was impatient. "Why do you continue to get my hopes up, Vasili? It's too painful to bear."

Vasili didn't move a muscle, but his eyes darkened, and I could tell he was angry.

"Very well, I will continue my search."

"And this time, don't return until you have what we need."

"Yes, my queen." Vasili bowed. He marched over to me

and gripped my elbow. Not hard, but I could tell he was disappointed in me.

"I'm sorry," I muttered.

Vasili froze, turned to me, and his eyes softened. "No, I just made a mistake. I thought you could help me." He sighed. "Let's go. It's best if I don't show my face around here for a while."

"What do you mean?"

"I'm technically banished until I return the stolen treasure or convince the Kingdom of Isla to help ours."

We took a different route out of the palace and headed down a small path, passing various coral gardens, and like the rock inside, these were dead.

"Vasili, what happened here?" I pointed to the fossils.

"Our world is dying." He pointed above at the sea, and it looked even closer than before. "The magical sphere that protects us is slowly collapsing. The queen's magic is the only thing keeping the Undersea from disintegrating, but she is old and weak. Even our people, the naiads, selkies, and mermaids have gone above ground to the Overkingdom. And unless we can find the lost treasure, all will be lost."

I felt sadness at the loss of his home, and now that I knew what to look for, I could see the patches of coral and life that were dying away. Structures and buildings were eroding as the magic was fading.

We came to a different whirlpool, this one just outside the palace sea gardens. He placed his ring on the stone again, and the statue moved, revealing the whirlpool.

"Come, we must get back."

I hesitated. "I don't know if I should. I'm not exactly welcome there."

"Nonsense, like I said, you'll be my guest, and enough time has passed that all will be forgotten."

He grabbed my gloved hand and jumped into the whirlpool. We hit water and fell and continued to sink. Then we weren't sinking but swimming to the surface. The pressure in my ears popped, and a roaring sound echoed in them underwater.

CHAPTER SEVENTEEN

T his time, we didn't come out from one of the fountains. I coughed and swam over to the edge. Vasili gracefully swam next to me and helped me out of the water. I wrung out my hair as I glanced up at the mystical waterfalls of the palace.

The air was cool, and the sun had set. Vasili pulled out his flute and played a few notes, and our clothes instantly dried without a single wrinkle, my hair perfect.

"Come, we mustn't be late. Much time has passed since we left."

"What do you mean?" I looked around at the darkness that still surrounded us. "It's still night. It's only been a few candle marks."

Vasili's eyes dropped to his feet. "I didn't explain fully, and for that I'm sorry. Time passes differently in the Undersea."

I stopped and stared at him, panic filling my voice. "How much time exactly?"

"What is only a few candle marks in Undersea, is days in Isla."

"No, Vasili. Please tell me you're wrong!" I grasped at the

long glove and pulled it down to reveal the white veins along my arm, which had moved above my elbow.

Vasili took my hand, placed it over his arm, and escorted me through the mists and toward the palace, which was lit with lights and the sound of music. With practiced ease, he navigated us through the maze of paths and fauna and came to an outdoor banquet.

"What are we doing here?" I asked.

"The king is having a minor celebration."

I couldn't contain my frown of confusion. "Why?"

"You'll see."

Paper lanterns hung from the nearby trees, creating a kaleidoscope of color on the ground. Tables scattered across the lawn with enough seating for a few hundred people. Humans, elves, gnomes, water sprites, and all races sang and drank in the celebration. Servants in white dresses moved between the tables, bringing out trays of food.

My stomach was making the most unnatural noise from hunger, and I immediately made my way through the mass of people to a gnome and took a skewer from his tray. Learning from my lesson with Vasili's food and penchant for raw fish, I gave it a cursory sniff.

It smelled sweet, fruity, like pineapple with some spice. I took a tentative bite and wanted to cry with joy. I quickly devoured the morsel and hunted down that gnome for a second skewer. Now, if I could only find some cookies, I would be happy.

In my search for food, I became separated from Vasili but wasn't worried as I found the buffet table. I grazed on sweet cakes, grilled fruit, and fish wrapped in leaves. I was about to reach for what looked like grilled softshell crab, when my skin prickled with warning.

Slowly, I turned and surveyed my surroundings, but there were too many people to pinpoint the evil magic I was feeling. Maybe I was mistaken. I grabbed the crab in my gloved hand, and the magic came again like a slap to my face.

"Oh, come on." I sighed and dropped the crab back on the plate. "I'll be back for you later," I promised the delicious crab and tried to open my senses to track the magic user.

"Talking to the food, are we? I wonder, does it talk back?" Someone chuckled behind me.

I turned around and saw Brennon. Gone was his swash-buckling pirate gear, and instead he wore a green fitted jacket trimmed in gold, white pants, and polished black boots. His blond hair was slicked back, and his earring was gone. He looked fantastic.

Brennon's eyes widened in surprise when he recognized me. "Meri. You're alive?" He grabbed my arm and pulled me aside. "I thought you drowned. I've had men searching the cove for you."

Was that relief I saw wash across his face? Maybe for a second, and then it disappeared, hidden behind a mask of stone.

I had to remind myself that I had been missing for days. Not hours.

I couldn't hide my irritation and roughly pulled away from his grasp. "So you could turn me over to the royal guards? If I had known you would be here, I wouldn't have come," I said between clenched teeth.

Gripping my dress, I lifted the skirts so I wouldn't trip and quickly tried to make my escape.

He rushed after me, his long legs easily catching up to me, and he stepped in front, cutting off my path.

"What do you mean, if you had known I would be here? Of course I'd be here."

"Leave me alone," I snapped. "I'll leave."

"And go where?" He scoffed. "I admit, I was angry and rash with my words the last time I saw you. But I know you don't have anywhere to go...." He trailed off as Vasili came up to me and placed his hand on my back lightly.

Brennon's eyes narrowed. He looked ready to rip Vasili's hand off.

"You were saying? I have offered Merisol my protection," Vasili answered. "She will stay with me."

"Like hell she will," Brennon roared. "Over my dead body."

"And what are you going to do?" Vasili lowered his voice and stepped toe-to-toe with Brennon. Vasili was thin but tall. He was one of the few men I saw who could meet Brennon eye-to-eye. "Keep her tucked away as your mistress? Hmm? How noble of you, Brennon," Vasili sneered. "And what would your future wife have to say about that?"

Future wife? It couldn't be true. I felt sick to my stomach. Not once during our voyage had he mentioned being engaged, but why would he?

I looked to Brennon for confirmation, and his shoulders fell. He looked ready to strangle Vasili, and yet he wouldn't meet my eyes.

"I've heard enough," I whispered.

Brennon wasn't finished. He lifted Vasili up by the collar of his shirt and punched him in the jaw. The crack echoed, and I instinctively winced, but the impact didn't seem to faze Vasili. His head fell back, and he laughed.

"Now that's more like it!" He kicked Brennon, who

doubled over and then tackled him, knocking him into an hor d'oeuvre table.

The two wrestled. Vasili wrapped his legs around Brennon's thick neck. Brennon twisted and grabbed a handful of Vasili's long hair.

"No fair!" Vasili howled.

Brennon's face was turning red, but the fight continued, and they rolled into two nearby guests, who quickly side-stepped the fighting duo.

I stood by and watched them fight, but yet it wasn't to kill, and by the crowd's attitude toward the entire affair, this scene may play out often. A gentleman appeared next to me, drinking out of a gold goblet, and the fight thoroughly amused him.

"Get him in an armlock!" the stranger shouted in encouragement. Vasili and Brennon broke their hold but not their fight.

A quick glance at the man's dark-blond hair, thick arms covered by green velvet, and his gold circlet revealed that I was standing next to King Roald of Isla. The king handed me his goblet to hold and clapped his ring-covered hands. He kneeled down and gave the two men fighting critiques.

"Vasili, you're quicker; use your speed. Brennon, don't leave your side open. Oh, too late!" King Roald groaned as Vasili landed a punch to Brennon's right side.

"Can you make them stop?" I pleaded with King Roald, who was now mimicking the fight with his own fists, sending jabs into the air.

"Why ever would I? This is how the two of them have been handling their differences for years. It will all be over as soon as one of them draws first blood."

"First blood," I repeated.

Crack!

Brennon's fist connected with Vasili's mouth. Vasili stumbled, shook his head, and spit a mouthful of blood on the ground. He held his hand up in surrender, and Brennon backed off.

"That's it, Brennon!" King Roald cheered.

Brennon offered an outstretched hand to Vasili, who took it, and they gave each other a brotherly slap on the back.

They disgusted me—by the display, by the encouragement, and by the fact that they forgave each other so fast. Brennon flashed me a victorious grin. I glared at him and stormed away.

"Meri," he called after me, but I ignored him, my fury growing with each step I took. He harmed Vasili. He harmed my friend. Brennon grabbed my elbow and spun me toward him.

"Leave me alone!" I pushed him in the chest. I was feeling hurt at being rejected. He didn't react to my push, for he was an immovable wall of muscle.

"I want to apologize," he said, "for not telling you about my engagement."

"What does it matter to me?" I asked bitterly. "I'm just someone you used to entertain yourself."

"That's not true. It was wrong. I should have more control, but whenever I'm around you, I seem to lose what little I have."

My eyes betrayed my anger. "You knew. You shouldn't have kissed me."

"I know, and all I can do is beg your forgiveness." Brennon seemed sorry. "Please, Meri. Please say you'll forgive me."

I was a sucker for his blue eyes. "Yes, I forgive you. But not for what you did to Vasili."

"What?" Brennon became indignant. "Vasili had it coming."

"Vasili was protecting my honor, which is more than I can say about you."

It was a low blow, and he stepped back. "Yes, I understand. But I can't allow you to stay with him."

"Why not? I find the Undersea appealing."

"You've been there?" It shocked him. "Is that where you've been the last few days? I can't believe he took you there. I will kill him for sure now."

"Stop!" I snapped at him. "You have no say in anything regarding me or my life. I can go with him if I want."

Brennon's eyes twinkled with mischief. He leaned down close, his lips inches from my ear. "That's not true, my little Meri. For you are mine. No one can take you from me. Not even Vasili."

"What do you mean?"

"I have you under a binding contract."

"That was when I was your cabin boy. As you can see, that is no longer the case." I held my hands out to show my dress.

"I admit, I miss the tight-fitting boy clothes, but I much prefer you in dresses. You look ravishing, by the way. But you are still in service to me. I'm still your captain. You signed on with me for a year and a day."

"You can't be serious," I snapped. The curse was slowly consuming my life. I needed to find a way to break the spell, not play servant to him.

"Get used to being by my side." He was enjoying tormenting me.

My mouth dried out. Images of me cleaning his room daily and pressing his shirts filled my head.

My mouth pursed, and I wanted to stomp my foot like a

little kid and scream out at him, because that left me stuck at his side. Instead, I channeled my inner Rosalie. I became calm and collected. "And if I refuse?"

"Then I have no qualms about having you punished for breaking my contract and thrown in prison."

"You're a pirate," I grumbled.

"Why thank you for the compliment," Brennon breathed as he grasped me around the waist, pulling me closer. "I have a tendency to take the things I want." He pressed his forehead to mine. "And right now, I really want to kiss you again."

The curse and his betrothed disappeared from my mind, for I became weak in the knees. He made me hate him one moment and then want to kiss him in the next breath. His lips brushed against mine, and I turned my head as he kissed along my neck.

"Am I interrupting?" A deep voice chuckled.

I pulled away from Brennon's grasp and let out an embarrassed squeak. King Roald stood over us, nonplussed by the embarrassing circumstances we were caught in.

Brennon rolled his eyes, groaning loudly, but his grip on my arm didn't lesson. I tried to wiggle free, but he held firm. I stepped on his foot, and Brennon grunted and let go. I snatched my skirt and tried to curtsey.

"How can I help, Your Majesty?"

"I hoped to have a moment with Captain Pike," King Roald answered.

Feeling irritated, I took a jab at Brennon. "Maybe you can teach this pirate some manners, Your Majesty."

Roald roared with laughter. "Not likely. My son is pretty hardheaded. It runs in the family."

"Son?" I gasped in surprise, as a flush of embarrassment rose to my face.

King Roald addressed his son. "You really do have a way with the ladies. Come now, Brennon." He held his right arm out, and Brennon begrudgingly followed.

Brennon scowled over his shoulder, shot me a look, and mouthed, *Stay there.*

I rolled my eyes. As soon as he was out of sight, I took off. I needed to figure out the source of the magic I felt earlier.

I walked along the edge of the palace grounds and didn't feel much of anything other than the magic that sprung up from deep within the mystical waterfalls, which was a fountain of renewing magic. I continued to walk through the mists and found a hidden set of steps that led down the sides of the falls. The steps were slim, no deeper than a hand, and a black chain was the only handrail available. But this seemed to be where I felt the magic, and the closer I came to the ocean, the surer I was. The falls poured right into the ocean, and there was a small sandbank along the side and a man-made ocean breaker.

But it was what lay beyond the breaker that gave me chills. I self-consciously touched my heart and felt it flutter in fear. In the deep ocean, highlighted by the moon's rays, I could see them.

Seven silhouettes floating in the water, watching and waiting.

CHAPTER EIGHTEEN

"There you are. I was worried," Brennon's voice echoed above me.

I had come up the treacherous trail from the ocean and didn't notice him pacing by the pools, waiting for me.

He ran a nervous hand through his hair. "It just so happened that Howland had seen you head off in this direction. That path isn't safe. The steps are eroding, and the safety chains are loose in some parts."

"I'm fine," I said numbly.

He looked down the path I had come up. "What were you doing?"

"Nothing," I breathed. Seeing the mermaids in the ocean, knowing they were just waiting for me to die so I could break their curse, was very depressing.

"Well, the gathering is almost over, so I think I should show you to your room."

"I don't want—"

"It's not about what you want, but what your captain orders."

I had no fight in me. Not tonight. I was emotionally beat and really wanted to be comforted. I looked to Brennon's firm arms and decided on the second option.

"Fine," I said without arguing. "As long as you bring me cookies."

"Is that all it takes to keep you happy?"

"Cookies make everyone happy," I added.

"I will remember that."

Brennon must have noticed my change in mood, because he became somber as he led me through gardens and into the palace. I barely noticed the marble floors, white sandstone walls that sparkled with bits of colored glass, and how most of the windows were stained glass in ocean shades of blue, green, and white. Another fountain stood in the middle of the foyer as we headed up the stairs to the second floor into a private wing. He stopped in front of a door and unlocked it. Pushing it open, he waited outside.

"This will be your room."

"Where does the rest of the crew sleep?" I asked.

"Most of the crew is from Isla, so they returned to their families until we set sail again. The others stay at the inn in town."

"I could stay there," I offered. Not stepping into the room.

"No, it's not fit for a lady. Especially when I want to keep a closer eye on you. And like I said, I may need of your services."

"Then you should ask one of your many palace servants, Your Highness." I did a mock curtsey, and the corner of his lip rose in a half smile.

"But what fun is there in bossing them around, when it's you I like to rattle?"

"I'd rather be bossed around at sea," I muttered. At least at sea I knew what they required of me. I knew my worth, my value as a sailor, since I had fallen into a routine. In the palace, I wasn't prepared for what he would ask, expect, or... desire.

"Well, I usually spend ten months of the year at sea."

"What for?" I asked. "Looting, stealing, and what were you doing along the road when the transport picked you up?"

Brennon leaned against the doorframe and ran the back of his finger down my cheek. "A soothsayer told me I may find answers at an old fishing village."

"Did you find them?"

He smiled. "No. But I found you."

"I'm not a consolation prize."

He frowned. "I would never consider you second place—to anything or anyone."

I glared at him.

Brennon sighed and gave me a pained look. "We've been searching for the lost treasure of the Undersea for years. I hoped that by finding it, I could permanently postpone my coming engagement. I was even desperate enough to try to persuade a sea witch to help me."

"Why?"

"I've never even met her!" he yelled in frustration. "She's a complete stranger. An arrangement governed by soothsayers and seers to heal the Undersea. For if that kingdom falls, so does ours." Brennon's voice was laced with anguish. "The choice was never mine. I am but a puppet controlled by my father's wishes. But it is you, and only you, who pulls the strings of my heart."

He reached for my hand and placed it on his chest. I could hear the wild beating of his heart. My heartbeat picked up to match his, like two racehorses running toward the goal. But mine slowed, knowing I could never cross the finish line. I glanced at my gloved hand envisioning the curse beneath the material.

"Stop," I whispered, my voice full of emotion. I pulled my hand out from under his. "For I can never love you the way you want... or deserve."

Brennon's face fell with rejection. I feared he would ask more questions and suss out what I was hiding. I stepped into the room and slowly closed the door in his heartbroken face.

He knocked, but I didn't answer. I moved to the bed with its soft turquoise coverlet and slid across the top, burying my head into the pillows until I heard his footfalls leave.

I rolled over to take in the room and let out a lengthy sigh. The room was circular with no windows. Arched doors led to a balcony filled with potted plants. The shutter doors were open, and they let in a warm breeze. There was a fireplace, although based on the current climate in Isla, I didn't think they needed to use it but a few weeks of the year. A round table, two stuffed chairs, bookshelf, and an ornate wardrobe completed the room. But in every decorative piece or portrait, rug, sconce, and fire grate, the trident motif ran throughout.

I slid from the bed and moved to the balcony to look out upon the ocean, knowing that somewhere out there watching me were the mermaid sisters.

"I'm sorry, Mother," I whispered to the air. "I got myself into a bit of a mess, and I don't know how to get out of it. You taught us to use our magic, and twice now it has brought me nothing but trouble."

My lip trembled as I began a whispered confession. "I'm sorry, Aura, for losing control of my temper. I had only meant to help you, but I brought misfortune down upon our household. Maeve, I miss your sense of adventure. I'm sure you would have loved being at sea, flying with us above the *Bella*

Donna. Rhea, you were always the cautious one. If I had been more like you, I wouldn't be in this mess. You would have found the answer in a book, I'm sure. Honor, wherever you are, I hope you find what it is you're looking for, because I miss having you underfoot. Rosalie, I hope you and the baby are doing well, for I'm sure you must've had my niece by now. Oh, Eden," I murmured, "I'm jealous you found your family and have answers to who you are, where you're from, and that they love you so much."

"Families are overrated," Vasili's familiar voice came out of nowhere.

I followed his voice to see him sitting on the edge of a stone banister just around the corner, out of sight. How long had he been sitting there? But that's when I noticed that even though my room was circular, the balcony wrapped around to the next set of rooms, there was only a few feet of space between each balcony and could easily be scaled by someone with Vasili's long legs. He looked quite pleased that he made the jump.

"Is your room close by?" I asked.

"Nope, not even close. Brennon wouldn't hear of it." He grinned. "But that won't stop me from visiting you to make sure you're all right."

"I'm fine. But you shouldn't eavesdrop on people."

"I wasn't eavesdropping. I just thought it prudent that I join in on your one-sided conversation so people don't think you're crazy. And I still stand by my earlier statement that families are overrated."

"You only say that, because you know where you come from and therefore know your future."

"True, but knowing your future can be just as devastating as not knowing."

"Devastating. Is that because the queen is dying? Why can't you take the throne?"

Vasili nodded his head sadly. "Our kingdom is a matriarchal society. All the power lies in the female bloodline. And she is the last of her kind."

"Why can't she remarry and have more heirs? It seems like a simple solution to a world-ending problem."

Vasili looked uncomfortable. He pulled the collar of his shirt and looked away as he answered. "It isn't as easy as that. The queens are chosen by the sea. And as I'm sworn to secrecy, that is all I'm allowed to tell you."

I raised my eyebrow. "Then why bring me here?"

"There's just something about you. It's like we've met before, yet you said you've never been to the Undersea." He gave me a pat on the shoulder. "I wanted to see if that was true."

I shrugged. "I've never been there before but feel honored that you wanted to share your home with me."

"You are the only other person, besides Brennon, who I have taken to the Undersea. What you see is only a figment of its former glory. It's been slowly dying ever since that wretched day."

"I know this," I spoke up excitedly. "It's when a sorcerer and his army stole the heart of the Undersea. A magical treasure."

Vasili's head dropped, his hair falling over his eyes, and he seemed in mourning. "It was the day I failed our kingdom."

"Vasili you barely look over twenty yourself, you must have only been a child back then. How could you have failed?"

His eyes were glassy with emotion. "Meri, I am reaching my two hundredth cycle. I told you time passes differently in the Undersea. I was born to be a protector, a royal guard in charge of protecting the legendary treasure with my life. I failed my sworn duty when men from above broke into our palace and stole it. It would have been better that I died that day than to live knowing my failure would lead to the downfall of my homeland. The queen can barely look at me, and my own people despise me."

His hands clenched into fists, and they shook with anger. I went to Vasili and placed my hands on his shoulder. "I disagree. I'm glad you are alive. One day, you will find that treasure, return it to the heart of the Undersea, and it will thrive again. I believe it."

Vasili placed his hand on my head, his fingers so long that it was like wearing a hat. He gave me a crooked smile. "You are so young and so naïve."

I pushed his hand away. "I guess. But hope isn't a sign of being naïve. It's belief that we can change our circumstances."

"I tried. We tried. Brennon and I spent years searching for the treasure. Because if I can return it, there is the possibility its strength is powerful enough to keep our kingdom from collapsing. But I'm running out of time."

I glanced down at my arm and brushed my hand across the hidden mark beneath the glove. "We all are."

Sleep wouldn't come. I kept dreaming of the death omen, the shell I found weeks ago in my house dripping blood. My blood. The white cursed marks would finally move up my arm and onto my shoulder, engulfing my neck, and finally my heart. I dreamed of my lifeless body floating out to sea. Not dead necessarily, but living lifeless as sea foam, forever doomed to float on the sea, a shadow of my former self.

My dress that Vasili provided lay across the edge of the bed. In the wardrobe, I found a lightweight silk nightdress, which I donned before retiring, perfect for the humid temperatures. And I tucked the enchanted dagger under my pillow. The nothingness I felt was terrifying, and I awoke frustrated and terrified. I had to find solace.

I stood outside in my nightdress and stared out into the sea. Was this my future? To die before having truly lived? The stupid dagger hadn't glowed red; it was useless, and I believed it was just a ruse by the sea witch, designed to give me false hope, so they could syphon my magic without me fighting her.

I heard a rustle and scrape across the stone and assumed it was Vasili coming to annoy me with more hard truths.

"I want to be alone, Vasili!" I muttered as the sound drew closer.

"It's not Vasili," a deep voice answered. "But I think I should throttle him, for he's already been here to see you."

I turned to see Brennon standing in the archway of my room.

"What are you doing here?" I asked.

"I knocked, but you didn't answer." He hadn't changed out of his clothes, other than losing the cape. In his hands, he had a small satchel with a ribbon around it. He walked out to stand by me on the balcony. "Can't sleep?" he asked.

"No. I just feel unsettled here."

Brennon's brows furrowed. "Here, maybe this will help." He held out a piece of cloth and placed the object in my hands.

I unfolded the wrapping and looked at the smallest, most perfect seashell cookies dusted with colored sugar.

He took a star cookie out of my palm and held it enticingly in front of me. "Taste one. They just came out of the oven." He placed the cookie between my lips, and I bit down. It crumbled into my mouth, and I moaned at the flavor. It was soft, fresh, and not too sweet. A mixture between a cake and a cookie.

I caught him staring, Brennon's eyes watching my lips. He glanced away and put the other half of my star cookie in his mouth.

"Hey, I thought that was for me," I teased.

"Consider it my cookie tax," he answered. "Since I made them."

"Cookie tax? That is ridiculous. And you didn't really make them. Did you?"

"No." He flashed me a charming smile. "A servant did. But I oversaw."

"Oh, you mean you watched and ordered her about." I grinned.

"I had to make sure they were perfect. I even decorated a few." He plucked another cookie out of my hand, and before he could put it in his mouth, I snagged it back.

I spun, giving him my back, and ate the whole cookie in one bite. Which was a mistake, because I was laughing so much it was hard to chew.

Brennon's hands wrapped around my waist as he moved to grab the pouch of cookies. He pressed me close, and I heard his muffled laughter in my back as he lifted me up in the air.

I squealed as my feet lifted off the floor and made a play at running away. "Well, I guess I will have to taste something else just as sweet." He nuzzled the side of my neck, and I froze.

The cookies fell from my hands and crumbled on the balcony, the game suddenly over as I realized what was happening. He nuzzled again, moving his lips up to my ear as he nibbled on my earlobe. He pulled me closer, and I leaned into him, closing my eyes, enjoying being wrapped up in Brennon's arms and feeling his kisses trail up to my cheek. He spun me around, and I read the desire in his eyes.

Sugar still coated my lips, and Brennon leaned in; my mouth parted in anticipation. He slowly kissed my bottom lip and brushed his mouth across mine in the gentlest of kisses. "The cookies are sweet, but you definitely taste sweeter," he breathed.

My knees went weak.

My arms reached up around his neck, and our kiss deepened. He moaned, and our breathing quickened. His hand going to my waist, he lifted me up and carried me to my bed. I hit the mattress with a soft bounce, and he crawled up next to me, his eyes sweeping over me with yearning.

My body came alive at his touch, at the sight and smell of him, my hands eager to explore and running up his chest. Even pulling his shirt up to feel the muscles along his chest. A desire burned through us. It was a fire that couldn't be quenched with just kisses.

Brennon broke our kiss, and I could see it pained him to do so. I reached for him, but he pulled away.

"I'm sorry, Meri," he whispered. "I fear that if we continue, I will only hurt you in the end."

The rejection felt like a stab to my heart. The pain was intense, and I tried to move away, but he only dragged me closer to him, wrapping himself around me until he was cradling my small body. His chin rested on the top of my head, his leg over the top of my foot.

"What I wouldn't give to keep you forever," he whispered. I heard the heartache in his voice.

I wasn't blind or stupid. He never once said love. Because he had to save that for his betrothed. I tried to blink the tears away, but they silently fell. Brennon must have sensed my pain, because he stroked the back of my hair and kissed my shoulder.

This might be all we could have, and I suddenly realized it wasn't enough. I wanted Brennon more than a friend or captain. I wanted him as a husband, for I was falling in love with him.

I laid awake most of the night, my thoughts lost in heartache and a future that would never be ours. Brennon had fallen into a deep sleep, his arm wrapped around my waist possessively as if he, too, knew what we had wouldn't last.

Then I saw it. The softest pink glow across the sheet. At first, I thought it was the sunrise ebbing through the arched door. But the sky was still dark, and the birds hadn't begun their morning song. The glow pooled from under the pillow in front of me. My arm slowly moved up to reach under the pillow, inching along so as not to wake Brennon, but terrified of what I would find.

My trembling fingers found the hilt of the dagger, and I could feel a warm hum. I slid it from under the edge, and the ruby in the handle glowed. My head rested on Brennon's arm; I could hear his heartbeat as if it was my own. And the dagger was flashing in perfect sync with his heartbeat.

The heart stone in the dagger revealed its target.

The person needed to end my curse so I could live—was Brennon.

CHAPTER NINETEEN

I laid awake worrying, holding on to Brennon, and desperately trying to remember these feelings I had for him. But my worry led to exhaustion, and in the early morning, I fell into a troubled sleep. When I awoke, Brennon was gone. The sheets were cold and empty like my broken heart.

The sun's rays shone across my bed, promising a new day, but to me, it was a reminder that my time here on earth was short. I inspected my arm and saw a recent growth. The curse had claimed another inch of my life.

Instead of facing the day and facing Brennon, I curled up in the coverlet and placed the pillow over my head. Maybe if I stayed like this long enough, I would wake up and realize it was all a dream.

My door burst open with a thud. I peeked out from under the pillow, expecting to see Brennon, but I gasped as a large seal waddled into my room. His fur was silver speckled with black. He made a barking noise of protest at the foot of my bed, and when I didn't respond, he hopped up and fumbled, wiggling himself onto my bed. I screamed as the beast flopped around, circling and messing up the blankets until he was comfortable.

"Uh, hello," I said, turning my head to the side to get a look at the seal. I hadn't seen one this big or up close. They were all over the beach and the docks sunbathing. And I never expected to see one in my bed.

He flopped to his back and flapped his fin on his belly, as if asking for a belly rub. I tentatively reached out my hand and patted his stomach. He made a deep sigh. When I stopped petting him, he shuffled around in the bed and forced his head under my hand.

"Who are you?" I asked.

The seal gave me a lazy look and huffed before curling up, closing his eyes, and going to sleep.

"Uh, this is my bed." I pushed him in the side. He lazily opened one eye and then closed it.

A soft knock drew my attention to the door. A young woman with shoulder-length silver hair stood in the doorway. Her dress was simple, a dark-blue wrap dress with braided straps around her neck. She accessorized with white studded sandals and silver and turquoise bangles.

She placed her hands on her hips. "You just made yourself at home, didn't you, Lad?" She chastised him. "You need to ask permission first before you just adopt someone. Besides, you don't know where they've been." The girl gave me a sly wink.

She came and patted Lad's side, giving a whistle, and the seal just stuck his tongue out at her.

"Well, I guess there's my answer. He said he's not moving, so you're stuck with him."

"Does he bite?" I asked, slipping out of the bed and giving the seal a wide berth.

"Only when you stop rubbing his belly," she said, patting

him there. "But consider it an excellent omen, because he doesn't take to everyone."

"I need all the wonderful fortune I can get."

She stepped away from the seal and moved into the middle of the room, her hands at her sides, a wide grin on her face.

"I'm Lucy. I'm here to help you settle in, Miss...?"

"Merisol, but my friends call me Meri."

"What would you like me to call you?"

"Meri, please."

She grinned, showing small, even teeth. A light blush rose to her face, and she called out into the hallway. A few more servants entered with arms full of dresses and a jewelry box.

"We need to get you dressed for the day. What kind of dress would you like to wear?" She waved her hand, and I took in all the colorful silks, wrap dresses, and straps. A quick look at what the girls were wearing, and I became overwhelmed. I was used to wearing only dreary colors like brown and black with buttons. The thought of navigating those corsetless dresses gave me pause.

"Whatever you choose for me will be wonderful," I assured her.

Lucy pursed her lips and pressed her finger to them. "Hmm, your hair is a deep-red, and any pastel colors would accent your skin tone just perfectly." She rummaged through a few dresses until she found one that suited her taste. She picked out a soft-pink wrap dress and held it in front of me. Lucy helped me figure out the wraps that worked as a laceless corset, but what was most surprising was the extra length that split between the legs and tucked into a belt, giving me the illusion of wearing pants.

Lucy brought gold sandals that wrapped around my ankles. From the jewelry box, she picked out a gold armband.

She glanced at the white marks upon my arm and slid the band on.

"I think it's the perfect complement to your birthmark. It is so unusual." Lucy pinched the band and then grimaced when she looked at my hair. "Who hacked up your beautiful hair?" She tugged lightly at the uneven layers that fell just below my shoulders.

"It was a necessity." I shrugged.

Lucy took scissors to my hair and evened it out. It wasn't the waist-length hair I lobbed off, but it was still flowing and feminine. She then immediately braided sections and pulled them back, securing them with a yellow Islayan flower.

"There, beautiful." Lucy clapped her hands and then addressed the seal sleeping on my bed. "What do you think, Lad?"

The seal rolled up, gave me a look, and slapped his belly with his fin.

"Lad approves."

"I guess I got his seal of approval." I let out an unladylike snort and covered my mouth in embarrassment.

Even Lad sat up abruptly and gave me a peculiar look.

Lucy burst into her own odd laugh that sounded like a bark. Which only sent me into another round of laughter. The hilarity lightened the mood and my heart and was better than any of the medicinal tonic's Rosalie or Rhea would have given me.

I followed Lucy out into the hall, leaving the dagger hidden under the mattress. I wasn't ready to deal with having to look at that cursed piece today. I figured later on tonight I would chuck it into the whirlpool when no one was around.

When we came to the main foyer, there was a lot of commotion. Servants were running through the halls. And I could hear Brennon's loud, booming voice coming from farther within the palace.

Something was wrong.

"What is it?" I asked Lucy.

She bit her bottom lip. "It isn't my place to speak out."

I stood at the top of the stairs and watched as Brennon came storming out of the study a floor below.

"There must be another way." Brennon's anger was monumental. I could tell he was only seconds away from losing what little control he had left.

"It was our fault the thief snuck into the Undersea. We protect the entrance. It's our responsibility to bring new life to our home." King Roald chased after him. A smaller, less showy circlet embraced his noble brow. In his hand, he held the gold trident. He slammed the end into the marble floor so hard the room shook.

Lucy gasped.

"There must be another way." The show of authority from his father didn't faze Brennon.

"If there were, you would have found it by now. I let you search for an alternative for three years, Brennon. It's time to not be so selfish. As the future king, you have to think of others. Not your own wants and desires... no matter the pretty package it comes in." King Roald gestured with his trident in a wide arc that rose to point me out on the second level.

Brennon followed the trident, and when our eyes met, he froze. I knew what he was doing. He was fighting against the engagement. He was fighting for me.

"I can... not." Brennon's shoulders were shaking with uncontrolled rage, and he turned to face his father.

King Roald shook his head. "I'm disappointed in you, son. I thought I raised you better."

"Ask anything of me, and it will be done." Brennon kneeled before his father, bowing his head in supplication. "Just not this!" Brennon cried. "Please do not ask me to continue with the engagement."

"If you do not—" King Roald's volume dropped, and he spit with rage. "—you are no longer worthy to be my son. And you shall be forever known as the bringer of doom to both the kingdom above and the Undersea."

One of the handmaidens fainted at the announcement. Lucy's complexion was pale, and I saw her sway before another girl wrapped her arm around her for comfort. It seemed there was more history and dire circumstances than I truly understood for so many to react this way. I was so anguished that I balled up my silk skirts in my fists, ruining the fabric in the process.

My heart burst with joy at the thought Brennon was willing to give up everything to be with me. But then I was crumbling and dying inside with guilt, because he was turning his back on the kingdom, his father, his people.

The skin of my marks tingled, and I remembered my curse. I couldn't let him do this. I couldn't let him doom everything, when my future was ill-fated.

"King Roald," I called out and dashed down the steps, placing myself in front of the prostrate Brennon.

"You. When I first saw you, I thought you nothing more than a mere dalliance. Not someone my son would destroy two kingdoms over." King Roald's voice was dripping disapproval.

"I'm sorry, Your Majesty. I never meant to cause a rift in your family."

"Meri, what are you doing?" Brennon grabbed my hand and tried to pull me away from his father.

185

I wrenched my arm away. "I'm sorry. I can't let you do this."

Brennon's face became wary. He stood up. "What do you mean?"

Standing firm, I raised my chin and announced, "I won't stand in the way of his engagement."

"Now finally, someone with a speck of sense." King Roald looked pleased.

"This isn't just your decision. It's mine as well." Brennon turned to address his father. "And I choose to break this engagement."

"No!" I shouted louder than I meant to. My voice echoed among the halls. The stillness that followed was eerie.

Brennon looked completely baffled. He took a step toward me, and I retreated, turning away and hiding my face from him.

"Meri, what is going on? Don't you see? I'm doing this for us. I want to marry you."

My heart was breaking into a million pieces, the tears welling in my eyes. My chest burned as I struggled to take even a single breath. I knew what needed to be done, but I didn't have the strength. Drawing on every ounce of willpower I had deep within me, I locked away my love, hid the pain, and steeled my face to be cold and heartless. I had to or this wouldn't work.

"But I—" I put as much hate and disdain as I could in my voice, and I spun, directing all of my raw emotions toward Brennon. "—don't want to marry you!"

Brennon stood there, still as a statue, his face one of disbelief. His brows furrowed, his nostrils flared, and his resentment rolled across his face.

He shook his head. "I don't believe you."

I formed my words like poison daggers aimed at his heart.

"Believe it." I shrugged. "For I was using you. You were just an end to a means. I wanted to get away from the Brunes Guild. You were my ticket out. That is all."

The silence that followed was deafening.

Brennon stewed as my words slowly haunted him. His head dropped; his white-knuckled fists were shaking by his thighs. I had never felt more evil or cruel than I did in this moment.

When I killed the mayor's son, it had been an accident. I had never purposefully injured a person. But right now, I was trying to drive a wedge between Brennon and me. Not just a wedge, but purposefully create damage that could never be repaired.

Hurting him hurt me. But at the same time, I realized how powerful the pain that came with it was. And pain was power.

I was proud that I had hidden my tears, for Brennon slowly came forward and stood toe-to-toe with me.

Over Brennon's shoulders, I saw Vasili walk in from the bedrooms on the second floor, his hair a mess, his clothes wrinkled, and he was barefoot. He had obviously just woken up. Vasili stopped, leaned on the banister, and looked on with interest at the argument that was happening below.

"Meri, look at me," Brennon whispered so only I could hear.

I couldn't. What he was asking was too much. If I looked. He would see I was lying.

"Meri, please. Just look at me." Brennon reached out a hand to touch my face, but then it fell to his side.

Steeling myself, I met those sea-blue eyes and wanted to crumble. I could see his vulnerability and his love. He wanted reassurance, but I couldn't give that to him. Because one of us had to be strong enough to do what was right.

I stared up at him, didn't blink, and tried to pretend that I had somewhere else I would rather be.

"W-why?" he asked, his voice breaking.

"Because—" I swallowed and tried to think of something that would permanently end this. I glanced up, and Vasili yawned, stretching his arms. "—I'm engaged to Vasili."

"What!" Brennon roared.

Vasili choked in surprise. "What?"

I glared at him. Vasili gave me a wry, answering smile. He tried to straighten his wrinkled shirt. "Oh yeah, that's right." He ran barefoot down the marble stairs and put a hand around my waist. "We got engaged this morning. Sorry, forgot to tell you."

Brennon's jaw clenched. His hands raised for Vasili's throat, and I was about to witness another brawl between the two.

King Roald's deep laugh stopped them. "Well, that seems to settle it then. When Brennon's future bride arrives, we will have two engagements to celebrate."

"And when can we expect this young flower to join us?" Vasili tried to lay on the charm by giving me a wide smile and nuzzling his nose against my neck. I wanted to swat him away like an annoying gnat.

Brennon took a threatening step forward, but Vasili flashed him a stony glare.

"She arrives tomorrow's eve. The wedding will take place in three days."

King Roald clapped his hands, and the servants scattered. Brennon, Vasili, and I were the only ones left in the foyer.

I was going to faint. My knees went weak, and Vasili

sensed it. His grip tightened, but I was slipping. He pulled me into a fake embrace, giving me time to regain my composure.

"Why you had to include me in your game is beyond me," Vasili whispered. Wrapped in Vasili's arms, I didn't feel an intense rush of emotions like I did with Brennon. I just felt warm and safe. His lips brushed my cheek as he spoke. "But I will gladly play the part you have assigned."

I only squeaked a little in surprise and had to use all of my might to not hit him or push him away. It was a very chaste kiss, and it surprised me how different it was from Brennon's. I liked Vasili very much, but this kiss didn't give me butterflies or make my toes curl. And it seemed like it was the same for him.

He lifted me back up, and I cast a wary glance at Brennon. The prince's eyes were cynical, his hatred clear as he turned and silently stalked off.

"Well, love, if your goal was to make him jealous, you did it."

"I'm not your love," I corrected and punched him lightly in the shoulder.

Vasili stepped away from me and gave me a great bow. "As long as we're engaged, you will forever be my love."

"No."

"My sea flower?" he asked.

I shook my head.

"Sea horse?"

"Stop!" I panicked. "No nicknames."

"Nonsense, if we're going to pretend to be engaged, then I shall dub thee all the nicknames just to annoy you."

I raised a wary eyebrow.

"I have to get something out of this. So, I've decided to

have fun. Besides, you are the one who is being cruel to my best friend." He crossed his arms.

I sighed. "I'm doing this for him and for your kingdom." I sat on the second-to-bottom marble step. I crossed my arms over my knees and rested my forehead on my arms. Vasili moved to my left and sat next to me. He gave my back a reassuring pat.

"Believe me. I know what you are giving up and I'm grateful. I see the way he looks at you and the way you look at him."

"I don't look at him," I argued.

He laughed. "Excuse me. Should I say ogle each other?"

"I don't want to talk about it anymore," I whispered.

"Is there something else wrong?" Vasili asked. "You can tell me, you know."

I turned my head to look at him. The sincerity was written across his face in his raised eyebrows. I opened my mouth to explain and felt the burning begin. I swallowed and tried to speak. Her magic bound my words and scalded my tongue. I balled my hands into fists and tried to outthink the curse. Maybe I could be vague? I formed the words in my head and was surprised when they fell easily from my lips. "Do you know how to break a curse?"

He didn't overreact. He just asked, "What kind of curse?"

I was hesitant to tell him. "A very strong one."

"Who cast it?"

"I-I can't say."

Vasili tapped his chin in thought. "Well, if you won't tell me what kind of curse, or who cast it, you kind of limit my help."

"I know," I groaned, flopping my head back into my arms.

A few seconds later, he spoke up. "I have heard a tale of a

powerful sorceress who lives in a remote area. She may be able to help you."

My head popped up. "Really, who?"

"She goes by many names, but the one I'm most familiar with is Lady Eville."

"I was afraid of that," I groaned once more as he mentioned my adoptive mother.

CHAPTER TWENTY

It wasn't the worst idea ever. It just meant swallowing my pride and preparing myself for the tongue lashing and "I told you sos" that were sure to come. Not to mention my mother's wrath was legendary. She may tell me it is my problem to solve and that I brought this down upon myself.

Back in my room, Lad deemed my bed as his and only gave me a cursory glance before rolling over and giving me his silvery back.

"Nice to see you too," I said, closing the door.

I moved to the one gilded mirror in the room and ran my fingers down the side, searching for the runes and finding them etched into the side. I was in luck. It was an enchanted mirror. I frowned though, because there was a distinct lack of hum, of magical energy. It was cold.

The mirror was drained, or "dead," and as Mother would say, *"It needs to be recharged."*

We had a mirror in our home that Mother used to scry on the kingdoms, most notably, the royals. She knew about their economies, royal structures, heritages, and their enemies. She probably knew more than even the royal advisors.

Why? Because she was obsessed with her desire for revenge. Years ago, Lady Eville was engaged to the prince of Sion, but when her father lost their fortune, the prince lost his interest in her. Since then, she traveled for years with a magical menagerie, studying old magic, collecting secrets, and using them to gain significant power.

The kingdoms soon feared her. Since then, Lorelai Eville had done nothing but meddle in their affairs, showing up at their most inopportune times, preying on their weaknesses. When the Kingdom of Baist's son was bitten by a werewolf, it was Lorelai who cast protective wards around the palace to protect the world from his dark side.

Having met the sea witch and seeing my mother's revenge on her cursed daughters, it made me shudder. What if that had been me? What if it was the other way around and she cursed me?

Mother's grim omens and prophecies came true, and the current kings feared her and her power even more. She is unwelcome now at any court, and so were we by association.

Baist was anti-magic, as it had no ley lines of power that ran under the kingdom. Isla, Kiln, Rya were kingdoms that magic was abundant and widely accepted. I had seen the shops that sold charms, which included memory, fire, heat, and sharpening charms.

But it was odd that I would find a dead relic within the palace. I would have expected it to be charged and in working order. No matter, for I knew how to use any mirror or reflective surface.

I took a hairpin and used it to prick my finger. A deep-red blood drop swelled on the tip of my finger, and I pressed it to the cool glass as I whispered a basic enchantment. The reflection waved and spiraled outward.

"Mother," I whispered. And waited. I was hesitant to speak louder for fear that she would actually hear me—and at the same time terrified she wouldn't.

The reflection blurred and came into focus, and I saw her, Lady Eville. Her long black hair was braided over one shoulder, her pale skin shone, and her lips were as red as blood. Even in her midforties, she was one of the most beautiful women alive, and terrifying.

Her gray eyes looked up and met mine through the mirror. They narrowed as she took in my unfamiliar background, studying everything, missing nothing.

"So, you're in Isla," she stated, matter of fact. "I wondered where you had run off to." Her pitch hadn't changed. To the normal listener, they would have assumed it to be just pleasant conversation. Not to me and my sisters. We could hear the silent disapproval in her voice.

"Imagine my surprise when I got a message from Rhea that you murdered the mayor's boy." I saw the twitch of her lip and relaxed. No one in our family held any love for that monstrous family. "But to abandon your sisters like that was irresponsible."

"How do you know where I am?" I asked in amazement. I tried to search the room behind my mother and could only see a window.

"I'd recognize that gaudy decor anywhere." She pointed a polished nail at the trident sconce behind me. "You're in King Roald's palace, which means you've probably met the sea witch, Sirena. Or if you haven't, you soon will. Because there is a longstanding score between us, and I fear she will try to come after you."

I ran my sweaty palms down the side of my dress, out of sight of the mirror. "Well, about that. I seem to have already had a run-in with her."

Her eyes widened. "Oh, well, that's unfortunate. Are you okay, Merisol?"

Am I okay? I couldn't believe the words I was hearing. She sounded worried about me.

"No, I'm sorry. I thought I was doing the right thing, but she got the better of me." I slowly held up my right hand so she could see the silvery-white veins in the mirror, being careful not to explain or say anything but letting the curse mark speak for me. My mother would know right away what happened. This wouldn't be telling anyone, if she could see it with her own eyes.

Mother stilled; her eyes darkened with fury. Her lips pinched into a firm line, and by her silence, I knew it enraged her. "How dare she lay a hand on my daughter?" The mirror rattled with Lorelai's power that was ebbing through the glass. "She has already harmed my family once, and I thought I taught her a lesson. But this is too far. I can't believe she did this."

"What do I do?" I asked. "I'm limited in time."

The mirror shuffled as Mother dropped hers in her lap. Muffled voices came through on the other end. A few moments passed, and the mirror rose again to her face, but she was now whispering so the person in the other room couldn't hear.

"There's always a way out. Sirena only has covenant magic."

"Covenant magic?"

"Yes, it is binding magic that is created through promises, contracts, or agreements. She doesn't have many powers other than manipulation by unbreakable magical contracts. It always requires two parties, and there is always a clause written in on how to get out, but the problem with Sirena is that sometimes breaking the covenant's repercussions are worse than the actual curse."

My face must have given my mood away, because she caught on.

"What is it?" she asked. "What did she give you in exchange for the curse? Tell me everything."

"I can't." I pinched my lips and pointed to my mouth.

"Ah, oldest trick in the book. She bound you from *speaking* about it. Well, there are ways around it. *Show me.*" I stood and pulled the dagger from under the mattress and mimicked stabbing someone in the heart. I thought my acting was pretty good.

"Ah, a sacrifice." Mother let out a curse under her breath.

I pointed to the red ruby and made a flickering motion with my fingers.

"Of course, and it's probably heart-strung, so it is only someone you love. It's meant to be a double-edged curse. It will kill you or someone you care about. How long do you have?"

I looked down at my arm. "Not long. Longer *if* I don't use magic. Otherwise, it spreads faster."

Mother murmured to herself, and I could tell she was trying to think. In the background, I thought I saw my sister Rosalie, and then I heard it. The sound of a baby crying.

"Mother, is that...?" I asked hopefully.

"Meri?" Rosalie came into view of the mirror, holding a bundle in her arms. Her dark hair covered one half of her scarred face, from her battle with the evil sorcerer Allemar. She won and afterward sent him to another dimension. Unfortunately, he escaped and is in corporeal form, searching for a body. Searching for a way back.

Rosalie self-consciously touched her face to make sure her hair covered her scars and then lifted the bundle to the mirror.

"Meri, I'd like you to meet my daughter, Violet." She unfurled the blanket that covered her newborn to reveal an adorable pink cherub with a crown of raven-black curls. "Violet, meet your Aunt Merisol. Just wait 'til you meet her, and she will sing you the sweetest of lullabies."

Tears of joy filled my eyes and blurred the mirror. "Hi, Violet," I said her name, and she opened her eyes to reveal the most stunning eyes that matched her name. Violet. "She's beautiful."

Rosalie beamed. "She takes after you. She's always hungry and won't go to sleep unless she has a full belly or someone sings to her. Oh, I can't wait until you meet her. When can you come to visit? I miss you so much."

I got choked up, since I knew I wouldn't live long enough to see my niece in person. "S-soon. I'll visit real soon," I lied.

It was as if Violet could tell I lied, for she fussed and whined.

"Oh, you must excuse me! She's hungry," Rosalie exclaimed. She adjusted Violet and stood up. "It was good to speak with you, Meri. Please come see me soon."

"Give her a kiss for me and tell her that her aunt adores her and wishes her a happy life." Rosalie met my eyes. "And Rose?" My voice almost failed me, and tears blurred my vision, but I pushed through the pain. "I love you."

She gave me an enormous grin. "I love you too, silly." My sister moved out of view, and Mother's stern face filled the mirror.

"I must give it some thought. But I don't think there's a

way to break the curse. You'll just have to outthink her, daughter. And if anyone can, it's you. But Meri, remember this. You aren't my daughter by blood. But I chose you. You are the daughter of my heart."

A tear slid down my face.

"I told you how a fisherman and his wife gave you to me. But I never told you how they came to have you."

"I don't understand. I thought they were my parents?"

She shook her head. "No, the old fisherman found you floating in a bed of kelp and pulled you from the ocean after a storm. The sea protected you when you should have drowned. They raised you for a year, but then it was too dangerous for you to live so close to the water. Every time you cried or were hungry, you brought forth such a violent storm you almost destroyed their town. And Meri... you were always hungry." She smiled.

It was true. Even now, my stomach was growling.

"They feared your powers, so they brought you to me, so I could protect you until it was time for you to find your destiny. The farther inland you were, the weaker your powers. I refuse to believe it is because of Sirena your time will be cut short. You will overcome this. I know it."

"What can I do?" I asked.

"I believe you already know."

"I don't."

"I truly believe you are the one who will return the treasure to the Undersea."

"What? Even you know about it?" Then I remembered she spent much of her time scrying on kingdoms. She probably knew more than most.

She scoffed. "Of course, I even know what they lost, or at least I heard a rumor of what they are searching for."

"What is it?"

Her eyes were glassy with unshed tears. "The song of the sea."

"I don't understand."

"You will. Solve that, and then you will have the power you need to break the curse. In the meantime, I will speak with your sisters. Maybe there's something we can do." Mother Eville waved her hand in front of the mirror, and it went black as she ended it without saying farewell. A few seconds later, the glass shimmered, and I was once again looking at my reflection.

I wandered out to the balcony and looked out onto the vast sea as the white curls of waves came crashing into shore. I watched the crescendo of the waves and the ebb and flow of the rhythm of the water, and I was just as confused.

"A song," I spoke aloud to the ocean. "That makes no sense. How do I return a song to the sea?"

CHAPTER TWENTY-ONE

Vasili had taken his role as my fake fiancé to a new and annoying level. He appeared at my door shortly after my conversation with my mother and became my designated guardian from Brennon ever since. It seemed he knew what this kind of announcement would do to Brennon and the strain it would put on their friendship. He was willing to take the brunt of it, if it meant sheltering me from his friend's anger.

Brennon was stubborn and tried to get me alone. Each time, Vasili helped keep him at bay. During lunch, Brennon waited at the end of the buffet spread.

His blue coat was brushed, his hair slicked back, and he seemed nervous as he tugged at the buttoned collar. He didn't care much for the constraining clothes of being royalty. I much preferred the scruffy, wind-blown hair and the less refined Brennon of the *Bella Donna*.

"I wish to have a private word with you, my lady." Brennon tried to be formal in his request, his eyes pleading with me for answers.

My plate of food trembled as I struggled to contain my

emotions. I was about to spill the truth to him right there.

Vasili swept in, grabbed my plate, and announced loudly, "Come, my sea urchin, let's eat together on the overlook. We can finish planning our wedding there."

A sigh of relief escaped my lips, and I nodded. But as soon as we left, I felt a stab of remorse. It wasn't fair to either of us to deny our feelings. But I had to, for I was protecting him.

Vasili and I headed to the overlook, a seating area that had a perfect view of both the mystical waterfalls and the ocean. Here, I ate my lunch in silence, while Vasili went without food again. I wondered if he ate earlier, or did he sneak back into the Undersea for his raw fish?

After lunch, Vasili lazed on the stone bench, pretending to sleep, while I pondered the question my mother gave me.

In the midst of my thoughts, Lucy arrived with a message. She handed it to me, and I opened up the green envelope.

"What's wrong?" Vasili asked.

"Why do you think something is wrong?"

"Because you're frowning." He pointed to my forehead.

I held out the letter. "I've been commanded to escort His Highness into the city, because I'm still his cabin boy."

Vasili snorted. "I have to give it to him. He is persistent. That's just like Brennon to find a workaround to see you." He looked up at me from his prone position on the bench. "You don't have to go, you know. As my fiancée, I can decline on your behalf."

"Can you, even if I'm under contract?" I asked.

"Well, it will be difficult. I'm sure it will come to blows and such, but if I get the element of surprise, I can win and demand he break the contract."

I rolled my eyes. "Don't do that. It's no big deal." I turned to Lucy. "I'll go. Where am I to meet him?"

She pointed down a side path that was easily hidden by the palm fronds. "Just follow it until you get to the wall. Brennon will meet you there." She headed back to the palace.

I crumpled up the note and headed up the sandy path, the whole while working myself up into a quiet uproar. One, I didn't enjoy being summoned, and two, I had a feeling he would try to call my bluff.

Vasili caught up and fell into an easy step behind me, as the path wasn't very wide.

"I take it you've taken this path before."

"All the time. It's our secret way out of the palace."

We walked in silence until we came to the wall, and I stopped on the trail when I saw Brennon pacing. Even from a distance, I recognized those broad shoulders and that sun-kissed hair. He had a certain air of authority in his posture that spoke of royalty. I didn't know how I never noticed it before. Vasili, on the other hand, always seemed like he was hunched over, trying to hide, sticking to the shadows, and becoming invisible.

Brennon stopped pacing. He shot an irritated look toward the path, and our eyes met.

My breath caught in my chest, and heat rose to my cheeks. I looked away.

Vasili waited patiently behind me, and when I didn't move forward, he gave me a slight poke in the back before grabbing my hand and pulling me into the sunlight.

Brennon's gaze went right to our entwined hands. I tried to untangle my fingers from Vasili's, but he was having none of it.

"Brennon!" Vasili called out. "What a fine day to go into town. I'm so thrilled to receive your invitation."

"I didn't invite you," Brennon snapped.

"Nonsense, where my love goes, I go." He grinned and

held up our hands. I winced at the awkward angle he thrust my wrist, but he let go of my hand and patted me on the head. "Plus, I would love to pick her out some engagement presents. I'm assuming that's what you're doing, right?"

Brennon's scowl deepened, and he turned without answer. He went to the wall and ran his hands along the crevice until his burly fingers found an indentation. He pressed a certain stone, and the door slid open, revealing an empty alley. Vasili and I passed through, and Brennon closed the door behind us.

"What is with the secret door? Why don't you go out the front?" I asked.

"Because there're hundreds of women who stalk him." Vasili wiggled his eyebrows. "Some well-wishers, others who want to throw themselves at his feet, offering their love, their hearts, and their bodies."

My mouth dropped open. "Really?"

Brennon let out a snort. "No, he's exaggerating. There are not hundreds. Usually a dozen at most."

My mouth snapped close. I realized he was teasing me.

Brennon had dressed down out of his royal robes and was in clothes similar to what I had seen while on the ship—white sleeveless tunic, brown pants tucked into black boots.

Brennon was nervous as we walked side by side through the market, being a gentleman. He pointed out all the various treasure troves of goods that were only available in the kingdom of Isla.

"This is the only place in the world where you can find starfruit. When cut, it resembles a star, and we turn it into candy, which is a favorite among the children of our kingdom."

"And yours," Vasili added. "It was your favorite treat growing up. If I recall."

Brennon bought a handful and popped one in his mouth.

"Still is."

He handed me the yellow candied starfruit, and I chewed it slowly, savoring the slightly sour flavor of the rind and the added sugar coating.

"What do you think?" Brennon asked.

"I think it may be my favorite candy too," I added. "Although, I have had little candy in my life."

"Really?" Brennon exclaimed.

I shrugged. "Nihill isn't a place that sold those kinds of extravagant treats. The only candy we ever received was when Lorn would bring us a bag when he came and stayed with us during the summer months."

"Who's Lorn?" Brennon asked. I sensed his inner jealousy rising.

"He was our teacher. When we came of age, he would test us and give us our area of study. My sister Rosalie is a death seeker. She can dream of someone's death before it happens. Maeve is an Animagus. She can shape into animals, but the easiest for her are predatory birds. Eden has the gift of glamour."

"And you?" Brennon asked, stopping in front of a table full of necklaces. He fingered a beautiful glass shell and without looking up, he added, "What is your gift? Besides putting hapless ship captains under your spell and annoying people."

My cheeks felt warm. "Um, well, that's what is odd. Most of my sisters can tap into magic by using words or incantations. I struggled with them. I found it easiest when I...." I tucked a strand of my hair behind my ear.

"Yes?" Vasili leaned forward, placing his elbow on the table in front of us. Both men looked at me expectantly, and I became nervous. Even though they both experienced what I can do firsthand, I couldn't say it out loud.

"Never mind," I answered. When they tried to press for more, I became silent. When Brennon couldn't get any more out of me, he dropped the subject. We soon became lost in the market and dress shops.

"Buy an arm cuff, my lady." A fairy flew in front of us. She was one of the larger fairies I had seen, her slim body held aloft in the air by blue-and-purple wings that looked too small to keep her body afloat.

When she had gotten our attention, she flew back over to the table of arm cuffs manned by a brownie. His short, stocky form sat on a tall stool that put him eye-level with me. Dark, beady eyes peered at me over a long nose. Shoddy overalls covered his thin limbs. He didn't speak but nodded gruffly to the table of beautiful arm cuffs.

Not wanting to be rude, I stopped to peruse the matching sets of cuffs. Most had a trident motif or circular patterns. Many were inlaid with expensive jewels, but those weren't the ones that caught my eye. I instantly fell in love with the double swirl pattern that reminded me of the whirlpools to the Undersea. It wrapped around the arm twice and had the matching pattern on the bottom, both inlaid with aquamarine stones.

I carefully perused with my eyes, because I lacked money.

Vasili whispered into my ear, "Would you like one?"

"I do, but I can't afford any of them. I lost all my money weeks ago at the inn."

"Doesn't matter. I'll buy one for you. Just pick the one you want." Vasili reached for his money pouch.

I couldn't hide the excitement. It was my first genuine gift not bought by a sibling. My eyes went back to the cuff with the matching swirls.

Before I could point to the cuff I wanted, Brennon snagged it and its larger counterpart off the table. He dumped a handful of gold coins in the brownie's lap, who sputtered at the gross overpayment. The cuffs disappeared into Brennon's satchel, and he gave me a blank look.

My joy left. The other cuffs were beautiful, but none spoke to me the way the other one did. It was as if it was meant for me, and now it was gone, and Brennon didn't even care.

"Oh, uh..." It seemed a waste to buy a cuff now. "On second thought, maybe you could get me something else." I tried to keep my voice light, but I was feeling disappointed.

"As you wish," Vasili said. He noticed my sudden mood change and the reason. He glared at Brennon, who already moved on to the next stall filled with books.

Well, that would make me feel better. I edged up next to Brennon and was looking at the colorful leather-bound books, when I felt a prickle of warning along my back. I glanced over my shoulder and saw nothing, just a group of women who stopped at the same cuff booth I did, a faun and an Islayan woman passing by, and someone pulling a cart.

Maybe it was just me being paranoid. I tried to go back to enjoying the day with Vasili and Brennon, who seemed to be constantly challenging each other and bickering like brothers. Each street we traveled, I had the distinct feeling I was being watched.

"We need to stop at Mosca's." Vasili pulled on my elbow, and without telling Brennon, we parted ways. "You haven't lived until you've tried Mosca's treats."

"What is it?" I asked, craning my neck to see if I could figure out who was tailing us and if they were following me or Brennon. Someone in a cloak passed the street and turned the opposite way.

I let out a breath I didn't know I had been holding.

"It's candy snow."

"But it's a tropical island?" I held up my hands, signifying the warm breeze.

Vasili grinned, showing off his pointed canines. At first, when I saw them, they made me uncomfortable. He knew that and was very careful to hide his smile. Whenever I spotted them now, it was a rare treat for me, because I knew he was truly happy.

"Just let me show you." Vasili was like a kid, running in front of me and making an enormous deal out of a woman covered head-to-toe in fur and gloves over her hands. Even in the intense heat, her nose and cheeks were red as if she was close to frostbite.

"Mosca, I presume." I eyed the woman who stood over a pail of fresh water. She dipped her finger in the water and swirled it around, and it instantly froze. She then chiseled out a section of ice, ran it through a grater and into a cup. She poured candy flavoring on top and added sugar candies in the shape of seahorses.

Mosca saw Vasili, and her chubby face lit up. "Hey, Vas, the usual?"

"Yes, please." He waited eagerly next to the tub as she ground up the ice, and instead of adding the sugar candy to it, she reached below that counter, pulled out a glass jar, and uncorked it. A whiff of fish hit me hard, and I had to cover my mouth. She slathered the ice with it and then added a sardine to the dish, handing it to Vasili.

"Mmm, my favorite." He took a bite, and his eyes rolled back in pleasure. He shoved the fish-smelling ice under my nose, and I wanted to gag.

"No, thank you. I'll just take a red one." I pointed to the safe colored candy ice the child next to me had, his lips and cheeks painted red from the dish.

"You don't know what you're missing."

"Uh, I think I do."

Mosca handed me my ice, and it almost slipped from my hand when I caught a familiar face staring at me from across the way.

His hook nose and mangled ear were hard to miss. A group of soldiers passing by hid him from my sight, and when I looked again, Fang was gone.

"What's the matter?" Vasili asked.

"What happened to Fang and Thorn when we landed?" I questioned.

"They're imprisoned at the wharfs, awaiting their trial. Sea crimes are tried by a maritime court." He licked up the last dregs of his ice then tilted the cup back and slurped up the fish-based sauce.

"Are you sure?" I asked. The uncomfortable presence was back. I was definitely being watched, and now I knew who it was.

"Of course, he had them delivered to the guards to await their trial for crimes at sea." He finished his treat and ate the hard cake dish it was served in.

I looked over my shoulder. Maybe I'd been mistaken. Maybe it wasn't Fang.

The ice candy suddenly didn't seem all that appetizing, and I felt worried as the feeling of being followed intensified.

"Vasili, I think we should leave."

"What's wrong?"

"Someone is following us." I was anxious and feeling exposed. I didn't know why, but something was wrong.

"Are you sure?"

I nodded.

Vasili sensed my mood and looked around. A worried

expression came over him, and he nodded. He grabbed my hand, and we hurried through the streets at almost a run. We zig-zagged, double backed, and even hid in an alcove, not even sure what we were running from. But I saw Vasili's eyes glint with excitement as he thought this was another game.

The second time traveling through the city and taking the back streets, I noticed a different side to Isla. It wasn't as vibrant and fruitful as I originally thought. I had only been on the major thoroughfare. Now, I saw fountains that were no longer flowing with water. They had dried up and were filled instead with refuse.

As we ran, I finally heard it. Heavy footsteps following us. There was no mistaking we were being chased or hunted. A stitch in my side slowed me down.

One second, we were in town, with sandstone buildings and colorful roofs and shutters, and the next, we were in the dense forest and running and branches snagged my hair.

"Vasili, where are we going?" I cried out.

Vasili came to an abrupt stop. He flung his arm out to catch me as I almost went over the cliff.

"This is wrong." He leaned over and looked at the cliff and the rushing river below. He pointed across the vastness to the remains of a rope bridge that had been severed and lay useless on the other cliff.

The crashing and footsteps slowed, and we turned. Vasili bravely stood in front of me as Fang and Thorn stepped out to address me.

"What do you want?" I asked from behind Vasili's back.

Thorn unwound his whip and flicked it, sending a spray of dirt our way.

"Revenge, for one," Fang answered. He pulled his cutlass from his belt and tested the edge of the blade against his finger.

"But it seems we aren't the only ones looking for you." He beckoned to the woods behind him. "Told you I recognized her from the wanted poster in the prison."

Three more shadows came into the light, and I froze. My hand reached for Vasili's arm.

The Brunes Guild.

"Very good, Fang. I knew posting your bail was a magnificent idea. Never have we had such issues tracking someone," the tattooed leader spoke up. "Something keeps hiding her from us."

My mouth went dry with fear. It must be all the mists from the waterfalls from within the palace grounds that hid my presence. But now that I was in the open again, they could track me.

"Give her to us," the leader called out.

My heart plummeted. Five against two. There was no way Vasili could take them alone. My hands trembled as I knew what I needed to do. I stepped from behind Vasili and moved toward Fang.

"Always knew you were trouble." Fang held his cutlass out at me. His lip curled, and he warned, "Leave her be, Vas. We have no beef with you. Just the girl. Go, and we will let you live."

"Now, Fang, as appealing as that offer sounds—living and all—death seems way more exciting." Vasili smiled, his hands reaching for the two short swords holstered on his back.

I dropped my hands to the side, lifted my chin, and was about to open my mouth to sing, when a blur dashed out of the woods. Steel clashed against steel.

Brennon appeared out of nowhere. He rushed forward and met Fang's sword with his own. He quickly overpowered Fang and began an offensive attack, an overhead strike, followed by an underhanded punch to Fang's gut. The older man crippled over in pain.

"Aaah!" Thorn cried out, coming to Fang's rescue. He released his whip, and it wrapped around Brennon's sword arm. With a yank, it went flying out of his grasp to clatter in the dirt.

Brennon, head lowered, raced forward and tackled Thorn to the ground. Brennon was bigger, stronger, and quickly gained the upper hand. With a single punch to the jaw, he knocked Thorn out. He raced to his feet and placed himself in front of me.

The Brunes Guild was not as easily intimidated. Their leader looked on with interest, while their assassin selected a weapon from his bandolier. He shuffled his knife from hand to hand.

"Vas!" Brennon cried out, reaching for his own sheathed knife. "What are you doing, taking bets? Get her out of here."

"Fast way or slow?" Vasili asked, his voice lighthearted despite our circumstances.

Brennon gave a quick glance over his shoulder to take in our surroundings. His face became grim. "Fast. And if something happens to me, promise you'll take care of her."

Vasili nodded.

Fast? Slow? I didn't understand Vasili's question, but I wasn't going to leave Brennon.

Vasili grabbed me around the waist and lifted me into the air.

"No!" I screamed, trying to fight him. I had to help Brennon.

Vasili spun us around and jumped off the cliff. The wind tore at my hair; I kicked my legs and screamed as we took the fast way down the cliff.

CHAPTER TWENTY-TWO

Cold enveloped me as I crashed into the rushing river below. Vasili and I separated during our freefall, and now I was bobbing and turning in the water. The rapids were tossing me about like a toy. I didn't know which way was up. I gasped. Water crashed over my head as I fought to stay above the torrents. It wasn't slowing down but going faster as a soft roar filled the air, and I realized I was about to be swept over the largest of the three waterfalls.

I fought to swim against the current, swimming at an angle. It was no use. I was quickly running out of steam. I opened my mouth to sing, but water rushed in, choking me. The rapids pulled at me, and I closed my eyes and knew this was it.

A rocket of flesh hit me in the side. Arms wrapped around me in a cocoon as we tumbled over the falls. I became weightless, lost in a white cloudy mist, the roar of the falls dulled to a soft hum. And I wondered if this is what death felt like.

Then my vision cleared, sounds came back like a crash of thunder, and we hit the rocks at the bottom.

My mouth was dry, my eyes crusted with sand, and my body felt broken and disjointed as I tried to lift my head. The rust-colored sky swam above me as I rolled to my side and blinked. I could see Vasili sprawled out next to me, his back covered in dark bruises. He grabbed me as we went over the falls and positioned himself to take the brunt of the impact as we hit the rocks. He protected me.

"Vas," I croaked out, kneeling by his battered body.

Blood dripped from his mouth, and he was struggling to breathe. His lungs rattled, and his eyes were as big as moons.

"You stupid fool!" I cried out as I gently shook him. "Risking your life for me."

His lips opened to make a sly retort, I'd bet, but he coughed, and more blood came out. He was dying, and I was losing him.

I couldn't let it happen. I wouldn't let it happen. I gathered him close to my body, his head pressed against my heart, and I sang.

First, the soft, wordless lullaby of my childhood I used to sing to comfort my younger sisters, and then I formed the notes of healing. My magic was a blend envisioning the sigils and singing them into existence, and I focused on the word *healing*. Healing was not my strength and was almost impossible, but I wouldn't let that stop me.

Nothing was happening, and I could feel Vasili's life slipping away. I sang harder, poured my soul into my words as they echoed into the sky. The sea became violent as my sorrow and doubt built. My arm burned as the curse siphoned my powers from me even as I used them to heal. I felt his lungs rebuild and repair; the bones of his ribcage reknit.

I wasn't fast enough. Even as his body healed, his soul slipped away.

His last breath rattled in his body as he went limp in my arms. It wasn't fair that even now the sea witch was stealing from me. He sacrificed himself for me.

"No!" I screamed and let my anger fuel my power and not my voice. I grabbed onto the essence of Vasili's soul, used my magic, and sang.

Come to me. Obey.

I flung his soul back into his body.

Vasili's eyes opened and he gasped. He sat straight up, his hand over his heart as if he was in pain. He blinked in confusion and looked around at his surroundings, the rocky beach and the waterfall that was twenty yards behind us.

"What was that?" he murmured, wincing in pain.

"Are you okay?" I asked fearfully. Maybe I hurt him more instead of healing him?

"I think so." He closed his eyes and drew his face toward the sky. "I was dead. Or at least I think I was, then—" He blinked at me. "—you pulled me back. It's impossible."

"No," I quickly denied what I had done, knowing I overstepped my bounds. "I only healed you. You came back on your own."

He rubbed his chest and gave me a slight smile. "Well, thank you for healing...." He trailed off as he looked out along the shore.

I followed his gaze, and we both froze. Dozens of shark were marooned on the beach, fighting against the sandbanks. Hammerhead, tiger shark, and even the gentle nurse shark, species that wouldn't normally swim in a pod together were scattered across the beach.

"I've never seen anything like this before in my life." Vasili painfully pushed himself to his knee and struggled to his feet. He rushed out to the water and began to grab the nurse shark by its tail and worked on dragging it back into the deep. Once there, the nurse shark swam in a circle and then, with an impressive leap, marooned itself on the beach again.

Together, we worked at pulling the smaller species back into the water, but we couldn't handle the sheer numbers that were recklessly beaching themselves.

"No!" Vasili cried out in despair as the beautiful creatures suffocated.

I felt a tear fall down my cheek, and I understood what the sea had done. I had unsettled the balance. Vasili was one with the sea. He died, and I stole his soul back, so others had to take his place. It was the life cycle of the sea. And even though he wasn't their ruler, they were sacrificing themselves to fix what I had done.

I knew it, and so did Vasili.

"No, brothers." Vasili collapsed, his arms wrapped around the nurse shark as it gasped for breath. "Please, don't do this. I'm not worth it." He sobbed loudly.

I placed a comforting hand on his shoulder and looked out at the sea, trying to figure out what to do.

"Do something!" he yelled, turning to point a finger at me. "Save them, you must. You have the power to do something."

"There is a balance that has to be restored."

"And you messed with it," he accused, his eyes glassy with tears. "You should have let me die. I'm a failure. I'm not good for anything, and it was a good death. A noble death, and you stole it from me."

I heard his pain, and I understood. Felt it within my own soul. The longing to atone for his failure years ago.

"I was selfish," I said out loud. "I am selfish. And I'm not ready to let you die." I ran my left hand up my arm, tracing the mark that was now near my shoulder. I had only a hand span left before the mermaids stole my life. "But I'm not ready to let them die either."

I walked into the ocean, let the cold water swirl around my fingers, and I sang, forcing the waves to do my bidding. To sweep in and carry the sharks back out to sea. With every incoming wave, they tried to beach themselves, but I refused to let them. Like a conductor, I used my voice and hands to control the waves, moving them and driving them back into the ocean. It was a battle of wills, mine versus the sea. I sang until my throat was raw, my body shivering in the cold, and demanded that the ocean hear my will and obey. I stumbled in the water as the sea tried to knock me from my feet, time and time again.

Each time, I struggled to stay upright to continue my spell.

Warm hands clasped my waist and held me still as I sang. I felt a renewed strength as he joined his will into mine. My body grew warm, and I felt the power like the sun and sky push through my body, giving me strength. The arms wrapped around my waist, and I leaned into him as I faced the sea.

My protector at my back.

Finally, I felt the ocean give in. Like a petulant child, she sent a last wave of destruction toward me, and I pushed it back playfully. The sharks turned back to the deep ocean; their gray bodies shimmered as they disappeared.

I had won, but at what cost?

I shook with cold. I had stayed in the ocean until night had fallen, exhaustion took hold, and my knees buckled.

Sturdy arms swept under my knees, around my shoulders, and lifted me out of the chilled water. My head fell against his shoulder, and we turned toward the beach, where I saw Vasili on his knees, watching me in awe.

I looked up at Brennon and wanted to weep with joy that he was okay. I focused on his strong, clenched jaw with the faintest bruise forming along his cheek. A slight cut marred his perfect brow. Signs that he tangled with the Brunes Guild and won. He must have jumped over the cliff shortly after we did.

I enjoyed the possessive way he held me in his arms as he waded through the still waters. Deep down, during the turmoil, I knew it was Brennon. He was like the other half of my soul. I recognized it, and so did he.

I didn't understand until now. The power of the royal line of Isla. Brennon's power was untrained, and not an offensive magic but an inherited one. His was one of strength, determination, like his personality.

I understood the connection between the royals and how their magic fused with the kingdoms above and below. The male royal line of Isla was their own ley lines of power, and when I needed it, when I could give no more without sacrificing myself, he fed me his power. Brennon became my ley line. He was my strength.

And for the moment, cradled in his arms, I knew I was safe. I buried my face deeper into his shirt, breathed in the scent of his magic. It smelled like earth and a sky after a thunderstorm. He leaned down and kissed my brow, and I let the exhaustion take hold.

CHAPTER TWENTY-THREE

I awoke in unfamiliar surroundings. I wore a clean white wrap dress, and pillows were tucked carefully around me. Brennon slept uncomfortably in a chair pulled next to my bedside. His hard face looked at peace, and I wanted to reach out and brush a stray lock of hair out of his eyes, but I was afraid I'd wake him.

I studied the contents of the room. Furniture inlaid with gold and a white table in the center of the room piled high with books, and the wall fountain had trident painted tiles of blue and gold. The room suited Brennon.

I glanced back to Brennon, and he was awake. He leaned forward, reached out, and threaded his fingers through mine. Our palms touched, and I could feel the electricity of our attraction run through me.

"Are you okay?" he asked.

"Yes," I said breathlessly.

"Meri, we need to talk." His eyes fell on the mark on my shoulder, and he ran a finger along it. "What is this? I watched as it glowed and spread when you used your magic."

I pulled my hand out of his and lowered my head. "It's nothing that concerns you."

"If it deals with you, it concerns me." His jaw clenched. "And I don't believe you are engaged to Vasili one bit."

"It doesn't change what needs to happen." My heart ached, as I had to ask the questions that needed answering. "Who is she?"

His brows furrowed. "Who?"

"Your fiancée"

"I don't want to talk about this now." He reached for my hand again, and I pulled back.

"We will. For this is everything," I said firmly. "For I understand what you are now and how important your match is for the success of the two kingdoms."

He looked away. "When the treasure of the Undersea was stolen, so was their future. It was a vessel of great magic that would sustain the Undersea like a ley line for hundreds of years. Queen Darya is fading, unable to sustain them much longer. So hopefully, my marriage to one of their own will be enough. My magic and bloodline can strengthen my future wife, and she can ascend the throne. For only a female can rule the sea. I can't. Vasili can't."

"And it is that union that brings new life to your kingdoms," I stated.

He nodded.

For once in my life, I desperately wished I wasn't a human born on land. I wanted to be of the Undersea. Even if it meant having pointed canines, or dark-green hair, or a sliver of scales along my body.

To save Vasili's home, they needed Brennon's marriage to work. I gently traced my mark on my chest. I had to not get in the way. No matter the cost. It was a sacrifice I was willing to make, even if he wasn't.

"Can you do me a favor?" I asked, hating myself.

He looked hopeful. "Anything."

"Can you book me passage on the first ship out?"

He looked aghast. "No," he said firmly.

"I would like to leave."

His hand balled into a fist. "I won't let you."

"You can't make me stay here. I'm not your prisoner." I pushed the blanket back and stood, raising up on my tiptoes to seem taller, my arms crossing across my breasts.

"The contract—" he started.

"To the stars with your contract. I would like to leave —now."

"Meri, you will not—"

A knock on the door interrupted us.

Brennon roared, "Enter."

A servant I didn't recognize poked his head in. "Your Highness, she has arrived."

Brennon's forehead creased. "Who?"

"Your fiancée. She's at the docks waiting to be escorted to the palace."

"I'm not going."

"Your father has demanded it, sire." The servant looked like he wanted to curl up and die. The door he was holding onto was shaking.

"Fine," Brennon snapped.

The door closed, and he spun, wagging a finger at me. "You will stay right here."

"I will not." I took a step closer and grasped his hands between mine. "We can't be together... ever. You may be selfish enough to sacrifice a kingdom, but I am not."

I had never seen a more defeated look in his eyes. He brought our hands up to his face, and he laid the gentlest kiss upon my knuckles.

"I would give you my everything if you stayed," he breathed out.

"I'm selfish," I whispered. "It wouldn't be enough—" I looked at him from head to toe and knew my soul cried out for him. "—when I couldn't have the one thing I want. You." My eyes burned with unshed tears. His own looked glassy.

He nodded and cleared his throat. "I will look into finding a ship to take you wherever you want."

"Today."

His nostrils flared. "Tomorrow." He gave my hands a last squeeze and headed to the door.

I collapsed upon his bed and silently wept until I didn't have any tears left to cry.

Soft laughter came from the water fountain built into the wall. Fresh flowing water poured out of a vase a woman was holding and fell into the round tile basin. From within the fountain, I saw small beings swimming and diving beneath the water.

Slipping off the bed, I moved and kneeled by the fountain to get a closer look as undines played in the water, blue-skinned with webbed fingers and a soft spine on the back of their head with tails like mermaids. Their eyes like black marbles stared back at me as they chased each other below the water. Slipping above the surface, one placed their elbows on the side of the fountain and looked at me.

Their small doll-like features mesmerized me. The one on the edge of the fountain reached out a webbed hand and touched my cheek. I held still as the undine rubbed my skin and giggled. Then a second appeared, and a third.

I heard the bedroom door open but kept my focus on the magical undines before me. A loud bark came at my elbow, and the undines squealed and dove underwater. Lad shuffled across the marble floor in excitement and dove into the fountain, rolling over and forcing the undines to flee or get flattened.

"Lad!" I chastised as the seal gave me a lazy wink and waited expectantly. Seconds later, the undines played with the seal, running up his side and tickling him. I heard his joyful bark and soon realized they were great friends.

"I don't believe it." Lucy came into the room with a tray of food. It seemed she was never far behind Lad. "The undines have returned."

"They were gone?"

"We haven't seen an undine on Isla in ten years. We thought they were gone for good. Oh, I bet it's because she's here. This is fantastic news. It's just what our kingdoms needed." She sniffed, holding back tears. "Oh, by the way. You slept most of the day. I changed you. Your clothes were ruined." Lucy placed the tray of food on the edge of the table and moved the books so there was room for me to eat.

"Thanks, but why wasn't I taken to my room?"

Lucy put a stack of books on the floor and dusted her hands off. "You must ask Prince Brennon that. But he wouldn't leave your side, except for when I made him so I could help you change."

I blushed.

She shifted tray of food and looked up at me. "The entire palace is preparing for the future princess. There will be music, food, and dancing. I've laid out clothes for you already." She had been prattling about so happily that she only just realized what the arrival of Brennon's fiancée would mean to me.

My head dropped to my chest.

"I'm so sorry," Lucy gasped. "I mean no disrespect. It's obvious that the prince cares for you deeply. But we need this arranged marriage. It's the only thing that can bring life back to our kingdoms. I mean, seeing the undines proves it. Her arrival is just the beginning. Soon, maybe even Lad can change back."

"Lad?" I turned to look at the seal, and he bobbed his head at me and barked.

"He's a selkie. I mean, we both are. He's my brother." She ran her hands through her silvery hair. "He's been trapped in his seal form for years."

"A selkie," I breathed out. "I would have never guessed. But you don't...." I pointed to Lad in his seal form.

Lucy's smile fell from her face. Her eyes filled with sadness. "No, my fur was stolen from me a year ago. Without it, I can never return to the sea. But Lad's is different. Many of our kind can no longer become human. It's like we're forgetting our true form, or our magic has abandoned us." Her chin lifted, and her eyes brightened. "But I fully believe the prince's marriage to the daughter of the sea will fix all of that. We need to unite the Overkingdom and Undersea, and all will be well."

"You should speak with Prince Brennon. We just apprehended a black market selkie fur dealer and his furs. Who knows, maybe one of them is yours?"

"Really? I hope you're right. This is exciting news, I must go and find out," she gushed.

She left me alone with Lad, and I moved to the table and pulled out a chair. Sitting at the table with a whole tray of food before me would have normally lifted my mood. But a bad taste filled my mouth, and I knew it was the bitter taste of jealousy—that Brennon's fiancée was finally here and I had to face the cold, hard truth of my future and what little of it there was left.

It was extremely disheartening. Lad struggled and flopped out of the fountain and waddled his way over to me, leaving a trail of water. He pushed his head into my lap, his bushy white whiskers tickling my leg, and gave me the saddest eyes ever before turning his attention to my tray of uneaten food.

"You know, you're not as cute, now that I know you're human." I picked up what looked like a pastry filled with meat and fed it to Lad.

He was gentle as he took it from my hand and brought it to the floor, where he scarfed it down. He gave me a pleading look again.

"And forget about sharing my bed again." Lad stuck his tongue out at me, and I laughed. "Okay, well maybe the foot of my bed, since it really doesn't matter. I won't be here much longer."

He cocked his head and sneezed and then looked at me with a question.

"Don't worry, Laddy." I leaned down and scratched him under his chin. "I will be sure to never forget about the first selkie I met."

I fed him the rest of the food on the tray, which he gobbled down and then acted like he was still starving. He followed me out of Brennon's room, and it surprised me to see I was only one door down from my room. His balcony overlooked mine on the left. I marched into my room and headed straight for the bed; I reached underneath the mattress, and my hands clasped around the hilt of the dagger. I couldn't bring myself to take it, so I left it beneath the mattress.

I straightened the blankets and went to look at the dress laid out for me for tonight. Every fiber of my being wanted to run away and not face the future princess of Isla, but that was the coward's way out. I would meet her, and then I would make my leave. Use what little time I had left to break the curse and not worry about Brennon or his future wife.

The time passed slowly, and through much trial and error, I dressed myself in the green dress. It was another one that wrapped around, this time under my arms, giving the illusion of a strapless dress. I felt naked, so I wore my hair down, my dark-red locks flowing over my shoulders. I forwent the jewelry box, because Brennon provided them, and I wanted nothing that belonged to him. Instead, I plucked a purple flower from a vine that was growing along the balcony, using a hair pin to keep it in place behind my ear.

I knew when they had arrived, because the servants were running past my door in excitement, rushing to gather outside the palace doors to watch the prince escort her inside. I fell in line among the mob of servants lined up along the path. I found myself shuffled to the back and could only hear the excited oohs and ahhs as the company arrived.

King Roald's procession led the way. Ladies danced ahead playing tambourines decorated with ribbons, followed by the royal trumpeters and drummers. The fanfare was exotic, and fairies flew in circles dropping candies for the children. Next came the standard bearers flying the royal crest of Isla, and the king's bodyguards. King Roald waved to his people as he sat upon a great warhorse, while Brennon sat mounted on his dapple-gray horse, his face stiff and unsmiling, even though he looked dashing wearing his royal robe and crest. Riding next to him on a much smaller white mare was a dainty woman in a purple cloak that covered much of her head and body.

From where I stood on the front steps, I couldn't see her,

but I could hear from those on the ground their first impressions.

"She's so beautiful," a female servant whispered.

"They make a handsome couple," the butler added.

I stood on tiptoe, trying to see his bride.

They came to a stop in front of the palace. King Roald dismounted first. The staff bowed and curtsied. Brennon, his face void of emotion, jumped off his horse and handed the reins to a waiting stable boy. The murmur among the crowd stilled as people waited anxiously. He moved to the white horse and reached up. His hands grasped her around her waist, and he lifted her off the horse with ease. When her feet touched the ground, she pulled back her hood to reveal long, lavender locks.

I gasped in recognition as I stared at the woman before me.

Or should I say... mermaid.

Velora smiled serenely at the waiting crowd. She beckoned to Brennon, and he leaned down as she whispered into his ear. He gave a forced smile, and she blushed in response. Brennon put a gentle guiding hand on her back and led her into the palace. Up the stairs they came, and she slowed, stopping on the step next to me.

Her lips were plump and red, the color of fresh blood. She met my gaze and smiled. "Thank you for your sacrifice. It's because of you I could arrive sooner than expected." She ever so subtly licked her bottom lip.

I was shaking, my hands trembling with anger. I clenched my fists to keep from reaching out and attacking her. I couldn't believe what was transpiring.

I could feel Brennon's gaze on me, but I burned a hole in the ground with my own hateful glare. Refusing to look at him. Afraid he would see my anger and resentment.

He cleared his throat to get my attention.

I clasped my hands on my skirt and curtsied. "Your Highness," I said sourly, refusing to meet his gaze. The air became heavy with awkwardness.

"Come, my love," Velora purred. "I'm exhausted from my travels. I would like to rest awhile."

"Yes... darling," Brennon edged out, leading her into the palace, into his home, a place I would never belong.

CHAPTER TWENTY-FOUR

The outdoor gardens were filled with music, laughter, and speculation as guests from all over the city came to celebrate Prince Brennon's fiancée's arrival. Many saw her coming as the answer to their problems. I knew better.

Seeing her walking on two legs, dancing with Brennon on the outdoor patio under the moonlight, filled me with bitter jealousy. I heard her laugh, and my own voice felt shallow. It was my fault. She was here because of what she'd taken from me.

"You seem very solemn tonight." Vasili came out of the shadows and moved to my side.

"I'm sorry. I just don't feel like celebrating."

He held a flute of wine and took a sip before grimacing and rubbing his chest. "I know what you mean. Something feels off, and I can't put my finger on it."

"Are you okay? Do you feel any pain?" I asked worriedly, focusing on his chest.

He flashed me a fake smile. "No, I'm fine. Perfectly healthy, thanks to you." He raised his glass toward Velora.

"It's her that's giving me pause. I feel like I've seen her before."

"You have," I whispered.

"No, I haven't. I would have remembered someone that beautiful."

"On a certain island," I said vaguely.

Vasili's brows furrowed, and he stared at Velora. "I don't think so, maybe—" His mouth opened in surprise. "If you remember her, that means you *were* there on the island. Brennon was right."

I gritted my teeth and let out a forced sigh as the spell kept my mouth from speaking the truth about the curse. Instead, I opted for the truth. "That's the sea witch's daughter."

"So, we found the old hag. And yet, she failed to heed Queen Darya's royal ring."

I snorted. "She wasn't affected at all by your signet ring. She seems to only care for herself and implement her daughters to rule the seas."

"I have to admit, I never expected the sea witch's daughter to be so beautiful." He rubbed the back of his neck, and I could see the blush coming to his cheeks. He seemed smitten with the girl. Too bad he wasn't engaged to be married to her.

"Vasili, I know you can't rule, but can you marry her? Would that solve the problem between the kingdoms?"

He took another long sip, and I could see the effects of his drink were wearing on him. I had to wonder how many he drank before he showed up next to me.

"Don't think we didn't discuss it," Vasili muttered. "But alas, the sea has chosen the two of them."

"What do you mean by that?" I asked and waved down a house-elf. She stopped, and I took a glass of fresh-squeezed juice from her silver serving tray.

"I can't say, exactly. Just that it was deemed so."

Velora hung on Brennon's arm and pulled him to the dance floor. It differed from the music his crew played on the ship. It was a lively dance, and I watched as the guests created a circle around the two of them, and then an outer ring formed.

Her face came alive with excitement as Brennon easily guided her through the steps, his hand on the small of her back. When there was a lift he picked her up and swung her in the air, her silver silk skirts flowed in an arc. The circle of dancers lifted their hands, and an intricate chain began, and I became mesmerized by the patterns they made with their bodies. I couldn't help but watch Brennon and Velora, his tall frame and her lithe body with her long lavender hair, which looked to be made of moonlight. I could almost see it, the future king and queen, and I realized I was nothing more than a fading memory.

Melancholy slowly moved through my body, and Vasili sensed my somber mood, which now matched the slower song the musicians played.

"Will you dance with me?" Vasili asked. He held out his hand and bowed.

"I don't think it's a good idea," I whispered. I had no intention of being closer to Brennon.

"For a woman who pretended to be a boy, calmed a storm, jumped off a cliff, and controlled the sea, you sure surrender easily."

"I don't know what you mean," I snapped angrily.

"I know things are out of your control. I just never expected you to roll over and give up."

"Give up. Do you mean Brennon? He was never mine to begin with."

"I wouldn't be so sure about that." Vasili grabbed my wrist

and pulled me onto the dance floor. I hoped to stay on the opposite side of the outdoor terrace, but Vasili was maneuvering us right next to the engaged couple.

"Please, don't," I begged and struggled to get away from him.

"I can't help it. You know how I love to rile Brennon up."

"But I don't want to." I closed my eyes, and he spun me in a circle. I gasped and clung to Vasili for fear of falling and making a fool of myself. When I opened my eyes, it was to see Brennon's glued to mine. The muscle in his jaw ticked, and I knew he was angry.

Vasili leaned close and whispered in my ear, but to the curious bystander, it looked more like he was kissing up the nape of my neck. "Any moment now."

"Any moment and what?" I squealed as his lips brushed my neck accidentally, and I jumped.

Brennon stopped dancing in the middle of the floor. He looked like he was contemplating leaving his betrothed and attacking Vasili.

"You may think you know Brennon, but I know him better than he knows himself. He has always been a jealous person. He hates the idea that he can no longer have you. You're off limits. But you know what he hates even more?"

"Dare I ask?"

"That you may have feelings for me," Vasili whispered.

Now, I stopped dancing. Vasili grabbed me around the waist and pulled me close, uncomfortably close, and I tried to pull away from him.

"Relax, your secret is safe with me." Vasili smiled, ran the back of his hand up my face, and I shivered. Not from attraction, but from nerves.

"Which secret is that?" I asked breathlessly.

"That you love Brennon." His hand cupped my face.

"I don't," I exhaled.

"You do," Vasili teased. "And I'm about to prove that he loves you too."

"How?" I asked, fascinated by Vasili's green-gold eyes, and he leaned in as if to kiss me.

"By taking a beating for you." His lips inched closer, and he whispered, "Now."

Vasili was yanked back by the collar of his jacket. I heard a sickening crunch as Brennon's fist connected with his face and he was flung away from me. Brennon towered over us, his eyes dark, his face filled with rage not directed at me. He pushed me behind him and spun to face Vasili. "Don't you dare touch her!" he yelled.

Vasili was grinning ear-to-ear. He straightened his jacket and gave me an "I told you so" wink. "You okay, doll?"

"She's not your doll!" Brennon threatened.

"I'm not your doll," I snapped at the same time.

"Now, remember what I just said about proving something to you." Vasili shifted his feet from side to side, testing his balance. "I'm one hundred percent right."

"Vasili, stop this. This proves nothing."

"Stay out of this," Brennon ordered, using his captain's voice. "I will kill him."

"Why?" I asked.

"You need to ask?" He rolled up his sleeves. "Because he kissed you."

"No," I snapped. Stepping between them, I faced Brennon, my arms held wide, shielding Vasili with my body. I lowered my voice. "You have no say over me, Brennon."

"The contract—" he started.

"Doesn't control my heart," I stated. "It's not yours to take, but mine and mine alone to give." My words had the desired effect on Brennon. I could see my words crush him.

"Prince Brennon," Velora spoke softly. She came forward and placed a hand on his arm. "Is there a problem?" she asked, feigning ignorance.

"There's no problem." I was proud of how calmly I spoke, even though my emotions were in turmoil. I weaved my hand through Vasili's arm and batted my lashes at him. "Is there, darling?"

Brennon's knuckles cracked, and Vasili tensed before sweeping me with an adoring gaze. "No, Prince Brennon was just congratulating us on our recent engagement."

Velora's eyes widened, and her lips pursed. "Congratulations." She let go of Brennon's arm and raised a finger to my shoulder, tracing the white curse mark. "When exactly are you getting married? I'd hurry, if I were you. Unless you get cold feet."

"I'm not the one who has cold feet... or should I say fins."

Her eyes glistened, and she grabbed my elbow and waved at Brennon and Vasili, pulling me off to the side amongst the palm bushes.

"You shouldn't be here," Velora said. "You will mess everything up."

"What do you mean by mess everything up? It's already messed up. I'm going to die thanks to you."

When Velora wasn't focused on pretending to be a lady, her dialect slipped. Her words became sharper and sounded more foreign. "No, not me. Them. The bad men."

I shook my head. "No bad men, Velora. Your mother cursed me."

She was becoming impatient. "Only because she was

forced to by the... um..." She tried to think of the correct word-ing. "Malus, bad... evil one."

"Evil one?"

"Yes, all I want to do is to save seas from poison... dying. My home." She pointed to the sea. "One of the sea daughters —" She pointed to herself. "—must wed the sky prince." She pointed to Brennon. "It is written."

I was getting a headache from trying to keep up with her broken English. But how could I get angry with a girl who had only gained her voice a little over a week ago?

"Where is it written?" I rubbed my forehead.

"In the Undersea's temple. But it is gone. Destroyed. Many years ago."

"So now to save us all, you will marry someone you don't even love." I shook my head.

"No. I love him." Her eyes filled with tears. "I've always loved him. I used to sit on the rocks—" She pointed back to the breakers. "—and watch him play in the ocean when he was little. I would leave him presents. Shells. He wears my gift on his neck."

Velora gestured to her own neck, and I knew what she said was true. For I had seen the leather cord with the shells he wore. She loved him for her entire life. I've only known him a few weeks. There's no way to compare our love. I would lose.

"I don't want to die," I whispered.

"Then take the dagger. Use it." She mimicked stabbing with it.

"I can't!" I cried. "It only lit up for one person."

Velora brushed her lavender hair over her shoulder. "So, take that life in exchange for yours. Easy."

"Murder is never noble. And the person the dagger wants in exchange for my life... is Brennon's."

Velora hissed; her eyes flickered and became elongated slits. Her fingers and nails stretched into deadly weapons. "No. No one kills him. I will protect. I protect." She attacked, clawing at my face and my throat.

I screamed and used my hands to cover my face, trying to curl into a ball.

Velora became murderous, her eyes wild, and she ripped at my hair.

"Stop it!" I cried. "I won't ever hurt him. I can't."

"I'll protect him by killing you. Even if it dooms my sisters."

"I could never hurt him!" I yelled back. Her nails ripped at my throat. "For I love Brennon too!"

Velora backed off in her attack. No, not backed off. Vasili physically dragged her away. His arms wrapped around Velora's waist as he lifted her into the air.

"Let go. I kill her!" Velora cried out. "I will prove my love for the prince and kill her now."

My heart thudded in my chest when I realized we had an audience. Brennon stood frozen, his face filled with disbelief. *How long was he there? Did he hear my confession?*

Warm blood trickled down my neck and face. I wiped at my cheek with the back of my hand, and it came away bloody.

Brennon dropped to his knees next to me. He reached out to help me to my feet.

"No." I held my hand out, and Brennon froze. "Don't touch me."

"You're hurt."

I shook my head, knowing I couldn't bear to have him touch me after I foolishly declared my feelings in front of him. I was embarrassed and felt like a fool. "You can't. I can't. We... can't."

His hands dropped; he bowed his head. His hands clenched the fabric of his jacket instead. "I can't help how I feel about you, Meri," Brennon spoke slowly. "Please don't ask me to stop. It would be like asking me to stop breathing, and I can't."

"Duty before love," I said and met his eyes. They were pools of pain that mirrored my own. "Always."

I found strength I didn't know I possessed and got to my feet. Brennon wisely kept his distance, even though every beat of my heart told me to run to him. But it wouldn't do either of us any good, only hurt each other. I had to be strong for both of us.

I brushed the sand from my dress and palms and then headed toward the palace, skirting the larger groups of people. When I was halfway there, I noticed I lost one of my sandals in the scuffle. A servant saw me and gasped, running the opposite way, and I could only imagine what I looked like. I passed a mirror and slowed. Tangled hair fell across my face, and smeared blood coated my cheek. Fresh trails of scratches lined my neck and chest, and some were deep enough they still bled. My only consolation was that I kept my temper in check. I hadn't used magic, and I hadn't killed her.

So maybe it wasn't such a terrible day.

I held my stoic form until I made it to my room, and once inside, in solitude, I lost what little control I had left. I screamed. The doors on the archways blew open with power; the candles and all the sconces lit. The curtains on the bedposts blew wildly as if tossed by unseen hands. Even the cold fireplace roared to life and burned with such intensity that it was a molten white.

Rosalie could ground herself by touching the earth and releasing magic back into it. But it wasn't the same for me. I couldn't find balance that way. It always came out in a torrid of emotions and power via my voice. Then the scream lent way to a loud sob, and then a hiccup as I fell onto my bed, burying my cries and heart.

When I released all my magic and was finally numb to the pain, I reached under the mattress to search for the sea witch's dagger.

It was gone.

The shutter doors slammed open, and I went to the window to try to secure them closed. On the balcony, I saw fresh scratches across the ledge and ran my fingers into the deep grooves. They looked to have been made with a metal hook.

"Looking for me?" Fang taunted.

I spun and raised my hand, prepared to defend myself with magic, but he thrust a jar that smelled like sulfur under my nose, and I inhaled.

I felt dizzy, faint, and fell to my knees. Gagging and coughing, struggling for breath.

Fang's grinning face swam before my eyes, and he kneeled before me. "You'll be sorry, rat."

"Y-you pig," I spat, and I tried to raise myself to my knees to fight him.

Fang's fist connected with my face, and I blacked out.

CHAPTER TWENTY-FIVE

"How much are you going to pay me?" Fang's voice rang out. "I did most of the work, scaling the walls and bringing her to you, since you failed to capture her earlier. I should get some of that reward."

My eyes struggled to adjust to the dismal room. The earthy smell and dampness that permeated the floor and my clothes led me to believe we were in a cellar. The ground was cold beneath my body, moisture having wicked through my dress. The gag in my mouth tasted of salt and bitter herbs. I tried to work it loose with my tongue, but they tied it securely around the back of my head.

I moaned, as moving made me nauseous. My head throbbed painfully, and I tried to follow the shadows and movements with my eyes. There were four people—no, five— in the room with me. It was hard to count, because they were backlit, and moving halos blurred them.

"You will get the amount we previously agreed on. That's all." The hooded leader of the Brunes Guild moved in front of a table they were huddled around.

"Well, that was before I found out there was a hefty reward for this one."

"Fang, you are nothing more than backwater scum. A black-market smuggler and thief. You feed on the misfortune of others. You cannot see the big picture," the leader spoke.

"I'm not scum," Fang snarled. He pointed a meaty finger at him. "You couldn't find the girl. I did."

"That's because she's weakening. We could only get glimpses of where she was when she hit dry land." The speaker pulled a familiar stone out of his cloak, and I groaned.

The bounty hunters found me. But why would they traverse an ocean to find me? There must've been way more valuable targets than me.

"Still not my problem," Fang muttered. He took a drink from his hip flask and wiped his mouth on his sleeve. "I say, my fee has gone up. I want more money. Me and Thorn both. We have our own score to settle with that one."

"She is no longer your concern. We've settled up. Now go." The bounty hunter pointed toward the steps.

I laid as still as possible for most of the exchange, focusing on regaining feeling in my numb hands and legs with little movements, since they bound my arms and feet. With my mouth covered, I was at a serious disadvantage.

Another man came out of the shadows behind Fang. He leaned over the table, and the one lantern on the wall illuminated his ugly mug. It was Thorn.

He cracked his knuckles to show how powerful they were, like meaty hammers, weathered and calloused from working the lines and sails at sea for years.

"We want what's coming to us," Thorn added. "We'll take nothing less."

The bounty hunter became silent. He nodded to the other

two figures in the room, and they left up the stairs. I saw a trap-door open in the ceiling and then close after they departed. It sounded like a trunk was dragged over the opening.

I couldn't believe the bounty hunter's stupidity. He left himself alone with just Thorn and Fang. They had him by sheer size and numbers. And I almost felt sorry for the bounty hunter when Thorn reached for the snap on his belt to release his whip. He wound the end around one fist and snapped it, creating a garrote.

The man in the hood didn't seem intimidated by the whip or Fang, who sat at the table and placed his muddy boots on the top.

"Half." Fang tapped the table. "We want half of the reward money. Or we will kill you and take the girl ourselves."

"You really are foolish," the man said. "You do not understand who you are dealing with. I have no desire for the bond set on the girl."

He raised his hands, and I could see a glint of silver in his palms. It was the dagger. How did he get his hands on the enchanted dagger?

Fang gave a silent order, and Thorn attacked. He flicked the whip, and as the man raised his hands, I heard a silent whisper of power, "*Crescere,*" and it blasted Thorn into the dirt wall.

Roots grew out of the wall and wrapped around Thorn's neck, arms, and legs, immobilizing him. He tried to struggle against the enchanted roots, but they squeezed tighter around his throat, and he gagged.

"The more you struggle, the tighter they squeeze," the leader warned.

Thorn stilled, but his nostrils flared in fear, his body tense.

I struggled even harder against my bonds, fearful, because

the sorcerer seemed powerful.

"Aaah!" Fang attacked. He rushed the leader, trying to catch him off guard.

But Fang was old and slow. The other man spun with grace and ease, avoiding Fang's blow, and he unsheathed the dagger. Fang hit the other side of the cellar wall and, like an enraged bull, charged a second time.

"*Immobulus.*"

Fang stopped midattack. Everything but his eyes were frozen as he looked around and tried to cry out in frustration.

The bounty hunter lifted his hand and pulled back his hood to reveal a man with dark-blond hair and unfeeling green eyes. He held up the dagger, looked at the red stone in the handle, and murmured, "I wonder."

With deadly accuracy, he turned and stabbed Fang in the heart.

I turned away as Fang cried out in pain, and then the cry faded as he died. A thud followed as the spell dissipated and Fang's body fell to the floor.

"Oh, so not just anyone will do." The man sighed. He was studying the stone in the dagger and pulled it from Fang's dead body, wiping the blood on the edges of his cloak.

My body shook, and I struggled to inhale with the gag in my mouth. I couldn't take a deep breath, and I was choking on the cloth. My whimpers alerted the man to my wakefulness.

"Ah, so the sister is finally awake." He kneeled in front of me and held out the dagger, tapping the hilt on my forehead.

I recoiled at the touch.

"You continue to surprise me." He leaned back on his heels and cocked his head as he studied me. "But I should learn my lesson that anyone trained by her would have a few surprises up their sleeve. But I have a few of my own." He pulled back the sleeve of his cloak to reveal a firm and muscular arm lined with tattoos. I recognized them for what they were—blood magic runes. Which meant he was an apprentice, but who was his master? He was strong in magic and gaining power daily. Very strong, and part of his skin was still raw and red from his newest tattoo.

I mumbled through my gag and tried to talk. Maybe if he took it off my mouth, I could fight him.

"Ah, ah, ah. I know who you are. I know of your gifts, Meri, so I dare not take off the gag, but I fear it is unfair, since you do not know me." He sheathed the dagger and placed it on the lone table in the room.

"I've met your sister Rosalie, or should I say *my* sister."

I blinked and held my breath. I knew him, or had heard of him. He was Rosalie's half-brother Aspen, Prince of Florin. He was the sorcerer Allemar's apprentice, who had taken on the body of the late King of Florin, and Eden and Rosalie trapped him in the daemon realm. Until Allemar tricked Eden into releasing him. Now, Allemar was free—or at least his soul was free. His body was trapped in the other dimension.

"Ahh-en," I murmured.

He grinned. Aspen was easily one of the more attractive men I'd seen. He fled Florin by ship. No wonder he could follow us so fast. He was tall, not as tall or built as Brennon, but he had an air of authority about him. But I knew there was a chink in his prideful armor he wore, and that was his sister, Rosalie. I heard about their battle and how she easily defeated him.

"You *do* know me." His grin widened.

I knew how to play him against himself, and he never lived in a household full of girls like I did.

I rolled my eyes.

He scowled, his nostrils flaring. He leaned near me and grabbed the back of my hair.

I winced but kept from making a sound.

"Whatever my sister said, it's lies," he hissed. "I'm stronger now than I was a year ago."

I steeled my expression and pretended to look bored.

Which only set him off even further. His grip tightened, and I felt the hair rip from the back of my neck. Fire ran through my scalp, but I was the champion of playing cool. Well, not really, that was Rosalie; she was the ice queen. My emotions were usually as turbulent as the ocean, so I channeled my sister. I ignored him, letting my eyes glaze over and giving just the barest of shoulder shrugs.

His attractiveness disappeared into a mask of rage. "I will prove it to you."

He rolled up his sleeve and headed over to Thorn, who was trapped against the wall and for the most part still hadn't moved a muscle, hoping that he would be forgotten, but that wasn't the case.

Aspen reached for Thorn, and one of the tattoos on his arm glowed as he grasped Thorn's forehead. Thorn squealed in pain, his eyes rolling back into his head, and then he stopped struggling.

Aspen was breathing hard, and he pulled away. Thorn's head fell toward the floor, his entire body limp. Aspen rolled his head in a circle, shrugging under the new power he received from Thorn's life energy. Then I understood who he was and his motives.

He worked to gain power by killing. Blood magic. The darkest kind, and he did so under the guise of a bounty hunter. No one would think twice about the bodies he left behind or the money he collected as a reward.

Then I made the mistake of crossing his path and gave him a shot at revenge on his sister.

I thought Fang's death was terrible, but Thorn's was worse. I dry heaved and had to fight against the impulse. If I threw up, I could choke on my vomit and die.

Breathe, I told myself. *Breathe in. Breathe out.* Closing my eyes, I tried to imagine myself back at home. Safe in my bed. Safe from everyone, even myself.

Aspen was back with more abuse. His hand reached for my throat, and I could feel the power in his thumb, the one that pressed just enough to feel the frightened pulse in my neck.

"You're the weak one," he mused, pressing ever so slightly on my throat. "Beg," Aspen whispered.

I glared at him and shook my head.

"Beg, and I will think about sparing your life."

Never had I felt so powerless, useless. But I had pride, and a daughter of Eville doesn't beg.

I clenched my jaw and glared at him.

His thumb pressed on my jugular.

I choked. The pressure intensified, and I kicked with my bound feet at his stomach.

He released me for only a few seconds, but it was enough to catch my breath. I tried to crawl away from him. Then he was back on me. His sturdy hands grasped around my throat, and he squeezed again. He was playing with me, teasing me, trying to show me his power. And I hated him for it.

"Come on, I expected more of a fight from you. Sing your way out of this."

"Mmmff!" I cried, and Aspen's face drifted out of focus.

I was useless, my body gasping for air like a fish. I saw the trapdoor open, and light streamed down the steps.

"Enough," a voice called, and Aspen stilled in his assault. Someone had joined us and took a seat at the table.

Sirena.

The sea witch reclined in the chair. She wore a black wrap dress similar to the style of Isla. She looked almost normal. In her hands, she held the conch shell filled with my blood and that siphoned my powers and life.

"My daughters are not to their fullest yet. I need her alive until the counter curse is complete."

"No," Aspen argued. "I will kill her."

Sirena drummed her fingers along the conch in thought.

"You will get no joy in killing her, for she is barely a shadow of her former self. Or have you ignored the curse mark upon her skin?" She raised her eyebrows and pointed to my shoulder.

Aspen snarled, grabbed the lantern from the table, and held it up to my shoulder, inspecting the curse. "What is it?"

"I would have thought with all your training and tattoos," she teased, "that you would understand."

"Don't taunt me, old woman."

"Old woman?" Sirena stood up, and I could feel the crackle of energy about her. "Old woman. I am by far more powerful than you. You who pretends at magic. Who has no real affinity for it unless you do that?" She sneered and gestured to his blood runes. "I'm real. You are just a fake."

"I will kill you."

"You can try." Sirena placed the conch carefully on the table and picked up the dagger. "But then you will never get what you seek."

"It didn't work. You promised me—"

"It will work. It just needs the strongest magic of all to activate it."

"And what is that?" Aspen snarled. "I have no more patience for you or your riddles."

"Love." Sirena cackled. "You asked for revenge and a way to bring to power the one you seek. It will do both. If she plunges it into the heart of the person she loves—" She gestured toward me. "—she loses her love, and you get what you seek. Quid pro quo."

"Obviously, it hasn't worked yet. Because neither has happened."

"It's because she hasn't been properly motivated yet." Sirena stepped around to kneel in front of me. She ran her hand over my head. "You hold out, hoping there will be a way to save yourself. How very noble of you... and stupid." She slapped my face. Stars—bright, flashing stars—filled my vision, and the room spun.

"But there isn't. You will die, and for what? For a man who can't marry you but will always love you. Oh..." She clasped her heart. "It's so romantic. The true love kind." Her eyes narrowed and her lips pulled into an evil grin.

Sirena must have read the confusion upon my face. "This can't happen until after the wedding. Then, you will murder him on his wedding night, and my daughter will rule both the kingdoms and appease the sea and sky."

Did she not understand who Brennon was and the power in his bloodline? Did she only care for the title of queen and not saving the Undersea?

I shook my head.

"I thought you would say that. But what if he didn't return your love? What if he never knew who you were? Had forgotten all about you. Then, could you kill him?"

What was she talking about? She couldn't be serious. Why would Brennon forget me?

She moved back to the table and picked up the dagger. Sirena unsheathed it and cut at the bonds on my feet then my wrists. I immediately reached for the gag at my mouth, but she put the dagger against my throat, and I felt the slightest trickle of blood.

"I wouldn't do that if I were you."

My hands dropped to my lap.

"You will stab the prince through the heart on his wedding night. If you won't do it for yourself, then I will force my daughter Velora to kill Brennon, and you will die regardless. For she also loves him, but she is more afraid of me." She smiled cruelly.

"I will do it," Aspen said, reaching for the dagger.

Sirena pulled it out of his grasp. "Fool, you can't activate its magic within the stone. I told you only love can. You don't even understand that emotion. It's useless to you." The sea witch turned her attention back to me. "Now, don't get distracted or act all noble, because it will be done."

I rubbed my hand over my shoulder and the white mark that was growing toward my heart.

"Don't even think of trying to kill yourself by draining your magic to get out of the deal. You would really die over a nobody prince who has forgotten you?"

She snapped her fingers, and I felt the spell emanate from that snap. It shot out like a wave and hit me in the chest before passing through the walls and into the city. I wasn't sure what happened, but there was a feeling of foreboding afterward.

She waved at Aspen, and he pressed his finger to my forehead.

"*Somnus.*"

Sleep overcame me.

CHAPTER TWENTY-SIX

M y head was pounding, and I rolled over, the soft blanket wrapping around my feet. I opened my eyes and saw I was back in my bed in the palace.

Had I dreamed it all?

I sat up, wobbled over to the mirror, and gasped at what I saw in the reflection. Purple bruises covered my neck. A distinct four and one pattern in the shape of Aspen's hand. My jaw felt sore, and there was a distinct cotton-mouth feeling in my throat. I knew it was real.

"H-hel-lo," I rasped out and grimaced.

The angry prince did a good job of incapacitating me. I wasn't sure if I could sing a spell to save my life now.

"Just great." I winced again and reached for the pitcher of water, pouring myself a glass to try to soothe my throat, but it hurt to swallow, and most of the water ended up on my dress.

Opening up the wardrobe, I found a few more dresses Lucy added, and I quickly changed into a deep-blue one and made the most of my hair. But the bruises would need some glamour. I struggled to hold on to the spell. The bruises disappeared, and then every time I swallowed and felt pain, the glamour faded and reappeared. I was nowhere near as strong as Eden. I reached for an emerald silk scarf and carefully wrapped it around my hair and then draped it around my neck. It would do.

I headed to the door, saw the dagger on the bed, and contemplated leaving it. My hand went to my throat as I remembered being kidnapped by Fang and then his fateful end. Maybe it was better to be armed if I couldn't use my magic. Digging through the wardrobe, I found a belt and wore it under the dress. Tying the six-inch dagger sheath to the belt, it was barely discernible under the flowing skirt.

As I stepped into the hallway, I heard a familiar heavy tread, and my heartbeat picked up. I turned as Brennon came toward me. A blush rose to my face as he drew near then passed me without a second look.

He must not have noticed me with the head wrap.

"Brennon," I called after him in a croaky voice, and he stopped. Slowly turning, he gave me a curious look. I pulled the scarf from my hair, and he stared at me blankly.

"Do we know each other that you would address me so informally?" he asked and looked back toward the main hall. It seemed he was in a hurry.

The sea witch was right. It was as if Brennon himself was twisting the dagger into my heart. It couldn't be true.

"I just... uh, wanted to congratulate you on your upcoming wedding."

."Thank you," he said stiffly and turned.

"Uh, wait!" I called out in a panicked voice.

He pivoted around. His body language was stiff and formal. "Is that all?"

"I wanted to know if you love your fiancée?"

He frowned. "What kind of question is that? Of course I love her. She rescued me from the sea witch. If that's not genuine love, then I don't know what is. Now, if you are done pestering me, I need to return to my beloved Velora." He spun and left without giving me a second glance.

My feet were sinking into the palace floors as my world caved in on me. I leaned against the wall, pressing my forehead to the cool stone, and prayed to the stars above. This did not happen to me. The sea witch had truly cursed me. The man I loved forgot me.

I scratched at the mark on my shoulder and wanted to scream, but only a raspy gargle came out of my throat. I couldn't even release a single note that sounded close to singing.

"Vas." I pushed away from the wall, ran down the steps, and searched the palace for Vasili. I explored the study, the dining hall, the gardens and outdoor patio, and couldn't find him. One servant passed me by, and I recognized Lucy.

"Lucy." I waved her down. "Do you know who I am?"

She gave me an uncertain look. "Why of course, Miss Meri."

I sighed. "Have you seen Vasili?"

She shook her head. "I think he went home."

"Home? The Undersea?"

She nodded.

"Can you get a hold of him? Tell him to come back?"

"Why, after they closed the whirlpools, no one can go to the Undersea except those who were born there or have a royal signet ring."

"But do you know where an entrance is? To the Undersea."

"Those are closely guarded secrets. I can't tell you."

I chewed on my lip, resting my hand on the dagger at my hip, and wondered. I originally thought it was the same stone in Vasili's ring, but maybe the knife was made from a previous royal signet ring, and the only one I could think of was King Septimus.

I was running out of time. Plus, going to the Undersea would mean if I stayed too long, I could come back too late and miss the wedding all together.

I had to do it, and I had to find a mystical whirlpool to take me there. But I had only seen the one, somewhere in town. But Vasili said there was one in the palace.

"Are you telling me you've never seen him go somewhere then disappear for hours or days on end?"

Lucy shifted the basket filled with shells and dried Islayan flowers. "Well, that would be his bedroom."

"Okay, great. Where is it?" She gave me directions and I ran back through the palace and down the hall toward the door I assumed was Vasili's. I knocked.

No answer. I tried the handle. Locked.

I rubbed my throat and tried to sing.

"Lochni." I grimaced in pain.

The lock clicked, and the door swung open.

Vasili's room was laid out very similar to mine, except it was darker, painted and styled after the deep ocean and Undersea. And like mine, he had a built-in fountain.

I rushed to the fountain and searched the spout, the marble tile, and even the grout work. Kneeling on the ground, I ran my hands under the lip of the fountain, feeling for the symbol.

A shuffling and familiar huff came from behind me, and I glanced over my shoulder as Lad was making his way over to me. His curious and beady eyes appraising me.

"Lad, have you seen this Undersea symbol?" I dipped my finger in the water and drew on the stonework. The water darkened the stone and revealed the swirling vortex. "Have you ever seen it on this fountain or anywhere? I need to get to the Undersea."

Lad pressed his nose to the wet stone and sniffed, and I inwardly groaned. His human mind may have been too far gone. He might not have even remembered what I was talking about.

He shuffled his weight from side to side and then turned, hopping his way out the room and down the hall. I had a moment to decide. *Do I follow him or keep up my futile search?*

Lad turned and barked at me, waving his fin. *Follow him.*

For a seal, Lad was unexpectedly fast. I had to run to keep up with him. He led me outside, down the steps, and into the throne room. I hesitated upon entering and took in the vaulted ceilings, the blue-and-green sunlight that pooled in from the stained-glass windows, and the two thrones.

One golden and manly with a trident etched into the back of the throne. The second one, smaller and made of silver, and upon the backrest was the vortex symbol.

Lad stopped before the throne and then nuzzled the chair where the queen would have sat. Brennon's late mother. Or the future queen would sit.

Standing in front of the empty throne, I had mixed feelings. I understood the necessity of Brennon needing to marry Velora, but I didn't understand why, and there was only one person I could ask.

I pulled the dagger from under my skirt and stood upon the throne. Gently, I pressed the stone to the symbol and closed my eyes.

Nothing happened.

I groaned. And tapped it again and again. Each time expecting a different outcome.

"This is stupid."

I was about to step down, but Lad stopped me. He leaned his head back and gave a long bark that was awful. I clapped my hand over my ears and grimaced.

"What?"

He half barked and howled again.

"Sing?"

He nodded.

Maybe he was right. Vasili said the magic came from music, which was why all the royals held instruments in the paintings. It was why Vasili played the flute.

I licked my lips and closed my eyes. I hummed a few notes then hummed my childhood lullaby. The throne moved backward. I grasped the back of the throne as the floor opened up and a deep hole appeared. I could hear the rushing of water below but couldn't see it.

Was this a whirlpool to the Undersea or a watery trap? I clung to the throne in terror and decided against jumping. I would close the hole and find a different way.

As I made my decision, Lad had other ideas. He shuffled forward and dove headfirst into the darkness.

"Show off," I muttered. I couldn't let him outdo me. I took a breath and jumped after him.

Unlike last time. I was prepared for the cold, the darkness, and the abrupt ending. I broke the surface and wiped the water from my eyes, the dagger still held in my hand. I swam to the edge of the pool where Lad was shaking his fur and splattering water everywhere.

I was about to pull myself out of the water, when silver spears appeared in front of me.

"How did you get here?" Queen Darya decked in a slim black dress with a shimmering train sat upon her throne. Her face was pale and somber. "You shouldn't have been able to get here without an escort."

"The throne opened for me."

"Impossible." She didn't stand but lay slumped in her chair. "Where's Vasili?" She looked past me toward the pool of water I had just came out of.

"I don't know. I thought he was here, which is why I came."

"You really came here on your own?" She waved her hand, and the four royal guards wearing armor made of fish bones and tortoise shells stepped back into formation on either side of me.

I ungracefully pulled myself out of the pool, and the water dripped from my dress. I was still clutching the dagger in my hand.

The queen's observant eyes zeroed in on it. "Where did you get that dagger?" Her voice was harsh. The spears came out, and one jabbed me in the back.

"It's my bane," I admitted. I didn't have time to play coy. I had to get straight to the point. I placed the dagger on the ground and with my foot pushed it into the middle of the room.

One soldier brought it to her, and as she looked at the ring carefully, her face paled. "It's my late husband King Septimus's ring. I thought we lost it the day he died. How dare someone take his royal signet ring and curse it so? For they sullied it. I feel the darkness within." She hissed, revealing pointed canines. She tossed the dagger back to me. "It is dead to me now, and so are you. Begone."

"No!" I cried out and prostrated myself before her. "You're my only hope. The man I love will marry someone else."

"That's what happens with arranged marriages." She seemed bored. "My husband was from the Overkingdom. A prince of Isla."

"I didn't know."

"Why should you? We were married for over nine hundred years, before they murdered him."

"That's what I came here to learn more about."

Her lip curled in distaste. "What a horrible conversation topic. Begone, I tire of you and your prattling ways."

"No. I want to know more about what was taken all those years ago and why you blame Vasili."

She leaned forward, her fingernails digging into her throne. "Because he failed to do his duty. The royal males in our kingdom have one duty. They are born to protect the song of the sea."

"Vasili mentioned that. He said the ocean sings."

Darya rubbed her forehead. "It hasn't sung for a long time. She is in mourning."

"You mean *you* are in mourning," I said softly. "For you are the sea."

Darya's eyes turned glassy with tears. "I have lived a long time. The day they took the song from us was the day I started to die. All I had to do was live long enough to protect it. But I failed." She clutched her heart and sighed, leaning back in the throne. I could tell the crown weighed heavily upon her brow.

"Who took it?" I asked. "Who came from above and took the song?"

"He goes by many names," Darya muttered. "King breaker, Curse maker, I don't know the name he goes by now. Al—"

"Allemar?" I asked.

She nodded.

Her answer didn't surprise me. In fact, it only solidified my own fears. How else would he get the king's signet ring and give it to the sea witch? "He was the one who killed your husband, wasn't he?"

"Yes." She sighed again and closed her eyes.

Lad, who had stayed on the edge of the pool, chose that moment to make a loud and bawdy appearance. He flopped out of the water and came to stand in front of the queen. He barked, and she opened her eyes to listen then leaned forward with interest. "Is that so?"

Lad barked a last time and, like a dog protecting his owner, came and plopped down on my feet.

"The selkie says I'm not giving you the respect you deserve."

"I beg your pardon? You can understand him?" I nudged Lad and glared at him. "I'm sorry. I don't understand what his problem is?"

Queen Darya pushed herself off the throne and slowly came down the steps as if each movement pained her. Her back was straight from years of sitting on a throne, her neck long and elegant, and her eyes were the purest green.

"Yes, I do. I can understand him. In fact, he is of the Undersea. The sea grants the ability for its queen to speak to all of her many races. And he says I'm a fool."

"Lad." I nudged the selkie. "That is no way to speak to the queen of the Undersea."

"No, he may be right. He said you sang. That the ring didn't work for you, but you sang, and the doorway between our worlds opened."

"Uh, yes. He told me to."

"No, he said you sang a certain song. One he knows from his time as a guard here."

"I don't understand." I was feeling cornered, and I backed up. "Lad was a guard?"

"Before he became trapped in this form, he was one of the many guards of our treasure room. Vasili, my son, was the head guard. Follow me. Lad says I need to show you." She beckoned with a long, elegant hand and headed out of the throne room.

I wasn't sure what I was expecting. But Queen Darya led me down a hall. She paused before a set of blackened double doors scorched by magic. Her hand touched her chest, and she took a deep breath.

"I haven't stepped foot in this room in many years. There are too many painful memories." She waved her hand, and two more guards opened the doors. Queen Darya entered first, her black train trailing behind her. I waited, following at a respectable distance.

The room was circular, about a hundred feet across, with alcoves big enough for a person to stand every five feet. I could almost imagine Vasili standing in one alcove, armor and spear at the ready. Lad shuffled over to an empty alcove on my right and turned around, showing me the spot where he once stood guard.

I looked up and saw what was left of the dome glass ceiling that shattered. The room was frozen in time. Broken spears, helmets, and armor lay abandoned around the room. But I didn't focus on the aftermath. The object in the center of the room drew me. The epicenter of the guard's focus.

It confused me. I expected to see a podium, with a pillow or resting place for a great treasure. I was not prepared to see a cradle.

CHAPTER TWENTY-SEVEN

Something crunched beneath my feet, and I picked up the shells and crystal sea animals strung together and hung from a reed. I ran my thumb across the back of a crystal dolphin with a broken tail as I studied the other crystals, which included a blue whale and a green mermaid. Holding it up in the air, the light caught the mermaid, and she reflected a green glow across the tiled floor. I was holding a broken mobile, and my hands trembled.

"It's a baby," I spoke in awe.

Darya trailed her fingers around the edge of the bassinet. "Yes, a daughter born of magic."

"Who would want to steal a baby?" I asked.

"One who wanted to cripple two kingdoms," Darya said. "For only once every thousand years, the sea births a song. A female siren. That child is the embodiment of all the ocean's might and power. But it is too much power for one kingdom to hold, so the daughter is then engaged to the prince of the overland. The sea's magic is wild and chaotic and anchored by the magic of the Overkingdom. For only their line is strong and brave enough to survive our love. And then the couple rule and live a thousand years together in the Undersea until the next song is born. By then, many generations have passed in the overland, so a match can be made again."

"A song," I whispered. Holding up the broken mobile, I hummed the soft melody I had known for most of my life, ignoring the aching rasp of my throat until the pain was gone. No words, only a haunting melody that always comforted me. And in this confusing time, I knew I needed that comfort.

Darya sang with me, harmonizing to my melody. Our voices, both hesitant at first, grew in confidence as we sang together. And as we sang, the ocean above us came alive with sea life. Jellyfish congregated and showed off in an intricate dance. The bioluminescent lanterns flickered and grew brighter at our song.

Silent tears fell down Darya's face. "It *is* you. That is the song I used to sing to you every night."

I looked around the destroyed nursery and tried to imagine the room before the destruction. My eyes focused on a small rug, and I could almost remember a dark-haired man kneeling on it, holding a small stuffed seahorse over my head. Was it a memory of King Septimus? "It almost doesn't seem real."

"It's real. My prayers have been answered." Darya clasped her hands around mine. They felt so frail and cold. "How are you alive? I thought for sure when you disappeared that night that they had murdered you. I never once suspected you would still be alive."

"I don't know how I escaped." I closed my eyes and tried to remember, and I was getting flashes of memories. Of a great storm, a ship sinking, then floating in the sea. "I think the sea shipwrecked his boat. I washed up on the shore of a fishing village and later was taken to Lady Eville."

"The sea saved you when we could not. And brought you to the one person who could hide and safeguard you. I'm sad I did not get to see you grow up into a beautiful young woman. So many memories I missed out on." Her hand trembled as it reached out to cup my cheek. "I'm so sorry I couldn't protect you."

"How did I come to you?"

She closed her eyes as she recalled the day magic created me. "The tides changed, the sea groaned with the storms of her labor pains, followed by a mighty hurricane. One that does not bend to our will or magic. I traveled to the eye of the storm, and in the calm, cradled in a protective shell—was you. As with all the songs before us, we are born of storms and magic. And one day, you will have to brave the storm and find your daughter."

I leaned into her hand and tried to feel the connection that a child has with its mother. It was there, a small feeling of recognition and an even bigger feeling of unconditional love.

"I'm sorry I never found my way home sooner."

She shook her head. "No, no. Don't feel bad. It was meant to be. We have to trust in the ocean. She made her choice to not return you to me. She must have had her reasons. After all, you are the sea's song. You will bring the life back to both our worlds."

"I can't." I traced the mark on my shoulder that had almost reached my heart. "Do you know what this is?"

She shook her head. "Explain."

"I can't. There's a sp—" The words became stuck on my lips, and I cried out in pain.

Queen Darya stepped forward and pressed a finger to my mouth. "Speak," she commanded. I felt Sirena's spell not break but bend. As if Queen Darya was nullifying it with her magic.

Quickly, I fumbled out what I could not explain to anyone else. The curse, the deal, my inevitable death. She paled, and then she faltered. The spell wrapped itself around my mouth again.

Darya stumbled from shock. I reached out to catch her, and we both fell to our knees. "No."

Two guards rushed in to help, but Darya waved them off. She grasped my shoulders and studied the marks that now touched the top of my breast. "Sirena," she rasped out between clenched teeth. "She found an old scroll and convinced King Roald that the only way to gain the favor of the sea is for the prince to marry one of her daughters. By stealing your powers through blood, she is stealing your birthright and cementing their family on the throne. We can't let that happen."

"I don't know what we can possibly do. It's too late. Brennon has been bespelled to forget me, and if I try to fight them with my magic, I will only kill myself faster, and I really don't want to kill Brennon."

Darya stood up. Her face took on a faraway look as she tried to think. "I don't understand what the connection with the dagger is or how she put my husband's ring in it. But you are right. You have to stop the wedding. You have to fight them."

"I can't with my magic." I touched the mark. "I won't be powerful enough."

"Then you will have to use mine," Darya said adamantly. "Come, it's time." She signaled to the guards, and they came and stood around her. Even Lad, who had hung back, came up and pressed his head on Darya's leg.

She took her crown off her head and held it before me. "I, Queen Darya of the Undersea, by blood and song hereby appoint my adoptive daughter Merisol as my heir and Queen."

She placed the crown on my head and adjusted it. She stepped back and gave a stern look to her guards. "Do I have a witness?"

"Witnessed," four voices spoke up quickly in unison, and one seal barked.

I looked at the strange faces of the royal guards, and they looked grim. I didn't want to be the queen, but at the same time, I didn't want to die. I just wanted to live with Brennon at my side.

"Then you shall protect her as you would me. She is now the song of the sea and will gain all my powers and blessings upon my passing." Darya's hands trembled as she reached for the ornate silver ring on her hand. With a twist, she opened a compartment and pressed the contents to her lips, tipping her head back as she swallowed and released a contented sigh.

"What are you doing?" I gasped out, realizing too late the ramifications of her previous statement.

She gave me a stunning smile. Her eyes filled with tears. "I'm being selfish. I'm doing what I must do to save your life and to save my kingdom." She wobbled, and one guard wearing a helmet and visor reached out to steady her. She gave him a lovely smile. "I should have done more to look for you. I shouldn't have given up. But I was too afraid to leave the sea, never having thought you would be on land."

She grasped her chest, and the guard helped lower her to the ground. His arms wrapped securely around her shoulders, his head bowed as if he knew what was coming and accepted it.

I couldn't so easily accept her sacrifice.

"But to poison yourself?"

"It's belladonna, darling. I'm fading. My time here was almost to an end. I have grown weary, and once I die, the sea's power will no longer be contained. Do you understand? Her wrath is great. There will be typhoons, white squalls; hurricanes will be unleashed, and nothing on sea or land will be safe. Like it happened thousands of years ago."

"I don't understand."

"Then let me tell you a story, one that has been told to the daughters of the sea, and you will tell your daughter." She took a shaky breath and began. "The sea was lonely, and she wanted love, so she struck out against every man who ever tried to sail her waters and find her secrets. She capsized and crushed every ship that sailed her waters. Until one man, who sailed with the power of the sun and wind at his back. No matter how hard she tried to destroy him, he sailed through her storms. Storm after storm, squall after squall, the sea tried to sink his ship.

"Until her wrath was so great she destroyed his ship. It crumbled and splintered under her might and killed his crew. The man fell overboard, and she took pity on him, sweeping him to a nearby island for safety.

"The sea felt a closeness to the man, for no other sailor had braved her temper for as long as he did. She, with her soft, gentle waves and abundance of fish, would send him gifts on the island. She took care of him, fed him. But no matter how hard she tried, she couldn't communicate with him. So, she learned to sing. Every night under the moonlight, she would sing for him.

"And the man listened. Her song entranced him, and he slowly fell in love with the sea. But they could never be together, for she was the sea and he was a man. She used all her magic and created a human vessel of it. She created a siren.

"The siren walked out of the ocean, and the man knew it was his beloved sea by her voice. And since then, love calmed the sea's chaos. And now every thousand years, a new siren is born of the sea.

"When I die, my magic will pass on to you. And you will control the seas. Use my power to take back your love. Save your prince, kill the sea witch, and break that curse."

"But why?"

"Because, Meri, you are a siren. Born of the sea, your true mother. I was charged with raising you to take my place." Darya became weak, her head tilted back, and the guard cradled her gently.

"But what if I fail?"

"Oh, darling, but what if you succeed? When I pass, it will be your duty to protect the seas, as it will be your future son's duty to protect the future song born of the sea."

Her hands reached for mine, and I clasped them softly as she struggled to breathe. "I only wish... that Vasili knew... how much I loved him." Her eyes were glassy, and she choked.

The guard holding her threw off his helmet. His glorious dark-green hair came cascading down his shoulders, and Vasili pressed his forehead to Darya's. "He knows, Mother. He knows."

Darya looked up at Vasili, and her smile brightened as she pointed to me. "You have a second chance. Protect her, son. Protect the song of the sea."

"I will not fail you a second time, Mother." He rocked her in his arms.

"I'm sorry for—" Darya's eyes fluttered, and in one last exhale, she died.

Vasili pulled his mother into his arms. His shoulders shook as he silently cried. His grief was immeasurable.

The crown upon my brow felt heavy upon her death, and my limbs tingled as a song pierced the air.

Darya's body glowed like the sun, and the sweetest of songs echoed through the chamber. Like a curtain being raised, the glow lifted from Darya and floated like a cloud to ascend around me. The music grew louder in my ears as the magic settled into my body. I could hear them—the chorus.

They sang as one. All the sirens of the past, all singing their song at once, and I immediately knew them as my sisters, all of us born of the same mother, the sea. There was Allegra, the sea's first daughter, Cadence, and Harmony. Hundreds of sirens, all singing together at the passing of their sister, all of them welcoming me.

The music settled into my soul, and then the song ended. And there was an absence, a nothingness. Where moments before I was happy at meeting my sisters, now an empty feeling settled over me. I felt irritable, alone and abandoned.

I glanced at Darya's body, and all I felt was discontent. She was right. The power of the sea flowed through my veins, yet not only the power but her fury, and right now, I wanted to destroy the sea witch, Sirena, for cursing me, for trying to steal my birthright and my love.

Three guards kneeled before me, all of them verbally pledging themselves to me as their rightful queen. Vasili still cradled his mother, and I looked at them both as I saw them for what they were.

Weak.

Everywhere I looked, I was surrounded by weak, pitiful creatures. All of them would be nothing without me... the sea.

I looked down at my dress I was wearing and decided it wasn't appropriate for a wedding. I sang out my desire, my voice and throat no longer hoarse, and the sea answered with magic. Darkness moved across my skin as my dress lengthened into a black cloud before reforming as a long-sleeved dress with strips that flowed like tentacles from my waist down. My hair turned white as the ocean's power rushed into my body, which was nothing more than a vessel.

Above the protected ceiling, dangerous creatures came to do my bidding—sea snakes, sharks, sea lions—and from beyond, I could hear a creature deep beneath the ocean. It stirred awake at my power, and I could feel his hunger.

Come to me, I mentally called. *And we will feast on death tonight.*

Vasili brushed his fingertips across his mother's eyes, closing them in death. He glanced up, and he was shaken.

"Merisol, what is happening to you? Your eyes, your hair. They're not the same."

"I am not Merisol." My voice sounded hollow. My mouth was moving, but the words were not my own.

"Who are you?" Vasili stood up and took a tentative step toward me.

"I am the sea," I said. I ran my fingers down my dress and smiled at the beauty of it. The ominous black dress and dark coral that decorated my shoulders, like deadly bracers, my black crown upon my head completed the look.

It was time to go. Not to a wedding, but to a funeral.

CHAPTER TWENTY-EIGHT

I didn't need the fountain to return to the upper world. All I had to do was close my eyes and imagine another body of water, and instantly I was there. I was stepping out of the enchanted waterfalls and stared down at the pitiful scene before me.

Time had passed quickly while I was in the Undersea, and the wedding was already in progress. The burning in my breast as soon as I arrived back on land told me the curse was quickly taking hold. I would not let it happen.

The *Bella Donna* was anchored out at sea to have the palace and the setting sun as the perfect ceremony backdrop. A trail of white flowers led from the beach to the anchored ship. Soft music flowed and echoed across the waters, its melody a painful ache in my ears.

"Fools," I snarled. Leaving the whirlpools, I marched down to the beach. Following me out of the enchanted pools was my army from the Undersea. I recognized Vasili as the head guard, and Lad was on my left, waddling to keep up.

When I came to the ocean, I sang a note, and it answered as I stepped out onto the first wave. It swept me up, the foamy swell carrying me seamlessly toward the ship. The salty air was relaxing, and my ears were in tuned with all the voices of the creatures of the sea. The seagulls flying about the ship were even cawing out a cry of celebration.

I frowned as I feared I was too late.

In seconds, I was at the ship. The wave crested and lifted me up to the railing, and I stepped onto the *Bella Donna*'s deck to a chorus of surprised gasps.

The wedding party was small, comprising the ship's crew and a few of the courtiers and royal guards. A longboat was lowered and ready to take the rest of the party back to shore after the nuptials.

I spied King Roald standing on Brennon's right, and the sea witch was on Velora's left, the conch clutched in her hands. Sirena spied me, and her face went pale. She clutched the shell to her chest and glanced at her daughter fearfully.

I followed her gaze to look upon the couple. My heart hurt, as my love stood before me, a glorious godlike statue in gold, his clear sea-blue eyes unfocused as I passed the priest and stood in front of him. Even now, in all my power, he couldn't see me. I turned my hatred toward the mermaid and her sisters, five who stood next to Sirena, and one I sensed waiting in the sea beyond the ship.

Opening my mouth, I sang out a simple note, and the power of the ocean answered. The waves churned and rolled, their foamy mouths picking up the *Bella Donna* and tossing her about like a leaf in a river. The sky turned black and winds blew sideways, scattering the petals that covered the deck and the colorful ribbons that hung with the sails.

People screamed, some dashing for cover. The crew raced for weapons. I didn't pay them any attention. It was the sea witch who I turned to. She grasped the conch shell in her hands, and her mouth mumbled as she held the conch higher in the air.

A pain ripped through my shoulder as the curse burned through my breast.

No! I would not give in like this. My singing grew louder, the ocean answering my calls.

Brennon drew his sword. He raised it to attack me, and I almost wished it would strike true. To end my pain. I closed my eyes. A dark blur brushed past me, knocking me aside, and collided with Brennon, knocking him down. Vasili attacked Brennon, and the two were in a familiar duel.

Roars and clashing of swords filled the air, and I turned to see the crew and King Roald's guards fighting my Undersea guards.

"What are you doing?" Velora cried out. Her hands trembled; the white bouquet fell to the deck.

"I'm taking back my birthright," I answered. "You knew. You both knew *who*, or should I say *what*, I am?"

Velora's eyes dropped guiltily. Her hands fumbled within her white silk skirts. She nodded. "We knew."

"And yet you still tried to kill me?" I hissed.

"Mother said it was the only way. That the sirens aren't the only daughters of the sea. That mermaids are as well," Velora fumbled out quickly. "And that it serves you right. It was justice for what Lorelei Eville did to us."

Roald was not at all phased by my show of power. In fact, he was grinning from ear to ear. "A siren? A true daughter of the sea. Who'd have thought you were still alive? Especially after all these years." He turned to Velora. "And you were nothing more than a poor substitute." He leaned back to watch Vasili and Brennon fighting each other, fully engaged in the outcome. He made a face when Brennon took a jab to the gut.

The king did not try to stop the fighting or pull back his men. He thrived on adventure and stubbornness.

I heard a sickening thud, and Vasili pulled away. Brennon was lying on the deck, motionless. A red blood pool formed beneath his body. The injury was to his shoulder and not life threatening. Vasili was just as strong as Brennon if not more and had maybe held back in his previous fights, but when it came to protecting me, he would fight to the death.

Vasili sheathed his sword. "You will not injure my queen."

Brennon reached for Velora, and she clung to him, her arms wrapping around his neck possessively, and she glared at me. I knew she would not give him up without a fight.

The wind picked up as my anger needed a place to vent. I spun on my heel and stalked Sirena. "Release him from the spell, now!" I screamed, pointing at Brennon.

Dressed in red and gold silk, her white hair was braided into a crown. She didn't look exotic or wild but cool and refined. Like a powerful woman. Her eyes closed to slits, and she held the shell in her hand. "No. You're too late."

My heart slowed, my mouth went dry, and I turned to look at the matching wedding cuff that both Brennon and Velora wore. The set I picked out. I looked at the spelled look in Brennon's eyes and how Velora clung to him, like she was drowning and he was the very air she needed to survive.

I felt sick.

Sirena grinned. "I see the change within you, Meri. Which means Queen Darya is dead. A noble sacrifice on her part to save you, but you forget that traveling to the Undersea takes time, and you lost. You may have gained more power from your attempt to seek help, but it will soon be gone as I drain the rest."

She held out the shell, and the last of her mermaid daughters climbed up the rope ladder and stepped onto the deck. Her hair was a saffron-yellow, her dress a simple white wrap. Her hands reached for the shell greedily, and Sirena handed it over.

With a single note, I sang, and with a powerful gust of wind ripped the shell from the mermaid's hands and blew it into the ship's mast. Unbelievably, the shell didn't shatter.

"It can't be broken or destroyed." Sirena cackled. "Your time as the sea queen will soon be over, and it is my daughters who will inherit."

I understood how the sea in Queen Darya's story felt and her warning about her anger. I was the sea, and my wrath was uncontrollable. How she wanted to destroy every ship that dared to sail her waters. She was in pain. I was in pain and wanted them to feel my own.

I sang, and the ocean answered. The water bubbled, and a humongous tentacle reached out of the sea and knocked against the sail.

A woman screamed. A second tentacle appeared and wrapped over the railing, searching along the deck until it found an unsuspecting soul. It wrapped around him and flung him into the thrashing waves.

"Finally!" King Roald roared. "Something worthy of me to fight!" He drew his sword and attacked my kraken, a much larger and dangerous cousin of Diesel.

The mermaids cowered, ducking their heads, as the kraken

was actively looking for the sisters. My pet found the one with sky-blue hair and flung her into the water. A mental cry of anguish knocked me to my knees. It was the kraken; he had received a wound from King Roald's sword.

Each stab felt like it was directed at me, and as I felt his pain, he fed on my anger.

"Now," I said. The kraken grabbed the king and flung him across the deck. He hit the center mast with a thud and fell to the ground.

I stared numbly at the unmoving body of King Roald. I had a moment of déjà vu. It was Armon's death all over again. I truly was a murderer. All around me, people were hurt or in pain, and their cries were like annoying gnats. I wanted to clear them away, wash them into the ocean.

I sang with the intent to not just wash them clean, but to bring the ship down. Then, and only then, would the numbing pain go away and I could feel again. Death seemed like a silent relief.

The waves stilled as the water pulled back in preparation, like a mighty hammer preparing for the final blow.

From the decks below, a young woman was struggling to come above and keep her balance with the help of a familiar cook.

"Meri!" she cried through the wind.

It was Aura. Her face a pale mask, her blonde hair whipping about her in a frenzy as she fought against the wind and sand. One arm covering her eyes, the other arm reached for me.

"What are you doing here?" I yelled. "Go away. I don't want you here. I don't want you to see me like this." I blasted her with wind, and she slid across the deck and almost went overboard. Howland grabbed her at the last second and pulled her back to safety.

She carefully got to her feet and approached me. "Never, ever disappear from me again!" she yelled over my violent wind. "Do you understand me? If you run, I will always find you."

My heart ached at seeing my beautiful and fragile sister.

"Oh, stop it. I'm not fragile." Aura made a face. "And stop blaming yourself for Armon's death. It was an accident, and you saved me. And I'm here to save you."

"You can't save me. No one can." I gasped, and my hand went to my chest. The white burning curse raced through me. "All I can do is make my death worth it. Make sure that my enemies pay for what they did and take them with me."

"Stop it, Meri. This isn't you. This isn't who you are."

"It is," I admitted. "I am not a normal girl. I'm the—"

"The sea," Aura interrupted. "Yeah, I know. Don't forget I can read your emotions. I've been reading your dreams for years. I suspected but it wasn't time to tell you."

"Secrets are poison," I spouted, feeling betrayed by her confession. "They slowly hurt the one person you want to protect." I looked over at Brennon, and my eyes burned with tears.

"I see," Aura answered. She slowly moved toward Brennon. Velora stepped in front of her, but Aura just laid a hand on her heart and whispered a word. "*Percipio.*"

The mermaid bride fell to her knees and sobbed. Aura reached out to Brennon, touched his temple, and whispered, "*Vide!*"

Brennon faltered and shook his head. He looked down at Velora with a confused look on his face.

Aura returned to face me. "There, his mind is clear. There are no more secrets between you."

Unbelievably, my sister, the empath, with a single touch had broken whatever spell the sea witch put on Brennon. But it wouldn't help me. It wouldn't save me from the curse. I looked down at the scar. White veins spread out over my heart, and I knew I had only minutes left.

"Oh no. Meri?" She read my mind and her eyes went to my heart, her finger tracing the scar.

"Stop, Aura. There's nothing you can do." I pulled her hand away. I winced in pain and fell to my knees.

The giant tidal wave I called and was holding back to destroy us all almost broke. The kraken retreated back into the safety of the sea. Lad was nudging Vasili. From within Vasili's jacket, I saw the silver handle of the enchanted dagger. The fool had brought it with him. I glanced away, trying to build the wall in my mind to keep Aura out.

"No, there is." She looked over at the dagger. "You just don't have the strength to do it." She grasped my wrists and glared into my eyes.

"I can't do it. I love him too much." I turned to look over at Brennon, who looked disheveled. Velora was crying and grabbing on to him, but he was trying to fight her hands and come to me across the deck.

"Meri!" Brennon cried out, his eyes clear and filled with love.

Velora knew she was losing him. She picked the conch up from the deck and began to drink greedily.

"That's for your sister!" Sirena cried out and tried to pull it away. "We must use it to save your youngest sister."

Velora didn't listen.

I gasped and sucked in a painful breath through my teeth

and looked at Velora who had placed the shell to her mouth and was now draining my life.

Aura focused her attention on the sea witch. Her head cocked to the side as she listened to the witch's thoughts and feelings. "You're a twin? The sea birthed two songs?" Aura looked to me for confirmation. "Whatever does that mean?"

CHAPTER TWENTY-NINE

S irena patted her white hair, and then I realized how similar she looked to Queen Darya. I closed my eyes and listened to the siren ancestral songs, and I searched for the sea witch's and heard a silent echo. A siren without a voice. Sirena's face turned dour with rage.

She raced for the shell and pushed Velora to the ground. She lifted it to her lips and drank from the conch.

Pain. Searing pain burned into my chest, and I collapsed to my knees in agony, the white curse mark digging deep into my heart. Her mouth came away bloody, and she wiped it with the back of her hand.

"Very clever of you, little sorceress. Yes, a century ago, the sea thought to spare her daughter from growing up alone, so she bore twin songs. And yes, I was mute. Cut off from all power. Cut off from my destiny. Never before had a mute siren been born. They didn't know what to do with me. I was an outcast, never to marry the prince of the overland and get my own happy ending. No, that was Darya's path, so I left the Undersea, met a sorcerer who gave me my voice and the power to create my own daughters, my own lineage. And I plotted for the day when I could take everything that matters from my sister."

A smile crossed her face. "And when you die, I will have my ultimate revenge and will kill the prince."

"No, not him!" With a mighty shove, Velora ripped the shell from her mother and knocked her overboard. The sea witch cried out as she fell into the sea. "I will not let you harm him. I will protect him by killing you." Velora drank from the shell, and I fell to the deck, my head hung low.

Brennon reached my side and pulled me into his arms. I felt so cold.

"Meri, please tell me what is happening?"

Aura answered. "That girl is killing her." She pointed to Velora. "With every sip, she is draining her life."

Brennon roared out a command. "Stop it now!"

Velora pulled her lips away, and a trickle of blood dripped down her chin. "Never. Not until she's dead." She took a final drink and held the shell upside down. "It is finished."

Lad let out a furious bark and charged Velora. She yelped as the seal chased her around the deck, leading her to the railing as a giant tentacle reached out and took a swipe at Velora.

She screamed as she hit the deck, narrowly missing being knocked into the raging sea.

My vision became blurry, and I grasped onto Brennon's shirt. "I'm sorry."

"Tell me! There has to be a way to save you."

"There isn't," I lied.

Aura ran toward Vasili.

"No." Brennon's eyes filled with tears. "I just got you back. I won't lose you."

A shadow moved behind Brennon, and a speck of silver glimmered in the air.

"No!" I raised my hand to stop Aura.

Brennon turned as Aura tried to drive the dagger into his heart. He blocked the blow with his forearm, and Aura cried out as she lost the grip on the dagger.

"No, let me save my sister. It's only right." Tears of frustration ran down her face.

"What do you mean?"

Aura pointed to the glowing gem. "The dagger glows near the heart of the one she loves. We can sacrifice them in her stead."

"Is this true?" Brennon looked at me.

"No," I whimpered painfully. My legs had now gone limp. "She lies."

Aura was beautiful in her righteous anger. "No, I read the sea witch's thoughts. It's true."

Brennon's jaw twitched, and he looked at me, love filling his eyes. "Then do it." He picked up the dagger and handed it back to Aura.

"Aura, don't," I warned. "If you do, I will never forgive you."

"It's my fault," Aura said. "If I'd been stronger, you never would have defended me that day and killed Armon. You wouldn't have run away. This wouldn't have happened." The dagger trembled in Aura's small hands. "I can make it right. I can save you."

"It is my destiny," I wept. "Please, don't kill him. I love him."

"Took you long enough to admit what I already knew." Brennon smiled. He brushed my hair out of my face and leaned down to give me a soft kiss on my lips. When he broke away, I wanted to cry. He turned and kneeled before Aura, unbuttoning his shirt to expose his heart.

Now faced with what she was about to do, Aura hesitated. She had never so much as harmed a fly.

"Here." Brennon pointed between two ribs. "Angle it upward and then twist it to make it quick and clean."

I slid to the deck, my vision becoming blurry. My arms stopped working; my lungs were struggling to breathe as paralysis took over.

"Nooo!" I sobbed as Aura adjusted the dagger, and her arm pulled back to strike.

A hand knocked the dagger out of her grasp, and it clattered on the deck. The gemstone in the handle went dark. From my position, black boots stopped in front of the dagger. A pale hand reached down to pick it up, and the dagger glowed brightly.

I followed the dagger's glow and looked up into the determined face of Vasili. The weapon thrummed and glowed in his hands as well, and I knew without a shadow of a doubt what he was planning on doing.

"No," I whispered as tears leaked out of my eyes. "Vasili, please, don't."

Vasili held up the glowing dagger. His voice was full of emotion. "Y-you love me?" he asked in disbelief.

I closed my eyes. I did. He was my best friend, my protector, and I realized there was a small spot in my heart reserved just for him.

"Then that is enough." He looked up at the sky and took a deep breath before meeting my eyes. "It has come full circle. Maybe you saved me just for this moment, so I could save you."

"No, don't," I whispered.

"It will be a noble death. I can finally protect you the way I was born to."

"Vasili, brother, give it to me," Brennon growled. He took a step forward. His hand reaching for the dagger.

Vasili shook his head and looked at me. "I failed to protect her once." His voice filled with conviction. "I won't fail a second time." The dagger's jewel pulsed in his hands. He turned its tip toward his heart.

Brennon rushed for Vasili, and they fought over the weapon.

With my last dying breath, I cried out, and my control over the tidal wave broke and it came crashing toward the *Bella Donna* as all hell broke loose.

"Meri," a voice sobbed.

My eyes fluttered open, and I looked up into the worried eyes of Aura.

"You're alive," she breathed out and pulled me into a hug. "I can't believe you're alive."

Aura was soaked, her hair plastered to her face, and I looked behind her to see the main mast had broken and crashed into the deck, causing major structural damage. Sails were torn and scattered, and we were taking on water, slowly sinking. The tidal wave crushed the *Bella Donna*, and most of the crew was gone. The few remaining had formed a bucket brigade and were doing their best to keep the ship afloat. Hammering was coming from below, and longshoremen were trying to evacuate the guests into the longboat and take them safely to shore.

The Undersea guard was working alongside the crew and were trying their best to save the ship.

I looked down at my chest and saw the white coral curse mark had disappeared, and in its place was a single white scar that looked like it was made by a dagger and had healed over.

"N-no," I muttered and grasped Aura's shoulder to help me stand up. Brennon stood over a still form. His shoulders were shaking, his head bowed in respect, and I knew what happened.

"I tried to stop him." Brennon's hands trembled as tears fell from his cheeks.

Vasili was dead, the dagger embedded in his heart. He looked at peace. Even though I was alive, I was still weak. Aura helped me over to Vasili, and I clutched his hand in mine.

"What were you thinking?" I muttered softly.

"He wanted an honorable death," Aura answered in his stead. "He wasn't really living after they stole you from the Undersea. He spent his life trying to atone for his mistake, and he found a way to do it." A single empathetic tear fell down her cheek. "He was truly happy in the end. A sacrifice of love, and because of that, his memory will live on forever."

"He shouldn't have paid that kind of price," I whispered.

"You did," Aura corrected. "You made a deal with the sea witch to save the crew."

Brennon's face filled with astonishment. "You did what? I can't believe you." He took a step toward me and reached to pull me into a hug.

I glanced at the gold marriage cuff on his arm and retreated. He wasn't mine. He belonged to someone else. And knowing that was killing me.

"Stop," I whispered. "Don't."

"Meri, I love you."

"And I, you," I said, tears falling from my face. "But this should never have happened." I pointed at Vasili's still form. "He should still be alive."

Brennon's eyes darkened. "Do you wish it was me instead?" He was angry. He finally realized I loved both of them, though not the same. Brennon was my true love; Vasili as my dearest friend.

"No. It should have been me. I should have been the one who died!" I cried out, and Aura reached for me. I waved my hand at her, and she stopped. "I wish you wouldn't have come." I turned to Aura. "This is all your fault." I pointed at Vasili's body.

Aura's lips pinched together, and her face filled with rage. "Look around you, Meri." She gestured to the ship and the wreckage that still floated around in the ocean. "You are the embodiment of the sea. Your death almost killed us all. If it wasn't for Vasili's sacrifice, we surely would have died. But not just us." Her eyes glittered with anger. "If you died, tidal waves, typhoons, and hurricanes would have destroyed the coasts of Candor, Sion, and Isla. Your death would have impacted the seven kingdoms." She touched her head. "I have seen it. Why do you think I followed you here? I mean, it took Maeve almost getting stuck in a mirror before Rhea figured out how to protect me during travel." She held up a bracelet that was a braid of silver, gold, and glass.

I couldn't believe what I just heard. Rhea figured out how to travel through mirrors. That was something the strongest of sorcerers couldn't do, and my sister had done it.

Her scolding only made me feel inferior. She was right. I could still feel the power of the sea coursing through my body, and her emotions were my own, and they were turbulent.

It was only then when I took a moment to look around the

deck did I see it was more than just Vasili who died. Other bodies had been wrapped in canvas and tied together, ready to be transported off the ship.

And the king. I killed the King of Isla.

I did this. I killed them. I was a murderer, and when I looked around, I didn't necessarily feel remorse. I felt anger and an intense and despicable feeling of pride.

Bitterness rose in my mouth as I felt my loathing overcome me. This was not right. The sea matched my mood, and the waves became choppy. *Oh stars.* I would hurt more people if I didn't get away right now.

I ran up to the bow and looked down at the water below.

"Meri, wait." Brennon rushed toward me, and my eyes locked in on the marriage cuff.

"Why? There's nothing for me here."

"I'm here." He touched his chest.

"But you are not mine." I pointed to the cuff and to a distraught Velora, who was a sobbing mess of tears.

His face fell as he looked at the marriage cuff and his wife in confusion.

I jumped, my body falling into the waves, becoming one with the water, disappearing among the sea foam.

CHAPTER THIRTY

My toes dug into the white sand as I laid out on the beach, listening to the song of the waves crashing into the reefs. It was my perfect island sanctuary. The sea revealed it to me, and I claimed it as my home. It was impossible to get to, and the waters were treacherous because of a ring of storms caused by magic, a hidden coral reef, and the fog that surrounded my island at night.

A perfect place for a sorceress to live in solitude, if I didn't have so many concerned babysitters.

"Coconut?" a male voice asked.

Lad, in his human form, shoved a coconut under my nose. He expertly cut off the top and was offering me the milk. It turned out that by reclaiming my birthright it only amplified my powers, and Lad as a selkie was of the sea, so I could use magic to help him shed his coat. It was a painful process, but he said it was worth it.

Lad grinned at me. His dusky-brown hair had hints of his seal spots in it, and he wore his seal skin as a cloak around his neck. He had become the captain of my guard after Vasili's sacrifice, and he took his job seriously. He was worse than a mother hen.

"No, thank you." I looked back out to sea.

There was something wrong. I felt a disturbance in the sea. It happened shortly after I jumped overboard from the *Bella Donna*. A great surge of power emanated around the ship, and then it echoed into the deep water.

Lad described to me what transpired after I dove into the sea. He said Vasili's body disappeared in a flash of light and that a smaller ship was seen sailing away. He described the captain, and I knew it was Allemar's apprentice Aspen who had magically taken Vasili's body. They were shielding themselves from me. Or maybe it was because water diluted most magic, but either way, if they were on the sea, I would know it.

Every brigade, fishing vessel, or raft that touched the water or any river that spilled out into the ocean, I knew their location and even who was on it. Except for Aspen. I couldn't track him or Vasili's body. And four months later, I still couldn't find them.

He frowned. "Fruit?" A yellow banana followed the coconut.

"I'm not hungry."

Lad chuckled. "Liar. You're always hungry."

"Usually, but not right now."

He sat cross-legged in the sand next to me, sighed dramatically, and peeled the banana. I almost preferred him in his seal form, because then he was less annoying.

"He's close, isn't he?" Lad asked. He pointed the white tip at me. "You always get testy like this when he gets close."

I rolled my eyes and stared out at the sea. "Do not."

"Do too. And when he doesn't make it, you get angrier."

"Do not," I huffed, brought my knees up to my chest, and stared at the ship that was battling the storms, trying to make it past my protective circle. On my island, the wind was calm, the sun shining bright and warming the sands, but about a league out, the weather changed and became turbulent. Impossible to pass because of my magic.

"You could always, I don't know, lower the protective circle and let him through," Lad said while chewing.

I snorted. "There's nothing he has that I want."

"There you go again, lying to yourself." His dark eyes twinkled mischievously.

I took a handful of sand and tossed it on the banana.

"Hey!" Lad cried out in dismay. "You wrecked my banana. There should be a law against fouling perfectly good fruit."

I smiled. Lad got up and waddled away to get a new banana. Even though he was human, a few of his seal quirks were still visible.

There was something calming about Lad. He slowly became a trusted friend like Vasili, and he was the more talkative of my Undersea guards. Maybe it was because he spent years in a seal form, so he was making up for lost time. He wasn't at all surprised that I didn't want to return to the Undersea to live.

There were too many fountains and ways to get to Isla. I would constantly think about Brennon and Velora. Although, I used my new magic to bring life back to the kingdom. In fact, I was always hungry and eating, because I spent most of my days healing the seas.

Using what Lorn taught me about ley lines of magic, I scoured the deep pits of the ocean until I found them. I tapped into them, using them to clean the water, bring back the coral beds, and birth new life among the sea creatures. Sharks long extinct resurfaced. Lad pointed out three new breeds of seahorses and at least twenty new families of coral.

But I was irritable. All the time. My emotions were uncontrollable, battered about like a kite without an anchor. I frequently brought hurricanes to my island home. It was better if I stayed far away from everyone. I was too dangerous anywhere else.

Sirena returned to her island with six of her daughters. She seemed weakened. I wondered if there was a backlash for me regaining my power. Did it do something to the other daughters? I didn't know and didn't care.

My eyes focused on the black vessel bobbing along the horizon, and I wished he would go away. For I knew the person sailing that ship. It was Brennon, and he was relentless, fighting the high waters and wind, putting all the men's lives at danger. I would kill him myself, but Howland was on that ship. I wouldn't risk the lives of others so easily.

I sighed and left the beach, heading up to my island palace. It had grown overnight, made of lava that formed into a sanctuary and then cooled to create stone. My Undersea guards spent a week bringing items back from the Undersea palace to fill my island oasis. Even though I preferred to live in the sun above the land, they spent a good portion of their day in the water surrounding my island. Even now, there were ten guards swimming just out of sight from the ship. Only Lad was comfortable spending time on land with me.

I looked at the setting sun and knew that as the darkness rose, so did the tides, and the waters would become even more dangerous. But luckily, each night, he retreated, taking the ship to calmer waters.

I placed my hands on my hips and knew something had to be done.

My footsteps left watery trails along the deck that shimmered in the moonlight. The ship had sailed out of the treacherous water and was waiting beyond the fog wall to try again come morning. Battling the waves had worn out most of the crew, for only two were on watch.

I tiptoed to the captain's door and pressed my ear to it.

Silence.

I turned the handle, and it was locked.

"*Locherra,*" I sang, and it unlocked. I stepped in, letting my eyes adjust to the darkness within. The vessel was unfamiliar, since I destroyed the *Bella Donna*. This ship was smaller, the hull shallower, which meant it could travel faster and go up rivers if need be. But the layout of the cabin was almost the same. A four-post bed was off to the side, and I made my way over there to stare at the sleeping form.

A peek. That's all, I told myself. I would just take a quick look at Brennon and then send the four winds to push his ship out to sea.

He slept on his back in only his breeches. His tan muscles begging to be touched. The bedding kicked to the side, and he was even now tossing and turning in his slumber. Sweat trickled down his brow as he fought off a nightmare.

I couldn't help myself; I reached out and gently brushed his hair to the side. The feel of his skin beneath my fingers made my heartbeat pick up. His tossing subsided, and his breathing evened out. I rose to leave, and he moaned.

"Shhh," I whispered and sat next to him on the bed. He

calmed down immediately. Softly, I hummed to him, and his breathing deepened. Soon, he was in a deep sleep. Feeling brave, I reached out and gave him a kiss on his forehead before making my leave the same way I came.

The next morning, I sat on the beach and watched as Brennon fought against the waves. All day long, they battled, never once reaching any closer to their goal. Each day, Lad told me to lower the circle, and I told him to go jump in a volcano. But once night rolled around, I snuck onto his boat for the second time, once again watching him fight demons in his sleep, never leaving until I had sung him to sleep and kissed him goodnight.

By the third day, I was becoming impatient, pacing the beach, tossing shells into the water, waiting for him to break through the barrier. If he was such a skilled captain, he would have no problem sailing through the seas. But each day dragged on longer and longer as I anxiously waited 'til nightfall when I could once again see my love and steal a kiss. Which I always felt guilty for doing.

As soon as night came, I was waiting beyond the fog line for the crew to go to sleep. Same as before, I snuck onto the ship by using the waves to lift me up. When I went into Brennon's room, he was once again asleep, exhausted from fighting the storm at the helm.

His dream was more violent tonight. He was kicking and fighting someone. "No, Vasili," I heard him mutter.

I froze at his bedside and watched him relive his best friend's death repeatedly in his nightmare. I had already succumbed to the curse. I never saw the killing blow or heard his last dying breath. It was self-inflicted; Vasili sacrificed himself to save me.

Brennon, the strongest man I knew, was reduced to tears.

His breathing picked up, and he tossed and turned. He was a man haunted.

"Meri, please don't leave me!" he cried out in his sleep. I sat next to him and quickly sang to try to comfort him, my hands resting on either side of his cheeks. With my thumb, I brushed a tear away and felt a matching tear of my own slide down my cheek.

When he was calm, I leaned down to kiss his forehead in goodbye and pulled away. Brennon's hands wrapped around my body, pulling me down on top of him.

I gasped and looked into his very alert eyes. He rolled over, pinning me beneath him. "That's it? All I get, night after night, after fighting the waves to see you, and each night, you only give me a kiss on the forehead. Meri, you are enough to drive any sailor mad with desire."

My eyes widened in surprise. He had woken up when I calmed his dreams. My cheeks burned in embarrassment, and I struggled to break free.

"What kind of fool do you take me for? I finally caught you. You're not escaping my grasp. Do you know how hard it was to lay here night after night and not touch you? I'm not a patient man."

Brennon leaned down and claimed my lips. At first, I struggled, but was this not what I also wanted? He nibbled on my lower lip, and I moaned in desire. He took my cue and kissed me deeper before transferring his kisses to my neck and leaving a trail of them down my shoulder and to my collarbone. He gently pulled the neck of my wrap dress down a few modest inches to look at the scar over my heart, the one made by magic and Vasili's death.

Brennon kissed the scar before placing his ear on my chest

and listened to the beat of my heart. I placed my hand over the back of his head and couldn't stop the tears of grief and happiness that fell. He pulled away, and I felt his absence. It was like being abandoned all over again.

But not for long, because he pulled me close and wrapped his body around mine, his leg wrapping over my hip possessively. His lips searching for mine hungrily. A burning desire for more overcame me, and I could feel my soul cry out at the injustice. He was mine. I wanted him. The water matched my turbulent feelings, I could feel the boat swayed as my desire would surely drown us. That was the danger of the sea and my emotions.

Brennon's eyes filled with a yearning that matched mine, and I could see his confusion when I rolled away. "Where are you going?" he asked, sitting up in bed.

"Home," I said. I put my feet on the floor and stood.

"Meri," he groaned and reached for my wrist, stopping me in my tracks. "Don't leave."

"Brennon, I have to, for I have become too unstable and dangerous. I came to warn you to leave and never search for me again."

"Never!" he growled out.

"Then you will die out here. Go back to your wife, for I have nothing to offer you." I wrestled my arm from his grasp and moved for the door.

Brennon's feet hit the floor, and I knew he would not let me go. I sang a sweet note and it pushed him back into bed, the blankets wrapping around him, entangling his limbs.

"I will come for you, Meri," he promised as he struggled to break free from my binding spell.

"Don't, Brennon. Forget about me."

I slipped out the door, closing it behind me. As I did, I saw a familiar man sitting on the rolled-up sails, smoking a pipe. It was Howland.

"Thought that was ye, although ye look different." He gestured to my white siren hair.

Brennon cussed loudly in his room, and Howland's bushy eyebrows rose in surprise. "What did ye do to 'im in there?" he asked.

"I tied him up." I grinned. But then the smile fell from my face. "You need to convince him to stop trying to find me."

Howland took a few puffs on his pipe and pointed the wooden handle at me. "Maybe it's *you* who needs convincing. That man is in love with ye."

"I know that. But what can come of our love? It is forbidden," I said.

"Says who?" Howland looked confused. "When Brennon explained who ye were, it all made perfect sense. That boy has been obsessed with ye since he first laid eyes on ye. Ye two are meant for each other. Sky and sea."

I shook my head. A loud thump came from the captain's quarters. Brennon must have fallen out of bed. He would soon be out of the blankets.

My heart beat wildly, and it ached. "The sea does not want to be someone's second choice," I said speaking metaphorically and physically. I would not be Brennon's mistress.

"Girlie, you were ne'er his second choice."

The wooden door flung open so hard it hit the wall. Brennon looked like a caged animal that finally worked itself free, with disheveled hair and wild eyes.

He saw me and ran, his bare feet thumping across the deck. He reached for me, and I saw the pain in his eyes as I moved to the rail.

"No!" He reached out for me as a giant wave crashed into the deck, knocking him off his feet and sweeping him away.

The wave then swept me up like a mother carrying a child and carried me off into the fog and back to my island. His cry of fury and pain echoed after me.

"I will have you, Meri. I won't stop until you are mine."

I sat up, terror racing down my spine, sweat glistening my brow. My heart was pounding in my chest. Something was wrong. The sun's rays had barely crested the horizon. The sky was still gray.

A bark of alarm had me running to the balcony and searching the sea. I heard Lad alerting the guards in his seal form. He was out past the coral reefs. His dark nose poked out of the water, and then he dove back under as he was struggling to keep a large bundle afloat.

My heart stopped, and a chill of trepidation ran along my arms. I recognized the shape in the water as a body.

"No!" I cried, running barefoot out of my room, down the tower steps, through the main hall, out the doors, and onto the beach.

Peris, one of my guards, appeared next to Lad and was helping bring in the dead body. When they reached the shallows, Lad shed his skin and walked on two feet. They each tucked their head under his arms and carried him to shore. They laid him out at my feet, and I saw Brennon's pale and lifeless face.

"I'm sorry, my Queen," Lad cried out. "I couldn't reach him in time."

"What happened?" I cried.

"He couldn't breach the storm on the ship, so he attempted to swim here."

"That's over three miles," I said in disbelief.

My heart was breaking, and I was hiding it by focusing on my anger. I dropped to my knees next to Brennon and ran my hands along his cold face.

"Why would you do something so stupid?" I yelled in frustration and shook his shoulders. His head wobbled, but he didn't move. "You were always so stubborn, and now it's the death of you... and me." My tears freely fell as my heart broke. "I could've survived, knowing you were okay. It would have been painful, but I could've done it." I sobbed. "Please, don't make me live without you. I'm not strong enough."

The surrounding ground trembled as my emotions rocked the sea, thus disturbing the dormant volcano. Birds scattered, the waves pulled back, and my guards looked around in fear.

A hand touched my face, and I gasped.

Brennon sat up. He cupped my cheek, and he whispered, "Then let my strength be enough for both of us." He pulled me in and kissed me.

The island settled, the waves calmed, and Peris and Lad gave each other a sly high-five.

I broke the kiss and glared at them. "This was you!" I pointed at Lad. "And you!"

"He did it!" Peris elbowed Lad. "It was his idea."

"Lad, I told you not to interfere."

"No, you distinctly told me you wouldn't lower the magic circle and to go jump in a volcano. There was nothing about helping him get to the island."

"Meri." Brennon pulled my attention back to him. "Why do you keep running from me?"

I blinked at him and looked at my hands guiltily. "I'm not

emotionally stable. I can't control my powers over the ocean. I killed people. I killed your father. I can feel *her*... here." I tapped my heart. "I have thousands of years of the sea's jealous emotions to sort through and my own to process. I came here to protect myself, but also to protect the outside world from me."

"My father's not dead. It takes a lot more than a knock to the head to take out the men in our family. But you know the story," Brennon said. "The ocean needs the love of a man. He's balances her by being her anchor."

"I can't share you," I admitted, my fingers digging into my palms. "I'm too selfish."

Brennon grinned and pulled me into a hug, whispering into my ear, "You never have to. I am yours and yours alone."

"What about the wedding? Your wife Velora?"

"Never finished the ceremony. You interrupted it, remember? For which I am immensely grateful. Plus, I don't even remember how I got on the ship, or much of the wedding day, until the sea witch's spell wore off. The priest even agreed that the wedding wasn't legal or binding."

"You're not married," I said.

He grinned. "I'm not married... yet."

I frowned. "Yet?"

"Nope, but I am a captain of the *Sea Flower*, and by rights I can legally marry anyone on the ship. So as soon as I can get you on board, we're getting married."

It was very sudden. I pulled back, and Brennon lunged for me.

I squealed as he picked me up, slung me over his shoulder like a sack of potatoes, and walked into the surf.

I slapped his back and laughed. "What are you doing?"

"I'm not letting you out of my sight again. Not until we are married. And if that means I have to swim back to the ship with you, so be it."

Lad and Peris came rushing over to Brennon, running beside him in the water.

"What do you need?" Lad asked. "We'll help."

"Traitor!" I laughed as Brennon's grasp around my waist tightened. He gave me a playful slap on my rear. I squealed and kicked my legs. "What if I don't want to get married?" I giggled. The waves were up to Brennon's chest and soaked my dress. He slowly lowered me in the water, his hands wrapping around my waist and pressing me to him.

"Then I am in need of a cabin boy. I believe you have a contract to fulfill."

I wrapped my arms around Brennon's neck, staring into the eyes of the man I loved. "I'm done with contracts. Plus, I would rather be your wife than peel another potato."

"Oh stars, I'm glad you said that. You were a horrible cabin boy."

"I was not," I argued.

"Were too."

"Was n—" Brennon interrupted my argument with a kiss.

I sighed as our kiss deepened.

He broke away and whispered, "I love you, Meri."

The storm in my soul calmed at Brennon's words. The ocean rejoiced and sang aloud for all to hear.

Brennon pulled back from our kiss. His eyes were heavy, and he tilted his head as he listened. "Do you hear that? It's the most beautiful thing I've ever heard."

I grinned and kissed his lips again. "I do. It's the sea, and she is singing us a song."

Brennon looked out at the waves that surrounded us.

"Vasili used to tell tales of the sea singing. But I thought it was a myth."

"No, she was in mourning and had no reason to sing. But she is happy today."

"Is she?" Brennon asked, his face beaming with love.

"Yes, I am." I grinned.

"Me too." He pressed his forehead to mine.

EPILOGUE

My body felt cold, listless. The worn blanket against my skin felt rough like sandpaper and smelled like mildew. I wrinkled my nose in distaste. My senses were extra keen. A light shone from the candle on the nightstand next to me, and I heard a murmur of excitement as it swung closer to my face.

The light made me squint in pain. The voices grew louder.

"Devil's teeth," I groaned. "Shut up."

"Yes, sir," the man said.

I focused on the speaker and recognized Aspen and couldn't believe how much he had grown over the last year. I had to admit, if it weren't for him, I wouldn't be here. But then if it weren't for him, I wouldn't have been trapped in the daemon realm.

A cuss fell from my lips as I struggled to sit up. My legs and limbs were longer than I remembered. Why was I so cold?

"Get the fire stoked," I demanded.

Someone moved to stoke the small wood-burning stove,

and I didn't recognize the pretty female. Her hair was a soft lavender, and she had a fine figure.

I struggled to get up, my legs wobbling beneath me, but I was determined to stand, to get strong, to get my revenge on all those who wronged me. The boat swayed, and I grabbed the back of a chair to steady myself. Making my way to a mirror, I looked on my reflection and glowered.

"What's this?" I snapped irritably.

"There was a slight mishap," Aspen added.

· The reflection was foreign. I turned my head right and left to look at the angular jaw, the thin nose, and the abhorrent long, dark-green hair. I snarled and saw that my canines were a little longer than normal and had a sinister aspect I liked about them.

"Well, maybe this could work," I said, patting my new body and feeling the muscles underneath. I was hoping for the body of one of the kingdom's seven princes, but this would do until I regained my strength and magic. I turned, and the lavender-haired girl and Aspen both bowed.

"What was his name again?" I asked. Already feeling possessive over my new body.

"Vasili," Aspen said. "Of the Undersea."

"That explains the magic I feel in his bloodline. It's old and untapped, but it's there. This will do very nicely." I wandered to the map on the wooden table and looked at the seven kingdoms. Lorelai Eville and her daughters foiled many of my plans. I needed to get a stronghold.

"Where to next?" Aspen asked. He placed a silver dagger with a blackened gem in the hilt on the table next to the map. The red heart stone turned black after it transferred his soul into this body.

The transfer worked, because it was done as a sacrifice of

love. I could sense Vasili's feelings still stirring up in my soul. It sickened me. They would fade fast.

I picked up the soulless dagger and stabbed it into the map, in the heart of the kingdom I so desperately wanted destroyed.

"Set course for the kingdom of Rya."

Read Aura's tale in

(Coming 2020)

ABOUT THE AUTHOR

Chanda Hahn is a NYT & USA Today Bestselling author of The Unfortunate Fairy Tale series. She uses her experience as a children's pastor, children's librarian and bookseller to write compelling and popular fiction for teens. She was born in Seattle, WA, grew up in Nebraska, and currently resides in Waukesha, WI, with her husband and their twin children; Aiden and Ashley.

Visit Chanda Hahn's website to learn more about her other forthcoming books.
www.chandahahn.com

Made in the USA
Columbia, SC
01 July 2020